Diagnosis Dead

Also by Jonathan Kellerman in Large Print:

The Clinic
Survival of the Fittest

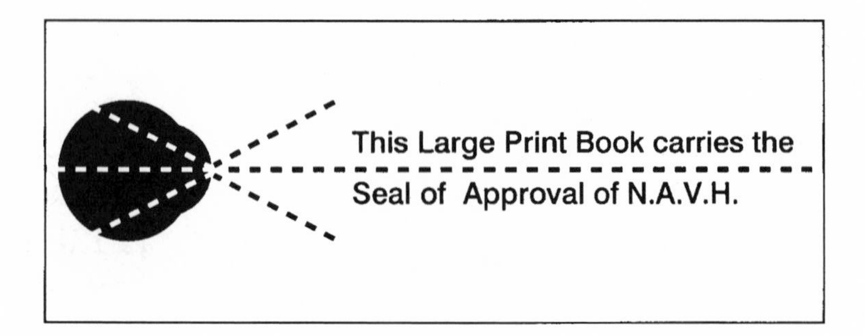

Diagnosis Dead

A MYSTERY WRITERS OF AMERICA ANTHOLOGY

Edited by

Jonathan Kellerman

G.K. Hall & Co. • Thorndike, Maine

Published in 2000 by arrangement with Pocket Books, a division of Simon & Schuster, Inc.

G.K. Hall Large Print Core Series.

The text of this Large Print edition is unabridged.
Other aspects of the book may vary from the original edition.

Set in 16 pt. Plantin by Minnie B. Raven.

Printed in the United States on permanent paper.

ISBN 0-7838-8956-9 (lg. print : hc : alk. paper)

Contents

Introduction

Jonathan Kellerman

Should you get a career criminal to engage in a rare moment of honesty, he may very well admit that crime is his *job,* and that he takes it as seriously as would any professional.

Likewise the business of *catching* criminals, an often plodding, picayune, migraine-inducing endeavor best left to those who get paid to do it. For, despite their shortcomings and limitations, and occasional displays of breath-taking incompetence, the boys and girls in blue and their plainclothes colleagues are almost always the sole solvers of mystery and mayhem. Private eyes are best left to squinting at adulterers behind keyholes, little old ladies in bulky cardigans wouldn't last a minute on the streets, and, when a serial killer is apprehended it's rarely — if ever — the result of a clever "psychological profile" expelled from the bowels of Quantico, but rather, plain, old-fashioned footwork by the unheralded local yokel gendarmes.

I am of two minds about crime stories that feature non-cops as detectives.

I despise those snotty productions where some effete, narcissistic rank amateur shows up the pros by manipulating the pieces of a silly, contrived puzzle.

Crime stories should feature cops.

All this from the guy who enlarged the theme

of Shrink Detective. But though the Delaware novels obligate the reader to assume a certain measure of suspension of disbelief — no psychologist could get in that much trouble — my intention from the moment I constructed the first Delaware, *When the Bough Breaks*, was to adhere to a level of realism that wasn't at war with what I knew about the so-called criminal justice system from my experiences as an expert witness. This meant that though Dr. D.'s intelligence and training would lend him a certain degree of insight, he could never wing it as a solo act, would always have to work with a cop and within the context of the "rules." Hence Milo Sturgis, and Alex's customary role as a consultant.

On the other hand, there is something extremely compelling and appealing about crime stories that feature naifs and other innocent amateurs — men and women caught up in Kafkaesque situations of life-threatening proportion, having to fight and/or reason their way to safety. Hitchcock exploited this theme frequently to brilliant effect, in films such as *Rear Window* — based upon a short story by that maestro of paranoia, Cornell Woolrich a.k.a. William Irish — as well as in *North by Northwest*, *The 39 Steps*, etc. Some of our finest writers, from James T. Farrell to Elmore Leonard, have taken us into the mind of the outsider grappling with the ugly side of life.

By abandoning the story restrictions and character limitations of police proceduralism, the skilful crime writer can be freed to create themes, situations, and paradoxes that pulsate with vitality and originality.

The stories in this collection possess that freshness and inventiveness. As a group, they tend toward tough-mindedness and a dark, brooding — but not despairing — spirit, well in-line with The Way Things Really Are In Contemporary America. Few, if any, can be termed dizzy or cute. Nearly anything in these stories could *happen*. That makes them frightening.

And shouldn't crime stories *be* frightening?

Because even the stiffening corpulence of Colonel Blowhard's livid corpse lying face up in the musty manor house drawing room during martini hour is a *terrible* event. The manipulated demise of *any* human being bears our serious attention, if not always in compassion, at least in horrified pause.

We crime writers have chosen to explore bad stuff. Sometimes we offer the illusion of solution (*I* avoid that nauseating pop psych cliché *closure* because terrible things never close.) Sometimes we leave threads unraveled because life is rarely neat and clean. Always we wrestle with the eternal and ultimately unanswerable question: why do people do evil?

This book is a compendium of significant talent plumbing the depths of bad stuff as it intrudes upon the lives of those *not* paid to deal with it — non-cop he's and she's cast, often against their will, in the role of fixer. Non-cop victims faced with conundrums they don't always solve. The protagonists in these stories occupy varied positions on The Mountain of Moral High Ground. Some you'll cheer on, others may cause you to look behind your shoulder a little more often the next time you venture out into the dark.

One way or the other, they're all doing their job.

What more can you ask?

Dream Lawyer

Lia Matera

"Picture this: a cabin in the woods, a hideaway, practically no furniture, just a table and a cot. Nobody for miles around, just me and her. I'm trying to keep her from collapsing, she's crying so hard. Her tin god's up and turned on her.

"She's got a gun there on the table, and I'm not sure what she's thinking of doing with it. Maybe kill herself. So I'm keeping myself between her and it. I'm up real close to her. Even crying doesn't make her ugly, her skin's so fresh. Tell the truth, I'm trying not to get excited. Her shirt's as thin as dragonfly wings, she's all dressed up expecting him. She should be hiding from him, but all day she's been expecting him. She's been dreading him but hoping he'll come, hoping he's got some explanation she hasn't thought of. Except she knows he couldn't possibly explain it away. That's why she's tearing herself up crying.

"She's so beautiful with the light from the window on her hair. But she's talking crazy — what she's going to do now, how she's going to tell everybody. Forgetting the hold he has on her, on all of us, how protected he is and how cool.

"And then . . . in he comes. She shuts up right away, surprised and terrified. I can tell by how stiff she gets, she's hardly even breathing. She's too freaked out to say any more. That's when I notice him there. But he's not paying attention to me. He's looking her over — her crying, the dress-up clothes she has on — and you can see he's making something out of it.

"She looks around like she's going to try to run. Big mistake. He goes cold as a reptile — I've seen it happen to him before. And then he picks up the gun and shoots her right in the face. Just as cold as a snake.

"That was my first thought, that it wasn't the person I knew, it was some . . . life-form, something outside my understanding with its own rules of survival like cockroaches. Because how could he just aim her own gun at her and blow her head off? Without blinking, without a word? After all she meant to him.

"I'm just about dying of shock right there on my feet. Compared to her, I'm nobody to him, nothing, just a bug that rode in on his cuff. Maybe that's why he says, 'I won't kill you. I don't have to.' He starts walking out. At the door he turns. 'If I have to kill you later, I will. But not like this. By inches. You'll see it coming a long way off, Juan. You'll see it coming for miles, so don't look back.'

"That's all. He didn't try to explain anything or change her mind. He didn't say a word to her, not even good-bye. He just killed her like she didn't matter. Like she was a fly and he was a frog. Zap. And then he left.

"By then I could hardly even stand up. I could hardly make my feet move to look closer at her. I wish I never did look. Did you ever have a bee get squashed on your windshield? That's what her head looked like. I wouldn't have expected so many colors of . . . Her face was blown right off except one part where there were still curls caught in a hair clip.

"I could barely keep on my feet much less figure out what to do about it. It was clear she was dead. Or wouldn't want to be saved if she wasn't. So it was no use calling nine-one-one.

"And as to him, well, my God, how was anybody going to believe me? With all his followers and his credentials — who's going to take my word over his? And what did he mean about don't look back? What would he do to me, this reptile-man who could blow away someone that loved him and that probably he loved, too. What would happen to me if I told anybody?

"I wish I could say I was confused over the trauma or something, but I was probably more scared than anything. That's why I left her there. I was too scared to do anything else, just too damn scared. Because I felt like I'd finally seen right inside him and found the devil there. I hit the road and stuck out my thumb, just trying to get some distance, trying to keep myself together.

"You probably know what happened after that. It took the police a while to catch up to him. They were looking for me, too; they knew I was there at the cabin from finding my fingerprints and hairs and like that. When they found me, I could hardly get any words out, I was still so scared. I guess they didn't trust me to stay and testify against him — they put me in custody, in jail. I wanted to get word to him, beg him not to do anything to me, beg him to understand it wasn't my fault, that I'd have shut up and stayed gone if I could. But I knew it was useless.

"When it was his lawyer's turn to do something, she had all these reasons I shouldn't testify. What it came down to was, I couldn't prove it was him and not me that killed Becky. I pointed at him and he pointed at me. And I guess in some legalistic way, we canceled each other out. However the technicalities worked, the jury never heard the whole story. So there was no way for them to figure out the truth, not beyond a reasonable doubt. I don't blame them the way some folks around here do.

"Some people wrote to the newspapers that they should have put me in prison whether I did it or not, because Becky was dead and somebody had to pay. And if it wasn't going to be Castle, it should be me because we were the only ones there in the cabin with her.

"And I can understand how people felt. It makes me sick to know he shot her and got away with it. And her, poor thing, all dressed up in case he was going to melt at her feet, hoping he'd come clean to everybody just to keep her respect. That's the part that hurts the most, that she was good enough to hope so, even with what she knew about him.

"I'd have twisted my life inside out to please a sweet girl like Becky Walker. I cry every time I think about her beautiful gold hair caught in that little clip. I couldn't save her, and I couldn't even get her a little bit of justice. Not even that.

"I tell you, it tears me apart."

The poor man looked torn apart. His natural swarthiness had paled to a sickly yellow. His graying hair was disheveled from finger-raking. His dark eyes, close-set above a hooked nose, glinted with tears. Prominent cheekbones contributed to the starved, haunted look of a survivor.

The walls of his small house were cluttered, even encrusted, with charms of various types. Mexican-made saints cast sad eyes on dried herbs and wreaths of garlic, rusty horseshoes were strung with rabbits' feet, icons of saints hung beside posters of kindly blond space aliens. And everywhere there were gargoyles. Their demon faces scowled down from the rafters, they brooded in corners, squatted on tabletops, leered behind rows of votive candles.

"Did you have a lawyer representing you before or during the trial?" I asked Juan Gomez.

"No."

"When the police questioned you, did they tell you it was your right to have a lawyer present?"

"Yes." He buffed the knees of his worn jeans, rocking slightly. "But what was the point? I was too scared to say what happened, anyway."

"But you feel you need a lawyer now?" Castle

had been acquitted of murder: the barn door was open, and the horse was long gone. Unless Gomez wanted some pricey commiseration, there wasn't much I could do for him.

When he nodded, I continued. "I gather this was a big case locally. But I just moved here, so I'm not acquainted with it." Having been fired from yet another law firm, this time for taking a too-strange case as a favor to a friend, I was once again on my own. Just today, I'd unpacked a parcel of business cards reading "Willa Jansson, Attorney at Law, Civil Litigation & Criminal Defense." I wasn't turning down anything until I got a little money in the bank.

The move from San Francisco to Santa Cruz had been expensive despite being only seventy-five miles down the coast. And I'd discovered that lawyers in laid-back Hawaii East charged only half the fees of their big-city counterparts.

Now my potential client, whose main selection criterion seemed to be counsel's willingness to make house calls, leaned back in his chair. It was painted white, like the rest of his plain wood furniture, and arranged on duct tape exes on the floor.

"You never heard of the case? You don't know about Sean Castle?" He resumed his anxious rocking.

"No. The name seems familiar." Maybe I'd read about him.

"He's famous for dream research."

"Dream interpretation, that kind of thing?"

"Prophetic dreaming." He continued to look surprised I didn't know. "Sean could lecture seven days a week about dreams and never run out of people wanting more. There's a waiting list for his workshops. He's a brilliant man."

"What does he teach people to do?"

"Recognize the future in their dreams."

I shuddered at the thought. Bad enough to deal with the future when it got here. "What did the dead woman threaten him with? What was she going to expose about him?"

He jerked back as if I'd slapped him. "I can't tell you that."

"I'm sorry?"

"That was up to her." He winced. "It's still up to her. I can't take it away from her."

"But she's dead." Was I missing something?

"A carpet doesn't stop unrolling just because the ground drops out from under it."

"Well, but . . . I don't know where this carpet's going." I did know I'd gone as far as I could with the metaphor. "You say Castle killed her so she wouldn't reveal some secret. And now you feel vulnerable because of it. Maybe you should share the information, if only for your own protection."

"You don't know this because you never met him." Juan looked more than merely earnest. "He means what he says, especially threats."

"You're afraid he'll kill you?" At least that part made sense to me. "Or however he put it."

"I'm not 'afraid' he'll do it, I know he will. Exactly like he said. By inches. It's already started." He watched me glance at the gargoyles. "Gargoyles are demons that switched sides. Because of who they used to be, they can see through any disguise evil puts on — it takes one to know one. They keep evil from coming close, like pit bulls in the yard. That's why they're all over cathedrals."

I glanced uncertainly at the snarling plaster creatures, some winged, some with horns and claws. They were daunting, but pit bulls barked louder.

"You need them when you're sleeping," he added. "You can't stay awake forever."

"No." I continued hastily, "So why do you want a lawyer?" An exorcist, a shaman, a psychic, even an acupuncturist would probably be more useful for counteracting psychological terror. When he didn't respond, I said, "Look, I'm no therapist, but it does seem that Sean Castle is playing on your fears. Manipulating them."

"You'd have to meet him to understand. If he wants something, it happens."

"Okay. But do you need counsel?" He seemed unclear on the demarcation between legal remedies and mythical talismans. And I still had plenty of unpacking to do.

"The lawyer sent me his will."

"He's dead?" I wasn't going to learn Juan Gomez was afraid of a ghost?

"No, he's alive — I'm absolutely sure. So why did his lawyer send me the will? Why does she think *he* lives here? Why did he tell her that? What does it mean?"

"Who's the lawyer?"

"Laura Di Palma." He watched me. "You know her."

"Yes." I don't know what showed on my face. But Di Palma had once cross-examined me in a murder trial. She'd tied me into incoherent knots and invited the jury to scorn my testimony. The experience had been akin to being repeatedly stabbed with an icicle. There was a lingering chill long after the pain subsided. "She didn't explain why she sent the will here? Did she send a cover letter?"

"Just the will. The envelope has her return address."

"Are you named in the will?"

The mention of Di Palma made me more curious than cautious. We shouldn't be discussing this unless and until we agreed I was his lawyer and talked about fees.

"He wants me to take his ashes to Becky's cabin and scatter them there." He blanched just thinking about it.

"You can refuse."

"No, there's a reason he did this. He's trying to tell me something. More than that." He resumed his neurotic rocking. "He's trying to trap me, do something evil to me. I need to figure out what. I need you to talk to his lawyer for me."

"You want me to find out her reasons for sending the will to your address? Or his reasons for wanting you to scatter his ashes?"

"Find out anything, whatever he told her. But don't talk to him yourself." He leaned forward. "Don't put yourself in his line of sight. Don't let him know you're against him. Okay? I have enough on my conscience already."

"Don't worry about me." If I could survive another encounter with Laura Di Palma, I was tough enough to face a mere assassin.

"And her, the lawyer. Be careful of her. Everybody that touches him gets some of the good burned out."

"Di Palma doesn't give him much of a target." I hastened to recover some professionalism. "What I mean is, she can take care of herself."

"No." He shook his head emphatically. "Against him, nobody takes care. You've got to sleep sometime."

I suppressed a smile, imagining Di Palma wrestling with nightmares. If anybody could get a restraining order against Freddy Krueger, it was her. "Why don't you let me take a look at the will?"

He rose and walked to a white velvet box on a white-washed table. From it he extracted a pair of latex gloves. He put them on, then carried the box over to me.

"Do you want gloves?" he asked. "I have more."

"No, that's okay." I reached into the box and pulled out a manila envelope. The return label was preprinted with Di Palma's law firm address.

The envelope was addressed in tidy type to Sean Castle . . . at this address. In block letters above were the words *Juan Gomez* and *c/o*, in care of. "It might just be misaddressed. A clerical error."

"I want to wish it could be so simple!"

I slid the will out. It looked like a Xerox or laser print of a standard-format will. I skimmed a page that distributed property and personal effects among a list of people, none with the surname Castle.

Juan's name appeared in a section about funeral arrangements and disposal of remains. It requested, without embellishment, that Juan take the urn containing Castle's cremains to "the mountain cabin formerly the residence of our mutual friend, Becky" and scatter them there.

I looked up from the will to find Juan standing as hunched and motionless as one of his gargoyles.

"Who owns the cabin he's talking about?" I asked him. "Are they going to want these ashes scattered there?"

"It used to be mine. But I deeded it to Sean so he could put Becky in it. She had to be isolated, and it's pretty far off the beaten path."

"Isolated?"

"That's what Sean said. Now I know what he meant, but then, I didn't think about it. She wanted to live there, so that was that."

"Did she realize it wasn't originally Castle's property? That you were deeding it to him for her benefit?"

He shrugged. "She knew I built it."

I hadn't been his lawyer then; this was none of my business. People signed property over to churches and foundations and gurus everyday. Scientologists bought enlightenment one expensive lesson at a time; Mormons tithed inconvenient percentages of their income; my father's favorite guru, Brother Mike, gladly accepted supercomputers.

"Who lives in the cabin now?"

"I don't know. I've never been back. I think of it as empty." He looked wistful. "If only . . . It could have worked out fine for everybody."

I waited, but he didn't elaborate. It certainly hadn't worked out well for the dead woman. Or, apparently, for Juan Gomez.

I returned my attention to the will, one of the first I'd studied since the bar exam. "Aside from being addressed to you care of Sean Castle, it's odd they'd send this out prior to Castle's death. You're sure he's still alive?"

"Yes. I wish he weren't, but I know he is."

"Well, it's not standard practice to distribute a living person's will, not at all. It raises beneficiaries' expectations, and that's unfair all around — the person might change his mind and revise the terms of the will or add a codicil. So I don't know why he'd want this mailed out now. It doesn't promise anything and it invades his privacy. It really might be some kind of mistake."

"He doesn't make mistakes."

"Neither does his lawyer. But a paralegal may

have screwed up. Maybe the wrong address in the Rolodex or a misleading scrawl on a Post-it . . . these things do happen." Bad enough Juan had been asked to scatter a murderer's ashes. He shouldn't have to worry about the will containing some hidden threat. "I could find out for you."

"Yes! But be careful. You don't know Sean Castle, you don't know what he does to people."

But I did know Laura Di Palma. And Juan Gomez was a good example of what *she* did to people.

"Willa, it's been years." Di Palma's law partner stood in the waiting room of her office, looking mildly surprised. "Are you still practicing labor law?"

I felt a little guilty saying, "No." I'd gone to law school to join the labor firm of illustrious lefties Julian Warneke and Clement Kerrey. Maryanne More had apprenticed there years before me, going on to the National Labor Relations Board before starting her own firm. But I'd stayed with Julian only two years before the lure of solvency seduced me into an L.A. business firm. I'd done a year of hard time there — despite my efforts to reinvent myself, I'd remained a hippie at heart, valuing my time above money. From a labor point of view, I'd been one sullen wage slave. "I just opened my own firm. Down in Santa Cruz. I'd like to pick up a labor clientele, but I'm barely unpacked."

In fact, that was why I was here now. As long as I was in the city to fetch the last of my boxes, I might as well get in Di Palma's face.

Maryanne nodded. With her smooth chignon and velvet lapels, she looked like a model in a Christmas catalog. "Are you here to see me?"

I glanced at the waiting room's dark wood walls, brocade couches, and Old Master oil paintings. All the place needed was a docent. The decor sure didn't match my impression of Di Palma. I suppose I'd envisioned shark tanks.

"I've been trying to reach Laura Di Palma. I've left several voice-mail messages and I haven't gotten a response. I thought I'd drop in and see if I could catch her."

Maryanne seemed to stop breathing, tensing as if she were listening for something. "I'm sorry, Laura's taken the week off to take care of some family matters. Can I help you?"

"Possibly."

Maryanne nodded slightly, motioning me to follow her down a parqueted corridor. Halfway down, a door labeled "Laura Di Palma" was ajar. In an office splashed with bright colors, a lanky man sat at a glass desk, holding his bowed head. Maryanne sped up, leading me to an office at the end of the hall.

I settled into a wing chair. Jeez, her office looked like a palace library.

"Laura Di Palma sent a copy of a will to Juan Gomez, my client. Among other things, the will asks him to scatter the ashes of her client, Sean

Castle. The envelope is addressed to Juan at his house, care of Sean Castle."

Maryanne shook her head slightly. "How odd." Neither of us stated the obvious, that sending the will to someone named in it denied Castle the confidentiality he might reasonably expect. "I assume it was misaddressed, and that she intended to send it to . . . Sean Castle, is it? I'm sorry if your client was disturbed by it."

I sighed. "Disturbed is the least of it. Mr. Gomez worries that Castle gave Ms. Di Palma his address. And he particularly wanted to keep his whereabouts secret from Castle. So I really need to check with Ms. Di Palma and find out what's behind this."

"Well, I can't speak for her. But perhaps I can find out whether it was a clerical error." She looked bothered. Because the office might have to notify Castle? Because she shouldn't have to clean up Di Palma's mess?

"I'd like to talk to Ms. Di Palma myself. My client really needs some assurance that Mr. Castle's not making any kind of veiled threat." After the creepy tale Juan had told, I could use a little reassurance myself. "You know Juan Gomez testified against Castle?"

"I don't know anything about Mr. Gomez. And I really don't know much about Mr. Castle, though I recall Laura represented him last year. But I'll ask her to —" She caught her breath, looking beyond me. "Sandy?" Her tone was bracing.

The lanky man I'd glimpsed in Di Palma's office was now standing in the doorway. A wide mouth and long dimples might ordinarily have been the focus of his thin face. But at this moment, gloom furrowed his brows and narrowed his blue eyes to a wince. He pushed sand-colored hair off his forehead, looking like Gary Cooper in some thirties melodrama.

"Did I hear you mention Laura?" His voice was deep and slightly Southern in inflection. "Anything I can help with?"

Maryanne glanced at me.

He continued standing there, so I said, "I've been trying to get hold of Ms. Di Palma."

The man entered, taking the wing chair beside mine. "About?"

"Sandy, I don't think this is —"

"What about?" he repeated.

"Are you an associate of hers?" I wondered.

"Willa Jansson, Sandy Arkelett. Sandy handles our private investigations." Maryanne's lips remained parted, as if she were on the brink of saying more.

I watched her uncertainly. Arkelett worked for her firm, this should be her call.

Finally, she told him, "Laura apparently sent Sean Castle's will to one of his beneficiaries."

Arkelett's brows rose.

"Juan Gomez. He's my client," I added. "He'd like to know why the will was sent to him. He and Mr. Castle were involved in a case she tried."

"I know Castle. I did the legwork on that case."

"Have you seen him lately? Do you know if the will was sent at his request?"

"Laura didn't tell me about any will." Arkelett was talking to Maryanne now. "You?"

Maryanne shook her head.

"Could it be a phony?" He reached a long arm across the desk as if to take a copy from Maryanne.

"My client didn't want me to make a copy," I explained. I didn't add that he'd nearly come unglued at the prospect of my becoming cursed by it. "It looked like a standard document with a number of bequests. It asks my client to scatter Castle's ashes."

"And it got sent to . . . ?"

"Juan Gomez."

He scowled. "I'll try and get a hold of Castle for you. Do you have a business card?"

I was a little surprised. It would certainly be more usual to contact Di Palma, wherever she was, before going behind her back to question her clients. Nevertheless, I fished two brand new cards out of my bag, handing one to Arkelett and one to Maryanne.

"Law school murders," Arkelett said, reading my card. "You were one of the witnesses."

I felt myself trying to scoot back the heavy wing chair.

"I worked with Laura on that case," he explained.

As the defense investigator, he'd have done a thorough background check of the prosecution's witnesses. He'd have given Di Palma details of my protest-era arrests and my two ghastly months of jail time. God knew Di Palma had gotten her money's worth, rattling my "criminal record" like a saber, using it to hack away at my credibility.

But, as lawyers love to say, that's why she got the big bucks.

Arkelett slipped my card into his pocket, and rose. He left without another word.

Maryanne said, "We'll try to reach Laura for you, of course."

Then she rose, too, resolutely shaking my hand good-bye.

Arkelett stopped me in the hall outside the suite of offices.

"Look," he said, "I want to ask a favor. I'd like to see Castle's will. Maybe ask your client a couple of questions." He frowned. "Because Laura . . . it wouldn't be like her to screw up. Not on a client matter, anyway."

"What would the will tell you?" And why didn't he just phone Di Palma, wherever she was?

"If you still have the envelope, the date and place it was mailed."

"I could call you with the information."

"I want to look at it myself. In case there's anything else."

Was he expecting blood? A coded scrawl? Juan had made this all seem strange enough. Having a man in a business suit get weird about it was even spookier.

"Some things you need to look at the original," he insisted. "I'd just like to make my own assessment. Take a few minutes of your client's time?" He tilted his head as if to figure me out.

"I don't know — he's a little high-strung." I couldn't resist asking: "Is there a problem? Some reason you're not waiting for Ms. Di Palma?"

He chewed the inside of his cheek. "Laura had to go deal with a . . . a sick cousin." Judging by his face, there was a hell of a lot more to it than that. "And well, we're not sure exactly where that took her. I don't mean to say it's a big deal — she'll be back soon enough. But in the meantime, guaranteed, she'd want me to check this out."

Check out the postmark on Juan Gomez's envelope? No, however Arkelett might try to soft-pedal it, he wanted to know where Di Palma had gone. I backed toward the elevator. Should I help him? If Di Palma wanted him to know her whereabouts, she'd have told him herself.

"I can maybe help your client out," Arkelett persisted. "If he's who I think he is . . ." He looked nonplussed. "Maybe I can help him get his head on straight."

"My client's afraid," I admitted. "Afraid of Castle. He warned me about him several times. And he expressed some concern about Ms. Di Palma, too. So I don't know how he'd feel about seeing you."

Sandy Arkelett leaned closer. I could smell

Old Spice on his lean cheeks. "If he wants you present, that's fine. No cost to him — I'll pay you for the hour, okay?"

"I'll see what I can set up." For a fee, I supposed I could fit it into my schedule.

When he opened his door, I said, "How are you, Juan? I'm sorry I'm a little early."

As I stepped in, he glanced outside, his grizzled brows rising. I looked over my shoulder. Sandy Arkelett had just pulled up to the curb.

Juan clutched his sweatshirt as if to keep his heart from leaping out of his chest. And I didn't blame him. Just as Arkelett had investigated me when I'd been a witness against Di Palma's client, he'd doubtless investigated every aspect of Juan's life before Castle's trial. I wondered how Juan would react if Arkelett alluded to any of it.

I closed the door.

"You don't have to do this," I reminded him. "Or, if you like, we can speak to Mr. Arkelett in my office. You don't have to invite him into your home."

"No." Juan's tone was more stoic than his face. "No, I understand what it is to love someone. Someone who's gone."

I'd told him Di Palma was apparently off on some private errand. I'd told him I thought Arkelett was trying to find out exactly where it had taken her. Now Juan had filled in the reason: Arkelett was in love with Di Palma. Maybe Juan was just guessing, but it fit, it made sense.

I looked around the gargoyle-protected room. It was somber with the curtains closed, lighted only with votive candles and a dim table lamp. He must not read much, not in this gloom. But there was no television in sight, either. Did he spend his days praying to the gargoyles leering in flickering candle shadows? "You've met Sandy Arkelett?"

Juan nodded. "He's by her side all the time. He puts himself between her and Castle. You can see that he understands more about Castle than she does. You can see it on his face."

I was a little taken aback. He couldn't have spent much time with Castle and his lawyer. Even his use of the present tense was disconcerting. He seemed to expect me to share some memory or vision.

Sandy Arkelett sighed deeply when Juan opened the door to him. It was a moment before he muttered, "Thanks for seeing me." The worry lines on his long face deepened, lending his words a somber sincerity. "Mind if I come in?"

I admired his thirties-movie silhouette, long and slim in a slightly baggy suit. Even his light brown hair was combed back like Gary Cooper's or Jimmy Stewart's. Di Palma was lucky.

"I was just asking my client if he felt comfortable doing this," I told him.

Juan was flattened against the door, staring at Arkelett.

The detective said, "I won't take but ten minutes of your time, Mr. um . . ." He eyed Juan so intently he seemed to be leaning toward him. "Is it Gomez?"

Juan edged away.

"I know I bring up some hard memories. So I'll make it real short," Arkelett repeated. "But it was a long drive down here — I'd appreciate ten minutes."

"I — I'm sorry. I have nothing against you. On the contrary. I just —"

Arkelett stepped quickly inside. "Thanks," he murmured. "I guess . . . would it be easiest to start with the will?" He glanced at me.

"Do you mind showing Mr. Arkelett the will?"

Juan caught his lower lip between his teeth. He walked to the white box on the white table. Arkelett looked around, his pale brows pinched. I watched Juan put on rubber gloves to open the box and handle the manila envelope inside it.

He brought it to me. Arkelett stepped up behind me, positioned to look over my shoulder.

The envelope was postmarked Hillsdale, CA. Central California, maybe Northern? Like most San Franciscans — former San Franciscans — I'd rarely bestirred myself to explore the outback.

I turned, handing Arkelett the envelope. It had been mailed on the sixteenth. Today was the twenty-second.

Juan reached past me, touching his fingertips to Arkelett's elbow. "Sit down," he said. "On the white pine chair. That's the best one for this. Do you want gloves?"

"No need." Arkelett chewed the inside of his cheek and stared at the postmark.

"Where's Hillsdale?" I asked him.

"North." It seemed to take him extra effort to look away from the word. Then his head lurched as if he were overcompensating. "Below the Oregon border on the coast. Laura's hometown. She started the trip there."

"So she did send it." So much for blaming a paralegal.

Juan hovered near the envelope, latex gloves poised to retrieve it. "Why does it have my address — *my* address with *his* name. How does she know my address?"

Arkelett said, "The firm has it on file."

"My address?" Juan blinked. "But how? Why?"

"You haven't been in contact with Laura lately?"

"No. As a discipline, I try not to think about it. About him. I would never call his lawyer. Never."

Juan was so shaken by the idea that he turned away, touching his hand to the snarling cheek of a candlelit gargoyle. Arkelett watched him.

When Juan turned back, Arkelett continued, "And except for the will, Laura hasn't been in touch with you?"

"Only through Castle. He's very much in touch with me. But not in the way you mean." Juan gestured toward the envelope. "This would be very crude for him. So blunt that at first I thought it was meant as an insult. But I begin to see the layers on top of layers."

"I expect I've stirred up a lot of worries, coming down here like this." Arkelett seemed to be memorizing every millimeter of the envelope. "But I'm just . . ." He glanced at me again. "Just trying to correct an office mistake, that's all. If I possibly can." He extracted the will.

Juan took a stumbling backward step, staring as if Arkelett had shaken out an appendage of Castle's. "I will go, go and . . . leave you for a moment."

He started pushing open the door to another room. Then he turned back to us, trotting to the whitewashed chair and scooting it behind Arkelett, virtually forcing him to sit. He left as if chased out.

Arkelett hunched over the will, giving it his full attention. I stood behind the chair, reading over his shoulder.

Arkelett turned to me. "You don't know much about Castle's trial?"

"Only what Mr. Gomez told me."

He seemed on the verge of saying something difficult. Then, with a shake of the head, "I'm not clear enough on client confidentiality to know how much I can say now." As Di Palma's associate, he was obligated to keep her client matters confidential. "I don't know if Castle's acquittal changes anything. Especially these days, with civil suits getting filed after not-guilty criminal verdicts."

Was he about to admit Castle's guilt? I'd already gathered as much. But he was right, the double-jeopardy rule protected Castle only from criminal reprosecution. It offered no immunity from a civil suit. So it wouldn't do for Arkelett to confirm Castle's guilt. Nevertheless, I was silent, hoping he'd say more.

With a shrug, he continued, "You should read the court documents." A half smile. "And take a look at the arrest report and booking sheet."

Castle must have priors I should know about. Or maybe something in the records supported Juan's fears. Everyone was so damn odd about Castle. I was ready to invest in a few gargoyles myself.

Juan returned then. Arkelett slipped the will back into its envelope.

"Thanks for your time." Arkelett stood slowly. "And thank you, Ms. Jansson. I'm a hundred percent sure Laura's going to phone you first thing when she gets back."

"You'd better find your Ms. Di Palma soon," Juan advised.

Arkelett stopped moving.

"She never understood what Castle is," Juan continued. "She was like a woman with dust thrown in her eyes. When he can blind a woman, he can take her away from anyone. Like he took Becky away from me. He can make her do anything."

Arkelett's face drained of color. "Can you elaborate on that?"

Juan shrugged.

"Are you saying she's in some kind of physical danger?"

"Mental danger, spiritual danger." Juan's eyes glittered.

Arkelett watched him for a moment. "Laura knew what and who she was dealing with — it's not a matter of dust in her eyes. But a lawyer's got to do everything she can for her client. You understand that, don't you? That it was Laura's job to win an acquittal? That's not to say it's necessarily the best result, not even for Castle. Maybe sometimes it's better to put someone away where he can get treatment, even punishment. But from the point of view of the lawyer, she's obligated to go for the gold. That's her pact with the client. Whether it's right in the long run . . . that's for the client to decide, that's for God to know. Laura did her job, that's all. You do understand that?"

Juan stared at his gargoyles. "Yes." His voice was a whisper. "But maybe Becky doesn't understand."

Arkelett handed me the will and walked out.

Until Juan mentioned them, I don't suppose I'd ever thought about prophetic dreams. But that night, I believed I'd had one.

I dreamed I was sitting in Assistant District Attorney Patrick Toben's no-frills office. Toben was the only local ADA I knew. I'd recently tried a case against him.

In my dream, Toben, dapper and well-groomed as in life, wore a gargoyle print tie. "I called you," he said, "because your business card was found at the crime scene."

At that, I awakened suddenly and fully, convinced Juan Gomez was about to be killed by Sean Castle. My dark bedroom seemed thick with shapes, lurking like Castle's curse. *I'll kill you by inches, Juan. You'll see it coming for miles, so don't look back.*

I sat up, clicking on a lamp. My new place smelled of carpet shampoo and fresh paint. The walls were bare and the corners piled high with boxes. I could hear the clang of metal pulleys on masts at the nearby yacht harbor.

I crawled out of bed, clammy with fear. I pulled a jacket over the sweats I'd slept in, and I slipped into my moccasins. I started toward the door.

I stopped with my hand on the knob. I was still half-asleep, showing a dreamlike lack of impulse control. What excuse did I have for awakening Juan Gomez at this time of night? He was scared enough without having me appear on his doorstep to relate a nightmare.

I took a deep breath. I'd gotten sucked into Juan's world of dreams and curses, complete with medieval gargoyles to protect the sleeping. But I knew better than to elevate mere worries into voodoo, misgivings into prophecies. Sean Castle could manipulate Juan only because Juan had done the psychological and emotional spadework for him. Juan himself had created the pursued, cowering man Castle had vowed to make of him.

Juan said Castle would harm me, too, if he became aware of me. But I could see Juan had it backward. Castle could undermine me only if *I* became aware of *him,* only if I let myself dread what he might do to me. Only if I frightened myself enough to awaken a client in the middle of the night.

I returned to bed and huddled there, trying hard not to imagine gargoyles, claws outstretched, in the shadows beyond the lamplight.

I hugged myself against the seacoast chill, thinking about the tale Juan had told, replaying his words in my mind. Having shared his horror, however briefly, I could move beyond smug pity. It scared me how much that seemed to change his story. Minutes before, I'd been proud of myself for breaking the chain of Juan's superstition. Now I feared the situation was much more complicated than that. How had Juan put it? *I want to wish it could be so simple.*

I considered Sandy Arkelett's reaction to Juan, his worries about revealing a client confidence, his advice that I read the court records and look at the booking sheet. I pondered the fact that Arkelett had recognized my name many years after my testimony, but hadn't recognized Juan's after only a year.

Once again, I jumped out of bed.

I cruised slowly past Juan's house, disquieted to see orbs of candlelight through his sagging curtains. It was nearly four in the morning. I'd hoped for the consolation of finding the place peaceful and dark.

I pulled up to the curb. I'd already promised myself: no debate. If Juan seemed to be stirring, I would knock no matter how foolish I felt. Maybe I had this figured wrong — unlike Di Palma, I made mistakes with disgusting frequency. Even if I was right, it was slim reason to bother Juan in the middle of the night.

But I just couldn't stop worrying about my dream. *Your card was found at the crime scene,* Assistant DA Toben had said.

Maybe it was a blessing not to be as perfect as Di Palma — I was used to apologizing. If I'd worried for nothing, fine, I would simply admit to being an idiot.

I looked over my shoulder as I approached the house. I'd feel like a flake persuading his neighbors I was no prowler.

When I knocked at the door, it opened slightly. Juan had left it unlocked, virtually ajar. Fear crawled up my spine. A man with gargoyles on every horizontal surface wouldn't leave his door open. Not unless he'd given up on protecting himself from Sean Castle. Not unless he'd tired of waiting in agonized dread.

I pushed my way in. "Juan?"

I almost stumbled over an object near the threshold. It was a gargoyle, shattered into lumps and shards of plaster as if dashed against the wall.

Only a few candles glowed, leaving most of the

room in shadow. Whitewashed furniture picked up flickers of color from glass votives. There was barely enough light to make out the remains of other gargoyles, their pieces strewn as if in a berserk frenzy. Their cracked demon faces, portions of curling claws, and remnants of reptilian wings covered the floor like macabre carnage.

For a moment, I let myself believe that the large shadow in the corner was another gargoyle, still intact. But I approached it with a knot rising up my throat. I knew it was Juan Gomez, sprawled dead on the floor.

My business card, I noticed, was lying in a pool of blood beside his hand.

Sean Castle had smashed all the gargoyles. Then he'd slashed Juan's wrists with the jagged slivers of plaster. Or perhaps Juan, sure Castle was coming for him, had beaten him to the punch.

Exsanguination was listed as the cause of death. Suicide was presumed, despite the fact that Castle's fingerprints were all over the house.

I spent the rest of the night with the police. Then I went to the office of Assistant District Attorney Patrick Toben. Toben had prosecuted Sean Castle. Now he had the paperwork for this case.

It was only right that he should. My client, I had come to realize, wasn't Juan Gomez, after all. He was Sean Castle.

"Yeah, Sean Castle killed Becky Walker, all

right." Toben ran a hand over his neat ginger hair. "Walker was living with Castle in his cabin. We think she freaked out over something he did — probably showing multiple personalities. So he got self-protective and blew her head off. From what you just told me, I guess there was a Juan Gomez inside him watching the whole thing happen. Whatever. By the time we caught up to Castle, he'd ditched the clothes he'd been wearing, gotten rid of the weapon, everything. We just didn't have enough for a conviction. That's how Di Palma played it. You ever seen her in court? Well, then you know. She's good."

"The name Juan Gomez never even came up?"

"Di Palma never let a psychiatrist near Castle. She told us from day one she wasn't going to argue diminished capacity or insanity, nothing like that. She completely removed it as a trial issue, precluding us from examining him ourselves. And from what you tell me now, I can see why. If the psychiatrists labeled him a multiple, we'd have used it against him, we'd have looked for a violent personality or at least suggested the possibility. But our circumstantial case was weak enough that Di Palma stayed away from all of that. She was smart. She must have known, but she let it hang on whether we had enough proof."

I reached out a shaky hand for the coffee Toben had poured me. "When Sandy Arkelett saw Gomez — Castle — I could tell something wasn't right. But I assumed it had to do with Di Palma, with Arkelett trying to find her."

"It's a long drive to look at a postmark," Toben agreed.

"I suppose he just couldn't imagine Di Palma sending a will to a beneficiary by mistake." Sheesh, nobody would take time to check it out if I messed up. "He knew something was wrong."

"Looks like Di Palma didn't screw up, after all." Toben didn't seem very pleased to say so. "I assume Castle had Di Palma write up his will, and that she mailed it to him while she was on the road."

I envisioned Castle receiving the will and writing "Juan Gomez c/o" above the address. He certainly knew how to scare his alter ego. By asking "Juan Gomez" to return to Walker's cabin, Castle was, in essence, making "Juan" assume responsibility, pointing out that he'd been present during the murder, too. Castle was reminding his better half, as it were, that the hand that killed Becky Walker belonged to both of them.

The real question was, had Castle killed "Juan"? Had he taken revenge on his cringing cohabitant? Or had "Juan" rid the world of Castle, killing Becky's murderer the only way he could?

"I should have known something was fishy as soon as I saw Arkelett's reaction to Castle," I fretted again. "He knew the score the minute the front door opened. He knew the problem wasn't with Di Palma, he knew she hadn't made a mistake with the address." I took a swallow of weak coffee. "I was so dense. Even when Arkelett told me to look up the arrest report."

"You'd have recognized Castle's booking photo." Toben tapped a pencil against a file folder.

"Arkelett could have just told me. The photo's a public record." But I knew Arkelett's reluctance involved not the photo but the conclusion to be drawn from it: that Sean Castle had multiple personalities, one of whom was willing to incriminate another. This wasn't an observation to be made by an associate of Castle's lawyer. Not in an era of civil trials following criminal acquittals.

I knew all that. But it didn't take the bitter taste out of my mouth. Maybe I could have done something if I'd figured this out sooner. I wished, not for the first time, that Di Palma and her PI weren't so damned competent.

"We talked to Di Palma this morning," Toben continued. "We tracked her down through an uncle — she's up north. She got real quiet when I told her what happened." His lips curled with disdain. "If she'd have let us do our jobs and put Castle away, he'd be a hell of a lot better off now."

And if Toben had presented a stronger case against Castle, Di Palma would have had to settle for an insanity or diminished capacity defense. But however she might feel about this result, Sandy Arkelett was right. She'd done everything she should for her client. She'd won him his freedom.

Then she'd left it to him to find real justice within himself and with his other selves.

I tried to remember what else "Juan" had told me about Castle. "Was he really a famous dream researcher?"

"Is that what he said?"

"Something about prophetic dreams. He had all those gargoyles to protect him while he slept."

"Sean Castle was the man you met in that little house. Did he look famous to you?"

"No. It's just that . . . I guess on some level, I figured this out while I was sleeping." I refused to attribute more than that to my dream. "I woke up in the middle of the night worrying about it."

"That's why you went over there?"

I nodded. The police had obviously considered my nocturnal call bizarre. Toben probably agreed, but he didn't comment.

He said, "For a living, Castle did a bit of everything. Gardening, roto-rooting, worked at the canneries when they hired extras."

"Castle, gargoyles — I suppose it was just the association of ideas. Gargoyles protect Castles."

"I guess gargoyles aren't protection enough."

"Neither are lawyers, not even the best of them."

The no-nonsense lawyer Laura Di Palma is the creation of Lia Matera, who has written several novels about her, the most recent being *Designer Crimes*. Her other Edgar- and Anthony-nominated series character is Willa Jansson, another California attorney whose approach to life is a little more laid back, as seen in the recent novel *Star Witness.* A former teaching fellow at Stanford University Law School, she lives in Santa Cruz, California.

Broken Doors

Brendan DuBois

My office is in a restored brick warehouse near the bustling Porter Harbor in New Hampshire, and there are tall windows in the east wall, windows that overlook the harbor and the Memorial Bridge that spans into Maine. There are days when I wish I could spend all of my time just sitting there, looking out the windows, as my patients sit behind me and unburden their minds and their troubles. But one of the cardinal rules in my work is Thou Shalt Pay Attention, and I can't afford to let my eyes drift.

However, as I listen to boring tales of domestic infidelity, amusing tales of odd obsessions, and terrifying tales of abuse, there are those times when I do wish I could just let my eyes look out into the waters of the harbor and the boats and tugs and the condos ringing the shore. And thankfully — not as often — there are also times I cannot tear my eyes away from my patient, as he or she sits there on the comfortable couch before me and tells me the dark tales of what is bothering them.

This happened to me one day as Ron Glover, a police officer for the city of Porter, came for a session after he was involved in a shooting incident the previous week. I have a long-standing contract with the Porter Police Department, with most of my work dealing with either pre-employment screening or stress counseling, ensuring that both the fresh-faced recruits and the tired-eye veterans of the Porter police don't have fantasies of leaving work one day and climbing the North Church tower with an assault rifle.

With Ron, I was to interview him and gain his reaction to what had happened the day of the shoot-out, to see how he was coping with those bloody few minutes, and then I was to give my recommendation as to when he could return to regular patrol duty. In the meantime, as the investigation into the shooting continued, he was taken off patrol and was placed on desk work, which meant sitting in the glass-enclosed lobby of the Porter police station and listening to complaints about parking tickets or conspiracy theories from the local drunks.

The week before our initial session, Ron had been the first officer to respond to a silent alarm at the Piscassic Savings and Loan near Trader's Square, a place in the center of town filled with gift shops, trendy coffee bars and restaurants with menus in Italian. In full view of scores of tourists and residents on a warm June day, Ron pulled his cruiser up about a half block away from the bank building, and then quickly got engaged in a gun battle.

Three armed and masked men, wearing body armor, came out of the Savings and Loan and started firing the moment they saw the parked Porter police cruiser. Ron returned fire, striking one of the gunmen in the head, killing him instantly. The other two fled in a stolen Toyota Camry, which was found abandoned in a parking garage six blocks over. The dead gunman was identified as one Charles McPhee of Charlestown, in the next state south, where robbing banks and armored cars has always been a neighborhood specialty. The other two gunmen remained unidentified, although the FBI claimed they were making progress in the case.

In my first session with Ron, he sat down on the couch across from me, hands defiantly placed on his legs. He had short brown-blond hair, a prominent nose, and his upper arms pressed tight against the fabric of his black polo shirt sleeves, hard muscles from long hours on the weight machines. He also had on blue jeans and black wrestler's sneakers. I have found that most patients' eyes tend to wander when they are talking to me, either looking at the framed prints of landscapes on the walls of my office, my certificates of education, or the ever-changing scenery of the busy harbor through the nearby windows.

But not Ron. He stared right at me and got to the point. "Any idea how long this will take?"

"Today?" I replied "Today it will take fifty minutes."

"Hah. Very funny. No, I mean, how long do I have to come to these meetings?"

I leaned back in my chair, hands folded loosely in my lap, trying to show a calm and relaxed demeanor. "However long it takes for me to come to a recommendation to your supervisors, that's how long. And a lot will depend on how well these sessions go."

He grunted and folded his arms and said, "Okay, let's get to it. Ask away."

"Fine," I said. "How are you doing?"

"I'm okay."

"Any changes in your diet?"

"Nope."

"Any changes in your sleeping habits?"

"Nope."

"Any feelings of guilt, of remorse, of shame?"

"Hardly."

"Nightmares, bad dreams, insomnia?"

"Nope, nope, nope."

I folded my hands. "Don't you think that's unusual?"

"What's unusual?" Ron said, still staring at me.

I shrugged, smiled a bit. "I mean, you did something last week that would cause trauma to most people. The taking of another man's life. Some people would find that very hard to handle, even though one was a police officer dealing with a bank robber."

It was his turn to shrug. "You know what it was like, Doc? It was like a training session back at the Academy. Except this time the bad guys weren't cardboard cutouts on a pulley system. They were real bad guys, armed to the teeth and wearing full body armor, almost head to toe, and when they spotted me, they opened fire first. They set the agenda, they put their own lives at risk, and I had nothing to do with that. It was their fault, not mine. And the guy I took down, he was a convicted armed robber, a suspect in a half-dozen other bank robberies and a couple of rapes, and I don't feel sorry that he's dead and gone and I'm still breathing. All right?"

"I hear you," I said.

"What about the notes," he said.

"Excuse me?"

"You're not taking any notes," he pointed out. "I thought all head docs had to take notes during chat sessions like this."

"Not this head doc," I said. "I make a few notes in my files after you leave, nothing too detailed, nothing too specific."

"And those notes go to my supervisor?"

"No, they stay here," I said. "The only thing your supervisor will get from me is the recommendation. Everything else is confidential. All my files remain locked in this office."

"Uh-huh," he said, like he agreed with what I was saying, but I could tell from his eyes that he didn't believe a thing.

"Look, it's Monday," I said. "Why don't we make another appointment for Wednesday. Is that all right with you?"

"Sure," he said. "Whatever it takes so I can get the hell off the desk. I need to get back on the street. Pretty soon I'll forget even which end of the police cruiser has the engine if I don't get back soon enough."

We spent another few minutes dealing with insurance and scheduling matters, and after he left, I did just as I said I would. I spent a few minutes with his file, writing up a few notes, and then I noticed something odd, something I tagged to be revisited the next time he came for a session. Then I spent the rest of the afternoon juggling paperwork and half-heartedly writing a guest column for the local newspaper on the importance of not stigmatizing the mentally ill.

When I was done for the day and I heard the five o'clock whistle from the shipyard, I conducted my usual, end-of-the-day routine. I gathered up all my notes, files, and papers, and put them into place, either in a desk drawer or in one of the wooden filing cabinets against the far wall. After setting those locks, I gathered the day's newspapers under one arm, went out into a hallway, and then carefully locked the three locks to my door. With each *snap-click* of the lock going home, I felt my breathing ease and my shoulders lighten. The feeling stayed with me when I got into my car and made the twenty minute drive home, to a condo on Tyler Beach.

I find the routine peaceful and reassuring, and I've never tried to examine it too closely, for I know I'm playing tricks with my own mind. What I do is to convince myself that in locking the door to my office, I'm leaving behind there all of the problems, nightmares, and obsessions that my patients have brought to me. By keeping everything locked away in my office, to be reexamined during the next day, this always guarantees a peaceful night at home, with no thoughts or dreams about what my patients have told me.

A silly ritual, I know. But it works.

It's worked for me for five years.

I hope it continues working for many more.

On Wednesday I started off by saying, "Tell me how everything happened last week."

Ron looked a bit defensive. "It's all there in my after-action report, and I know you got that paperwork."

"You're right, I do have it, but I just want to listen to it from your own perspective," I said. "Reading words on paper can be boring. I want to hear the real deal. I want to hear it from your own mind."

A shrug, and this time he did look out through one of the windows as an oil freighter eased its way into the harbor, shepherded by two tugs. "It was about ten A.M.," he said. "I was on Kendall Street, regular street patrol. Call came over from dispatch. Silent alarm triggered at the Piscassic Savings and Loan. I called in, saying I was just a couple of blocks away, and then I responded, just using lights. No sirens. I pulled up, about a half block away, and got out of the cruiser, and waited for backup. I was the first on the scene, and I wasn't going to do anything nutty or brave at that point. Right about then, the three bad guys came out the front door, carrying weapons and canvas sacks. They spotted the cruiser and opened fire. They had carbines, semiautomatics. Lucky for me they were in a hurry and most of the rounds went over my head. I returned fire and nailed one of the bad guys in the forehead. The other two hopped into a red Camry. I called it in that I was under fire, that I needed assistance, and backup started roaring in. I then went up and secured the scene. Made sure the bad guy was down for the count. That's it."

I nodded carefully. "Sounds just like your after-action report. And what happened after the scene was secured?"

He turned back from the window, a rueful smile. "Oh, all hell really broke loose then. Half of the backup that got there started looking for the bad guys in the Camry, while the other half blocked off the bank. State police came screaming in, and so did the FBI guys. In about ten minutes we had reporters and photographers everywhere, sticking their cameras and microphones in everybody's faces, plus tourists with their own cameras and camcorders. I didn't get home until two A.M. the next day."

"And what did you do when you got home?"

"Drank three beers and went to bed. Read for a while and then switched off the light."

"Sleep all right?"

Another shrug. "I guess I did."

"And the night after that?"

"Yep."

"So you've never had a bad night's sleep since then."

"Nope."

"Let's get back to the day of the robbery," I said, choosing my words carefully. "You were on Kendall Street, right?"

A nod. "That's right."

"Why?"

That question seemed to bother him. "What do you mean, why?"

I motioned to a stack of papers on my desk. "Among all the paperwork that the department sent over about you was the duty roster. Your patrol area that morning was in zone three. Zone three is the northeast, up by the malls and the business district. Kendall Street is zone one, downtown. Why were you out of your patrol area?"

His face looked defiant but I noticed that his hands were clasped tightly in his lap. "Had to run an errand. Some personal business."

"What kind of errand?"

"An errand, that's all," Ron said, raising his voice. "Look, what does this have to do with my state of mind, or whether I'm ready to get back to street work? You'd think you were from Internal Affairs. What's the big deal?"

I tried to keep a neutral look on my face. "I'm not sure. What is the big deal, Ron? What kind of errand were you doing?"

He muttered something and said, "Post office."

"Excuse me?"

"The post office. I had to get to the post office, mail some bills. I've been behind on some credit card payments and I wanted to mail them overnight, get those damn bill collectors off my back. That's all."

"Just a quick drive into the center of town, stop at the post office, and then back to patrol."

"You got it."

"Oh," I said, and then we talked for a while again about eating and sleeping habits. And through it all, his hands remained tightly together, as if he was afraid of what might happen if he wasn't holding them.

Before the next session, I did a more thorough read of Ron's personnel file, and I also made a few follow-up phone calls. I also took a long lunch and did some driving around Porter, just thinking and observing.

When Ron came in he said, "Are we making progress, Doc? I tell you, I'm getting sick of sitting on my butt for eight hours every day. I need to get back out on patrol, get some fresh air in my lungs."

I said carefully, "I do think we're further along than we were when we started. What's new? Any changes in your eating or sleeping habits?"

"Nope, not at all. Thing is, though, I've been staying up later because I'm not as tired when I get off shift. Out on patrol, you're moving, you're observing, you've got a half dozen things going on. Back at the station, it's just sit on your butt, do a little paperwork, listen to the radio hidden under the desk and give directions to tourists. Not much of a challenge, not at all. Can hardly wait for the day to end. Hell, I've become a real clock watcher."

We talked some about the department, about politics and who gained promotions because of who knew someone best, and then I said, "Tell me about your family."

"I'm single, you know that," Ron said.

"You're right, I do. But tell me about your family, growing up."

"Not much to say. Grew up in Porter. Dad worked in the shipyard. Mom was a beautician, worked out of the basement of our house."

"Brothers and sisters?"

"One older brother, Tom. A younger sister, Rachel."

"Did you get along with them?"

"As good as you could expect," he said. "Rachel was a typical little sister, always a pest. Tom was the typical older brother. Telling me to get out of the way, not to bother him, not to follow him if he left to hang out with his friends."

"And what are they doing now?"

"Humph," he said. "Last I knew, Rachel was living off the state with her two kids from two previous boyfriends, up in Dover."

"And your brother?"

"Don't know."

"At all?"

He glared at me, using that cop stare that they develop so well from stopping speeders, rousting drunks, and arresting drug dealers. "Why don't you tell me, Doc? Something tells me that you already know the answer to that one."

"I've looked at the files, that's all."

He crossed his arms, still glaring. "You're a stooge for Internal Affairs, aren't you?"

"No, I'm not," I said. "I'm just trying to determine what's going on. That's my job, and that's why you're here. And part of that determination is your family background, Ron. Your brother, Tom, he's been in trouble with the law ever since he was a juvenile, right?"

A nod, no reply. I went on. "Those records are sealed, but I did get some information about what he did after he turned eighteen. Some assaults. Burglaries. And one other interesting piece of information."

Ron kept his steady, deadly gaze at me. I said, "Your brother. He's also a suspect in a series of bank robberies last summer up in Maine. Correct?"

"You've been busy, Doc. Good for you. Anything else?"

"Oh, just something that raised a question or two. I went for a drive yesterday, up near the northern end of town. Between there and the post office near Trader's Square, there's a half dozen mailboxes someone could stop at. There's also two of those little postal centers, the kind of stores where you can drop off mail, packages, or buy stamps. Still telling me that you were on the way to the post office last week when that bank alarm came in?"

"Yep."

"Want to change anything else about your story?"

He glanced at his watch. "Says here I've been in this office for fifty minutes, Doc."

"We can go on for a little while longer."

A tight little smile as he stood up. "Sorry. The deal is I give you fifty minutes per session. Your time is up."

And he left the office, closing the door behind him, and two hours later, I left as well, again ensuring that everything was put in its place, all of the drawers shut and locks fastened.

During the next session, he quickly took the offensive after settling down in the office couch. "How do you do it, Doc?"

It was raining, the windows looking out to the harbor slightly obscured by the dripping water. "Excuse me?"

"How do you do it, day after day, listening to other people's problems," he said, one arm slung confidently over the rear of the couch. "Day after day about how my husband doesn't understand me, my wife doesn't understand me, my boss doesn't understand me, mom and dad never loved me, blah blah blah. How do you put up with it?"

Locks, a part of me whispered. Strong locks. "Oh, I get by, but let's talk about —"

He held up his hand. "Nope. C'mon, Doc, fair is fair. How come you get to ask all the questions? Scared of something?"

"No, not particularly," I said, not liking my answer. "What do you want to know?"

"Hah, that's a good one, a head doc inviting questions from a patient. Okay, why do you do what you do?"

In my mind I ran through a couple of replies, and said, "I've always had a feeling, even when I was younger, that I would become a doctor. But when I got older, I quickly learned that I couldn't stand the sight of blood, and then I took some psychology courses in college, and I was hooked on dealing with the challenges of the mind, the challenges of working with people who have such problems. I guess I turned out doing the same thing you do."

"And what's that?"

"Helping people," I said. "That's what we do in our jobs."

He laughed out loud and said, "Doc, for a guy who works with cops all the time, you've really got your head up your butt. What makes you think I became a cop to help people?"

Another person might have been insulted, but I was pleased. I had gotten him talking again. "Go on. What do you think police work is?"

He shifted in the couch, leaned forward, eyes staring right at me again. "Know what we are? We're glorified garbage collectors, that's all. We have better uniforms and weapons at our side, and better vehicles, and the garbage we deal with has two legs, but that's all we do. People in this city, they don't care about the homeless, they don't care about kids on the streets at two A.M. drunk out of their minds, they don't care about the people in the housing projects selling crack to each other. All they care about is that it's all out of sight, out of mind, and that we do our job, sweeping up the debris and dumping it somewhere. That's it."

"Why did you become a cop, then?"

"Excuse me?"

I made a slight motion with my hand. "Look at what you just said. Nothing I've not heard before from your fellow officers, but you obviously didn't become a cop thinking you were becoming a garbage collector. What drove you?"

"Let me ask you something," he said. "You an only child?"

"No, I'm not, but really, we should be —"

"C'mon, Doc. Let me have some fun here. Let's just say I'm curious. You got brothers and sisters?"

"No sisters," I said, not liking where this was going. "One brother."

That seemed to improve his mood. "Ah, a brother. Older or younger."

"Older."

"Ah, just like me. Did you get along all the time?" he asked, a mocking tone in his voice. "Did the young doc-to-be always have fun with his older brother? Did he always let his older brother borrow his toys, rat him out to his parents, and pour glasses of water in his bedding before bedtime? Did he?"

I cleared my throat. "He and I did all right," I said. "We had the spats here and there, but that's normal for growing up. Nothing out of the ordinary there. He had his interests and I had mine."

"What's his name?"

"Greg."

"And what's Greg doing now?"

"Greg's dead," I said. "He died when he was seventeen, about a month before he graduated from high school. He was in a car accident. I was twelve at the time."

"Oh," he said, slightly deflated, and I could tell that I had him back, so I pressed forth. "Let's get back to the topic at hand, shall we? Tell me again why you decided to become a police officer. Was it something you always wanted to do, or was it something you were compelled to do?"

He sat back in the couch, folded his arms, now silent.

I said, "Something to do with your older brother?"

No reply.

"You said earlier that you two didn't get along that well. Did you resent him? Did you dislike the fact that he was involved in criminal activities?"

No reply.

"Is that why you became a cop? To somehow get back at your older brother?"

A low voice. "You sure do ask a lot of questions."

"That's my job." And then, I knew I was making a major leap, something my professors and instructors would have been horrified at, but I tossed something out anyway. "The day of the robbery. You knew it was going to happen, didn't you. Maybe you got a postcard, maybe you got a note from your brother or a phone call. Telling you to stay away from downtown, telling you to stay out of harm's way. Is that it? Is that what happened? And you went there, intent on arresting him, intent on getting back at him?"

Ron stood up, his face mottled. "That's it. Time's up."

I checked my watch. "We've got fifteen minutes."

"Your watch must be slow." And he slammed the door on the way out, so hard that the pictures and certificates on the wall vibrated.

But still, later, all of the locks worked at the end of the day, and I managed to keep him out of my mind, all the way home.

And yet I couldn't help thinking about my brother Greg, no matter how hard I tried.

The next to the last time I saw Ron, he refused to talk about his brother, his family, or that day in Trader's Square when he shot dead a bank robber who was doing his best to kill him. Instead, we talked about the Red Sox, about the weather, about the challenges of dating when you're a cop — "I know it's a cliché, Doc, but it's true," he said. "Women love the uniform, love hanging around me when I'm on duty, but I'm invisible when I'm in civilian clothes" — and then there was a period of silence, about two minutes worth, before he spoke up.

"I'm getting tired of this," he said. "How about you?"

"Just part of the job," I said.

"Well, I'm tired of the damn desk duty, and I want back on the street. When are you going to make your recommendation?"

"Not for a while."

"Why the delay?"

I gazed steadily at him. "Because, Ron, I don't think you've been entirely truthful with me. And unless I know what happened that day and why, I won't be in a position to make a reasonable decision on whether you can go back to regular duty."

He sighed. "You want to know the truth?"

"I do."

"All right," Ron said. "It's all there."

"Where?"

He pointed to my desk as he stood up. "Right there, in my service record and the after-action report. Everything you need to know is in those papers. And another thing."

"What's that?"

"I'm sorry I gave you a hard time about your brother, the other day," he said. "It must have been hard, being twelve and losing your older brother like that."

"You're right," I said, keeping my voice even. "It was quite difficult."

Then, as he headed for the door I called out, "What am I looking for in your record?"

He turned back, grinning. "You're a smart doc, you'll figure it out."

So I tried, and luckily most of my afternoon was free, as I read and reread every scrap of paper contained in the official personnel file of one Officer Ron Glover. There was the initial application, the results of his written and oral exams, the three commendations he received for participating in some undercover work and the one letter of discipline for coming late to work one month on three different occasions. There was his yearly range qualification report and a series of certificates for completing certain police-related training, such as the use of a new nightstick and a high-speed pursuit class. There was also a letter of application to join the SWAT unit (denied because the unit was already fully-staffed) and a letter of application to joining the bicycle unit (accepted), and clipped to the acceptance letter was a photo of Ron standing next to a mountain bike, wearing a helmet, shorts and a PPD T-shirt.

I also read and reread the dry words of the after-action report, noting the robber who was shot once in the head, and the other two who got away. And when I was done, my head throbbed with exertion, and I felt like a fool for not seeing what must have been there.

During our last session, Ron was subdued. He

came in without the usual swagger and sat down on the couch and said, "It's over."

"I'm sorry, I don't understand what you're saying."

He looked up at me, his face bleak. "You haven't made any reports to Internal Affairs, have you? Or my sergeant?"

"No, I haven't," I said. "Everything we've said here has been confidential."

"For a while, right?"

"Well, until I make —"

"Look, Doc, I'm not that stupid. I know that there's no real doctor-patient confidentiality going on here. You're paid by the city and the department, and they're your real client. And whatever you've found out in these little sessions, well, I knew that eventually it was going to get back to my sergeant and the chief. But now I don't have to wait. It's over."

"They know about your brother?"

A nod. "That they do. A sister of the guy I shot, she came forward down in Boston. She doesn't want to suffer by herself. She wants the other two guys and their families to suffer as well, and she gave up the two names to the FBI. One of the two names is my brother. I have an interview this afternoon with Internal Affairs. The police union is sending a lawyer to go along with me . . . but, well, I know it's not going to go well. Probably by this weekend I'll be out of a job and scanning the want ads. Maybe I'll become a mall cop or something."

He got up from the couch. "Doc, like they said, it's been real, and it's been fun, but it ain't been real fun. Go ahead and make any kind of damn report you want. It's not going to make any difference at all."

As he started for the door I called out, "Ron, wait a moment!"

He turned, no longer the confident cop. Now he just looked like a tired man who was seeing a lot of the structure in his life begin to collapse, like old and decayed wood facing a terrible windstorm.

"What do you want? More insurance forms to fill out?"

"No," I said, a hand placed on top of his personnel file. "Your records. You said that if I looked closely at the records, I'd find out what really happened at Trader's Square during the bank robbery."

"And did you?"

My face was flush with embarrassment. "No, I didn't. I read everything at least three times. Nothing stood out."

"So why should I tell you?"

I struggled for something to say, and finally said, "I'd appreciate it. And I'd . . . well, in my final report to the department, I'll do the best I can."

"Trying to bribe me?" he asked, his voice now sharp.

"No, just trying to set you at ease."

He muttered something and came over, taking

the thick file folder and flipping through the pages. "Civilians . . . sometimes I wonder how you folks have enough sense to dress yourself in the morning. Here. It's right here."

Ron passed over a sheet of stapled papers, which I looked at, and then I looked up at him. "I'm sorry, I still don't understand. How does your range record have anything to do with what happened at the bank?"

He shook his head. "Man, it is true. The more educated you get, the dumber you get. Look at my yearly range scores, will you? Minimum passing score is an 80. Best score I ever got was an 82. Believe it or not, Doc, not all of us cops are Rambos. Compared to the rest of the department, I'm a lousy shot."

"And that means . . ."

He headed back to the door. "Figure it out, Doc. I barely get a passing score when I'm calm and cool and collected at the firing range, with nobody shooting back. Now, I'm in Trader's Square. There's civilians everywhere, diving for cover. Everyone's looking at me, everyone's depending on me, everyone's looking to see what the nice police officer is going to do, as those bad guys come out and start firing at me. And they're not using handguns or pistols. Nope, they're using semi-auto stuff that can punch a hole through a car engine. I start firing back, knowing who's there with the robbers, and in the middle of that, you know what I'm feeling? You know what's going on through my mind?"

My voice sounded weak. “No. Please tell me.”

Ron’s hand was on the door. “I was angry. I was angry at my brother, angry that he put me in danger, angry that he really thought I’d stay away that day. He always beat me, day after day, and this day, you’re right, I was going to get even. But I wasn’t going to arrest him.”

“You . . . you were trying to shoot your own brother?”

He opened the door. “No, you damn fool, I wasn’t trying to shoot my own brother. I was trying to kill him. And I’m such a lousy shot that I missed and hit somebody else. And I don’t feel bad at all. I just feel bad that I missed, and once again, my big older brother got the best of me.”

With that, he strode out the door and slammed it behind him.

Later that night, my mind was still racing through what had just gone on in my office. I left the office with my papers and my briefcase, and almost in a daze, walked out to my car. I sat inside the cool interior of the Volvo and yet I could not start the car. Could not do a damn thing except rest my head against the steering wheel.

I tried to think of what it must have been like, to be in the middle of the open like that in Trader’s Square during a bank robbery, knowing that the bad guys are there to kill you, that they are shooting right at you, that you are related to one of those bad guys, and that you shoot back, trying to kill the familiar man there, your brother, your relation, your flesh and blood. The man whose life you've shared, growing up and going to school and spending time together, this man, who should be one of your best friends and acquaintances, this man, you try to kill.

I try to think of what it must have been like, back then, as Officer Ron Glover. I try to do the best I can, as his doctor.

But I can't do that.

All I can think about is when I'm twelve, and my older brother, the golden boy, Greg. Straight A's in high school, star football player, someone who can do nothing wrong in the adoring eyes of my parents. Greg, my older brother, my role model.

Greg, my tormentor. Short-sheeting my bed. Tearing out pages from my favorite paperback books. Wrestling with me in the backyard and nearly choking me into unconsciousness. Breaking my plastic models of rocket-ships and airplanes.

Greg, my tormentor. One day he was furious at me for some little slight, and I was upstairs in our bedroom, the door locked, the door firmly locked, and I thought I would be safe until my parents came home from shopping. But Greg wouldn't let a locked door keep me safe, so he kicked it down and slapped and punched me, and later, my parents believed his story of falling accidentally into the door and breaking it.

Greg, my tormentor. Who said if I ever told my parents what he did, that he would come back a night later and make it ten times worse. And I lived in trembling fear, second to second, minute to minute, day by day, until that night, that glorious night, when he misjudged a curve coming home from a high school dance and wrapped the family Ford around a tree. For a long week he hung alive in a hospital bed, wires and tubes and monitors coming out of him, and I stood there next to my praying and grieving parents, praying as well, except I was beseeching God to take this tormentor away from me.

Which He did.

And the night of his funeral, I laid in bed, exulting at the empty and quiet and peaceful room that was all mine.

I raised my head from the steering wheel, and started my car.

And I was half-way home, still thinking of Officer Glover and his brother Tom and my own brother Greg, when I remembered that I hadn't locked a damn thing when I left the office.

And I realized it made no difference at all. No lock would ever again be strong enough to do the job.

Brendan DuBois' home is the New England countryside, and few writers know the ins and outs of their chosen backdrop so well. More of his short fiction appears in *Once Upon a Crime* and *Ellery Queen's Mystery Magazine*. His short story "The Dark Snow" was nominated for the 1996 Edgar award.

Four Views of Justice

Jon L. Breen

I. The Defendant

"I did shoot him, Mr. Alvarez," I said. "It was my gun, and I pulled the trigger."

My lawyer, a born poker player, showed no surprise. He just looked at me across the jail conference-room table for a moment with his kind, probing brown eyes. He was a small man, shorter than I am, very trim and athletic looking, impeccably dressed in a three-piece pinstripe suit. Luis Alvarez was well known locally as a specialist in high-profile lost causes, and mine certainly qualified.

"It's important to be honest with your lawyer, Ms. Cordell," he said at last.

"Call me Melissa, please."

"Though given the circumstances, it would be very hard to deny you shot him. But that doesn't mean you murdered him. Tell me what happened."

I drew a deep breath and told my story. "Getting a job with Stephen Ramsay seemed like a dream come true to me. I'd always been interested in architecture, you see, though I had no talent in that line myself. Becoming a great architect's office manager seemed to be the next best thing. I enjoyed my work and was good at it. And for a while, I enjoyed working with Stephen

Ramsay. He called me his 'girl Friday,' which I know seems an incredibly patronizing term today, but it didn't even bother me because I knew he relied on me, that I was valuable to him. When I'd been working there for about six months, things suddenly changed."

My voice broke slightly. I swallowed a few times and reached for a drink of water. Luis Alvarez waited for me to continue.

"Stephen Ramsay arranged more and more occasions when we'd be alone in the office together after hours. More and more frequently he'd find pretexts to call me to his home to work. It was so subtle at first; little comments that may have had a double meaning, seemingly accidental brushes. I fended his advances off, jokingly at first, then more firmly. I had no interest whatsoever in Stephen Ramsay on a personal basis, but it was important to me to continue to work with him professionally. I was making contacts that could benefit me later, and I really loved the work. I realize now I was the victim of systematic, long term sexual harassment. Finally he threatened me with the loss of my job if I didn't give in to his demands.

"It took me a long time, but I finally decided things couldn't go on this way. Stephen Ramsay's behavior was becoming more than annoying; it was becoming terrifying. And he announced his engagement. I wondered if his fiancée knew the kind of man she was going to marry. I think I had it in my mind that the threat of telling her the truth about him gave me some kind of leverage in stopping his harassment. When he called me to his office late that night, I went there to tell him once and for all that further advances and threats would not be tolerated."

"If you were afraid of him," Luis Alvarez asked, "why did you go to his office after hours when no one else would be around?"

"I wanted to confront him privately. It wouldn't help to have anyone else aware of the situation. I still thought I could salvage things somehow."

"You carried a gun."

"I always carry my gun to defend myself if necessary."

"And it became necessary, didn't it?" he said, a little sarcastically I thought.

"Don't you believe me?" I asked sharply. Tears came to my eyes.

"Please go on."

"The discussion didn't go as I hoped. I wanted to reason with Stephen. He became enraged. He came around the desk and charged me like a maniac; I felt threatened with being hit or raped or even killed. He was a powerful man. As he came toward me, I grabbed the gun out of my bag and pulled the trigger almost before I knew what I was doing."

I was sobbing now. When I composed myself, I looked up at my lawyer, who was nodding his head slowly.

"There are some details to work out," he said carefully, "but we have a defense."

II. The Juror

For many reasons I long felt confident I would never be chosen to be a juror. For one thing, I am intelligent and historically that alone has been enough to render one undesirable to manipulative advocates who prefer to make their arguments to the gullible and ignorant. To make my prospects even more unlikely, I hold a graduate degree from a major university. Another nail in my coffin of perfunctory dismissal is that I know a great deal of law for a layman and count a fair number of lawyers among my acquaintances.

Gordon Watts is my name, and I owe my legal knowledge to my occupation. I am a community college librarian, in which capacity I do a considerable amount of legal reference work and teach a course in legal research for our college's paralegal program.

My reaction to the juror summons was, as usual, irritable resignation. While I generally welcome a chance to do my civic duty, the result of the summons had always been the same: a few days of wasted time, sitting around that close, rundown jury assembly room through endless mornings and afternoons; trying to concentrate on my reading and ignore those around me; doing my best to tune out the unwelcome blare of morning television that assaulted my ears;

rarely even seeing the inside of a courtroom, and then only long enough for my unsuitability (call it stupidity deprivation) to be discovered.

I ought to have known this time might be different. Recent attacks on the jury system, the result of a series of clearly wrongheaded criminal verdicts and outrageously inflated civil awards, had led to nation-wide calls for reform, and part of that reform had been to widen the usual juror pool of misfits and retirees. Jury summonses at my college were epidemic as flu, and in contrast to past years my faculty colleagues were actually being chosen to serve, bringing back sometimes entertaining and usually boring stories of court and jury room dramatics. In my city, even the District Attorney himself, attended by much cunningly managed media coverage, had served on a jury recently. Obviously not in a criminal case, where he would have a conflict of interest, but in a personal injury suit, both sides of which loudly proclaimed him acceptable and unbiased.

Thus, there I sat that Monday morning, armed with the newspaper and backup reading matter, in the vast, overly warm, and generally dreary jury assembly room. To prove I was taking my obligation of citizenship seriously, I was dressed as I do for work, in dark suit, white shirt, conservative tie. Few of my fellow panelists lent dignity to the occasion in their choice of dress, but that didn't surprise me. Even at the college, an outpost of civilization and decorum one would think, there are no more than three of us on the faculty (outside of the administrative types, clearly a breed apart) who still dress like professionals, and the other two are decades older than my 35 years. The real mark of a gentleman, I always believe, is to uphold standards even when they are no longer standards.

Seated next to my aisle chair was a loud, potbellied salesman type who had brought no diversion for himself and repeatedly tried to make such of me via unwelcome conversation. I discouraged his attempts short, I trust, of outright rudeness. Two chairs down was a young woman I would certainly have laid aside my paper to engage in conversation, but there was little opportunity with the salesman seated between us. She appeared to be in her middle twenties, about the age of some of my students, but she knew better than they how to present herself: dignified, businesslike, no apparent tattoos or pierced body parts, but plenty of well-molded leg showing. She was reading a bestselling novel from that half of the bestseller list occupied by writers who can write. She may have had a brain in her beautiful head, another feature that would contrast her with most of my students. If I'd been the salesman, I'd have been expending my very limited charms on her rather than on me, but he probably sensed he would get nowhere. If he ever got up to relieve himself, which he would have to do eventually with the prodigious amount of coffee he'd been drinking, I would have my chance.

But before we could learn the strength of my seatmate's bladder, the jury gods intervened in the form of a flat voice on the public address system.

"Your attention please. Will all members of panel number six please proceed to Courtroom 41, Judge Kammerman presiding? That's on the fourth floor. Please be sure to wear your juror badges."

As I rose to my feet, I was pleased to see the young woman two seats down was also standing.

"Panel six?" I inquired.

She nodded, and with a courtly gesture, I invited her to precede me into the aisle. I was rewarded with a subdued but genuine smile. She was about five-nine, nearly my own height, in low-heeled shoes. Enjoying her muscular calves, shoulder length black hair, and everything in between, I followed her to the front of the jury room, coming abreast when we were out the door and on our way down the corridor to the elevator. By the time we had made our way through the labyrinthine hallways of the fourth floor to Courtroom 41, I had learned her name was Judy Conover, that she was already assistant manager of the jewelry store where she worked; that she hoped to go back to school for a degree in psychology; and that she hoped we would not be on a case that was drug-related. I heartily agreed.

In the front rows of the courtroom, nearly as drab, I must say, as the juror assembly room, I took a seat by Judy's side and gave my fantasies free rein. Selected on the same jury; sequestered in a city hotel; discussions of life and justice; subtle glances; midnight wanders down the hallway; conquest; bliss; wistful separation; exchange of phone numbers. That would be as far as it went, though; her number would never be called. At heart, I'm an incorrigible loner, and the next step would be to find another connection. Maybe in my legal research class, though establishing a meaningful relationship with a student was growing riskier as the years went by.

My wandering mind was a hard thing to control, especially when wandering on such paths, but it was time to concentrate on the present. If we didn't both get empaneled on this jury, I wouldn't have a chance to continue our relationship at all. As it happened, we had stumbled into a rather major *cause celebre,* the veritable juror jackpot if your employer and/or the state of your finances enabled you to stay away from work for a few weeks.

The case to be tried was first-degree murder. The defendant was Melissa Cordell, an unprepossessing woman in her thirties, pale-skinned, somewhat overweight, indeed looking like an elephantine ballerina in an ill-chosen frilly pink dress. She was accused of shooting to death locally prominent architect Stephen Ramsay, for whom she had worked several years as an office manager. Newspaper accounts — I had read them assiduously but if asked would say I hadn't

— said he had summoned her late one night to the office where they worked. That she had shot him with a small pistol registered in her name and carried in her handbag for protection, was undisputed. However, stories then, as they will, diverged.

She charged a pattern of sexual harassment. The prosecution, of course, disagreed. They would claim all the frustrated sexual energy had been on Melissa Cordell's side, that she had shot her boss in cold blood because he had spurned her, recently announcing his engagement to a wealthy (and, I might add, much more attractive) society debutante.

Through my reading, I must confess the prosecution theory sounded much more likely: if Melissa had reason to fear Ramsay, why would she even have come to the office that late at night? It was far more likely she would want to see him without other people around if the murder were premeditated. As for this trendy preoccupation with sexual harassment, to me that had all the credibility of the Twinky defense. If I were a successful architect, I could certainly fill an office with more appealing distractions than Melissa Cordell could provide. Probably he had hired her because she was an efficient office manager but didn't reckon with the mental unbalance that eventually would lead to his death.

Don't take me for a misogynist or a male chauvinist because of my politically incorrect view of the case. I'm all for young women achieving whatever career goals they have — why else would I devote so much energy pounding legal research techniques into the thick, if often lovely, heads of paralegal students? All my students, of course, but if anything I have redoubled my efforts for my female students.

Yes, I admit the case before us was fairly clear to me: the poor dead employer was the victim of an unbalanced person and now, no longer around to defend himself, was having his good name blackened in his turn. But that doesn't mean I'd prejudged the case. Not at all. I could approach it with an open mind. I could be swayed by reasoned argument to change my view.

I may seem to be getting ahead of my story in recounting all these specifics, but quite a bit of the circumstances of a case are at least hinted at during jury selection procedures. Some of the issues, the most potentially sensitive ones, need to be tipped off in order to detect any hidden biases, in this case those in the area of attitudes toward male-female relationships. The defense wanted a jury that was sensitive to issues of sexual harassment — indeed, they wanted more than sensitive; they wanted pushovers. We could expect questions about Clarence Thomas and Anita Hill.

If asked, I knew just what to say to prove my sensitivity — certainly, I've been to enough compulsory academic training sessions on the topic, as what college faculty member has not? You use the word *power* a lot, distastefully, as if it were one of the ugliest words in the English language. Nothing in the world, from mild flirting to out-and-out rape, is about sex. Everything is about power.

That I know the lingo and could deploy it in my own interest is not meant to imply I was somehow lying about my true views. I would be totally sympathetic to any woman, any person, who became the victim of genuine sexual harassment — I simply believe that the incidence of such activities has been grossly exaggerated by the media.

Following a round of questions directed to the whole jury panel, mainly establishing that none of us were personally acquainted with the judge, the opposing advocates, the defendant, or the victim, Judge Kammerman instructed the court clerk to begin calling names of panelists. I was heartened that Judy Conover and I were among the first twelve called to occupy places in the jury box. We were separated again, alas — I was juror number two and she number nine — but that would only be temporary. Surely if we both managed to make the cut, so to speak, I would have the opportunity to extend our relationship to its desirable end.

First the judge asked us a few questions about our experience with the criminal justice system: were we related to or acquainted with any police officers, prosecutors, other officers of the court? Had we ever been victims of a crime? Had we ever been victims of sexual harassment? Three of our number fell by the wayside in this part of the questioning, and three more were called to replace them, with the same questions repeated for the new occupants of the box.

Then we were individually turned over to the opposing lawyers, who did their best to probe our prejudices. I believe I performed well, convincing both advocates of my dedication to even-handed justice come what may. In the old days, of course, my degree of articulation and education would have doomed me to dismissal, but neither side wanted to be seen to denigrate the intelligent juror, especially in light of the D.A.'s recent sporting gesture, and I was deemed acceptable. Now I held my breath to see if the lovely Judy would join me for this several-weeks voyage on the high waves of good citizenship. If not, I would just as soon return to the classroom and the reference desk.

But Judy, to make a long story short, also made the grade, and a day later when the jury of six men and six women was finalized, she and I were among four of the original dozen sworn in to consider the People v. Melissa Cordell. Four alternates, also evenly divided as to gender, joined us. Much as I would like to have been sequestered on the spot, putting a jury away for the duration of the trial has fallen from favor since the O. J. Simpson case, so home we went. I might have tried to see Judy outside of the courthouse, but I guess it's my essential laziness that prevented it. I like to make my conquests in economical surroundings, and I could wait for those hotel corridors, which surely would be our hunting ground come deliberation time. So I went home to my usual bachelor pursuits, stopping at the video store on the way to pick up some relaxing adult films.

The next morning the trial proper began with the opening statements of the opposing advocates. It was a nice touch that the prosecutor was a woman: a big, solid, serious middle-aged amazon with the powerful delivery of an operatic diva but, alas, none of the feminine appeal of Marcia Clark. In a no-nonsense way, she invited us to reject the cries of wounded sisterhood and see a pure and simple murder for what it was. She was admirably brief and well-organized and I generally agreed with her position, though I knew, as defense counsel was bound to point out, no murder was quite that pure or quite that simple.

I had been looking forward to seeing Melissa Cordell's attorney, the famous Luis Alvarez, in action. But when the compact and nattily-attired advocate took to the podium for his opening statement, I confess I was too distracted to give close attention. Just before Alvarez had begun speaking, a blonde young woman in a very short blue skirt had come through the gates into the counsel area and leaned over the table to confer with him. She was extremely attractive and would excite the eye of any straight male she came in contact with — in fairness, some gay males, too — but I am not some love-starved juvenile who cannot put gaudy distractions aside and attend to business. In the library and classroom, rich as they are in beautiful women, I must do that every day. What momentarily took me out of the proceedings was that I recognized her.

I couldn't call her name immediately to mind. What I first remembered was where she sat in the classroom. And I remembered how she dressed, much differently from today, especially favoring torn jeans, that sexiest of student uniforms. I also remembered that she had been a distinctly unpromising paralegal student, one I would have pronounced unemployable in any law office — and yet here she seemed to be assisting one of the foremost criminal advocates in the state. Cynically, it occurred to me he might be employing her for other purposes than her paraprofessional talents, but if so, surely he would not have her running in and out of the courtroom with anything more important than sandwiches.

All of this flew through my mind in a matter of seconds. In those same seconds, our gazes met for a moment. I remembered her name, Holly McIntosh, and it was clear from her wide-eyed look of recognition that she had spotted her old professor.

III. The Paralegal

When I saw Mr. Watts, it was like being back in

school in more ways than one.

His class was worth one shitty unit, but you had to take it. He'd made some kind of a sweetheart deal with the director of the paralegal program to require their legal research class, and none of the other librarians wanted to teach it — or if they did, he knew how to prevent them from doing it. He was a dry lecturer who gave trickily unfair multiple-choice and true-false tests; he didn't know half as much law as he thought he did; he resisted fast and efficient online legal reference sources in favor of making us find statute and case law in dusty old books; and he believed the difference between the official and unofficial state case reports was of maximum importance — it is important, I guess, but not as important as he made it out.

Since I took his class, I've learned to talk. Then I was all, like, y'know, Valley Girl. But I could always write pretty well. My other paralegal teachers, practicing lawyers, praised my case briefs and legal memoranda and encouraged me to stick with the program, but old Mr. Watts made me feel like an imbecile. I pulled a C in his class and counted myself lucky to get that.

He was staring at me. Surprised to see I was working for a famous lawyer, I guess. But that wasn't the main thing seeing Mr. Watts brought to mind. I turned around and walked up the aisle out of the courtroom. I could feel his eyes following me. You always could.

That evening, I knew Mr. Alvarez — Luis, he

says to call him, but it's hard to get used to — would be behind his desk at the office preparing for the next day in court. He looked a little startled to see me walk in at seven P.M. Maybe it reminded him of the case he was trying and he thought I had a little gun in my purse — but he needn't have worried. Luis Alvarez was nothing but a perfect gentleman.

"Holly, why are you — ?"

"Mr. — uh, Luis, I have to talk to you. About one of the jurors."

He motioned me to sit down. "One of the jurors. Do you know one of them?"

"Juror number two. Gordon Watts."

"Oh, yeah, the librarian."

"What did you think of him?"

His eyes narrowed a little at that. It probably seemed strange that his paralegal was quizzing him about a juror, but I had my reasons, and he went along with me.

"He seems okay. A little cold and analytical maybe, but he certainly seems to understand women's issues." Luis grinned suddenly. "Why are you looking like that?"

"Like what?"

"Never play poker. Come on, Holly, what's the problem?"

"I don't think he's the best defense juror for this case," I said.

"What are you getting at?"

"Look, he was my teacher, okay? I sat in his class for a semester, and he was one of those guys who never look without staring. Whatever you're wearing, they make you feel naked. It's the way I imagine Stephen Ramsay looked at Melissa Cordell."

"It takes more than a look, Holly. Maybe it was deceptive. Maybe he had bad contact lenses or —"

"There was more than a look. I wasn't doing well in his class, A's and B's everywhere else, C's and D's with old Mr. Watts. So I went to see him in the library one day when he was at the reference desk, plenty of people around, and I asked him what I could do to improve in his class. He said I'd need to come see him in his office. I didn't want to go to his office. I wanted to talk to him with plenty of other people around."

"Still, it's a reasonable request, teacher to student," Luis said.

"Sure, sure it was. Up to that point, he hadn't done anything overtly offensive, and I could even kid myself my imagination was just over-active. I knew he gave a lot of the other girls the creeps, but I hadn't heard he'd actually done anything — I mean, you just don't expect that of teachers, do you? At least I didn't. Not then."

"So what happened?"

"I went to his office later that day. We looked over my most recent test. He sat too close to me, I thought, but it still could just be my imagination. Then he told me that I wasn't getting the key points, things he repeated over and over. He said I'd be lucky to pass the course at all. And

I'm like, 'What can I do?' and he's all 'I want to help you' and he invites me to see him after hours for some extra drilling. Work hard enough and I can get an A, he says. And all of a sudden he's got his hand on my thigh and I'm like 'HELLO!' "

I could feel the red in my face now, and Luis was looking at me, somehow sympathetic, concerned, and trying not to laugh all at the same time. I grinned at him to show I was okay.

"I'm, like, reverting, aren't I?" I said. "Reliving my student vocabulary. Don't worry. I'm not going to have hysterics in your office."

"I want to know what you did in Watts's office."

"What do you think I did? Screwed him on his desktop and got an A in the class?"

"I don't think so."

"Well, you're right. I pushed his arm away, got out of that office, never saw him again one-on-one, and got a C in the class. You must be a good judge of character knowing what I'd do."

Luis shook his head. "Nope. I remember that C on your transcript, like a sore thumb with all those A's. But what happened to Watts? Did you report him?"

I shook my head a little sadly. "I probably should have, but it was embarrassing, and it seemed like a lot of trouble, and it was just a one-unit course . . ." I trailed off.

"You mean if it had been a three-unit course you'd have filed a complaint?"

"If it'd been a three-unit course, I'd have screwed him on the desktop," I said.

It may sound callous, but Luis Alvarez and I have a similarly warped sense of humor. When we were through laughing, I asked him what we should do about Watts's presence on the jury.

Luis shrugged. "Not much we can do. He's on there now. If I'd known about this during jury selection, I could have used a preemptory. I guess I should always have a paralegal sit in on jury selection from now on."

I sighed heavily. "There has to be something I can do."

IV. The Lawyer

Holly's pretty face was a map of frustration. I could understand her desire to do something about Watts, but I knew it would be a mistake for her to try.

"I could go see him at the college," she mused, "threaten to tell what had happened if he didn't voluntarily get off the jury."

"Forget it!" I said, as harshly as I could manage. "You're called a paralegal, not an *extra*-legal. You try to tamper with a juror and you get in trouble, plus you get *me* in bigger trouble. Anyway it would be your word against his. He's an arrogant character. He'd probably call your bluff."

She looked crestfallen, but I figured appealing to her loyalty to me might do the trick.

"Holly, there's plenty else at the office for you to work on. I want you to have nothing more to do with this case. Remember it was Perry Mason who skated on the thin ice, not Della Street."

That got a smile out of her anyway. "Are you sure? Look again. Della cut some fancy figures of her own." Then she scowled. "But I'm not Della. I'm just a paralegal."

"Don't put down paralegals. You'll find them of immense help when you're practicing law yourself."

Her smirk was half proud and half sardonic. "That'll be the day."

When she left the office, I hoped I had dissuaded her from doing anything silly. I thought I had. She was smart enough not to endanger her own future, and I thought she was loyal enough not to endanger me. I never asked her to come to court any more during the Cordell trial, and she never did.

Now she's in law school. I finally convinced her that was where she belonged. I think there may be a place for her in my office when she gets her degree and passes the bar, but I haven't promised her anything. And anyway, it's possible she'd prefer to prosecute.

But you probably want to know what happened with the Cordell trial and the juror, right? I'll hit the highlights.

During the first week of deliberations, while the jury was under sequestration, one of the female jurors accused one of the male jurors of unwelcome sexual advances. Judge Kammerman talked it out with the parties involved — we didn't even find out who they were, but obviously we had our suspicions. Both were allowed to stay on the panel, and deliberations continued.

Not entirely to my surprise, the jury didn't buy the sexual harassment argument. Melissa Cordell was convicted of first-degree murder. We're appealing it, of course, but losing doesn't bother me too much. I did my job, did the best I could with what I had to work with, and it was the right verdict. From the first time we talked, I figured she was guilty. Not that people hire me to have an opinion on that topic.

Holly was unhappy with the verdict, telling me Watts's presence on the jury tainted it. I reminded her that six women, including one who had herself charged sexual harassment, had to have agreed with him. It's the system, I assured her sententiously — nothing's ever perfect, but justice is usually done.

V. Another Defendant

It was two years after my service on the Cordell jury that I had occasion to schedule an appointment with the celebrated Luis Alvarez. Though I hadn't voted his client's way in the trial, the job he had done with absolutely no case had impressed me tremendously. Now that I was myself the object of legal action, the defendant in an absurdly frivolous accusation of sexual improprieties by one of my students, I knew that he was the kind of advocate I wanted to present my case.

"This is not in my usual line, Mr. Watts," he said. "I specialize in major criminal work. Also, your best choice in defense of a claim of this kind, particularly if it goes to trial, would be a woman lawyer."

I had to agree, remembering that kind of, shall we say, casting against type had been helpful to the Cordell prosecution.

"I have a young female associate who has just passed the bar but is one of the most promising lawyers to join this firm in years. In fact, I believe she's a former student of yours. She often remarks on how you challenged her."

Of course, I found that gratifying.

Alvarez reached for the phone on his desk. "Shall I arrange a meeting with her?"

"Very well," I said. After all, what did I have to lose?

Jon L. Breen has written six mystery novels, most recently *Hot Air*; over seventy short stories; contributes review columns to *Ellery Queen's Mystery Magazine* and *The Armchair Detective*; was shortlisted for the Dagger awards for his novel *Touch of the Past*; and has won two Edgars, two Anthonys, a Macavity, and an American Mystery Award for his critical writings.

The Bad Boyz Klub

Doug Allyn

They drifted in by twos and threes, some carrying coffee cups from the vending machine in the hallway. The classroom's metal chairs were arranged in a semicircle facing the desk and they slouched into them in no particular order. It was only the second meeting for this group, too soon for cliques to form.

The men were a mixed lot, mid-twenties to late thirties, a couple of biker types in denim vests, autoworkers in coveralls or flannel shirts, a few professional men in sport coats and slacks. One man was in uniform: a rent-a-cop. A typical crew.

"Good evening, gentlemen. Welcome to the Domestic Violence Program, under the aegis of the 14th District Court, city of Flint. I'm Dr. Colleen Mackenzie, Assailants Counselor —"

"Doc, it's only been a week. We haven't forgotten your name. Not yet, anyway." Charlie Weeks. Car salesman, fortyish, tweed sport coat over a maroon turtleneck. He'd thrown his wife through a screen door into the street. At her interview she told me he was a devoted husband and father. Her medical records showed a long pattern of minor injuries typical of abuse.

"Actually we don't *all* know it, Mr. Weeks," I countered mildly. "We have a new member tonight, Mr. Florian Woytazek, the gentleman on the end." Woytazek nodded warily at the others. An autoworker, he was wearing dungarees, a brushcut, thick glasses, and an owlish look.

"Welcome to the Bad Boyz Klub, Flory," Jojo Lassiter said. "What's your beef? Goose your old lady in church?"

"We'll deal with specifics later, Mr. Lassiter," I said. "Everyone's specifics." Lassiter was a biker, compactly built with a dark, shaggy mane, a Fu Manchu moustache, jeans, leather vest. He seemed affable enough, but his girlfriend had gone underground, refusing to testify against him. A bad sign.

"Mr. Woytazek will be the last new member of this therapy group, we're at our limit, so from here on —"

"Actually, I think we're already short one, Doc. Vic Manetti won't be coming." The voice was one of the group's two blacks. Martin Cleveland, a TV cameraman for Channel 18, mid-twenties, shaved head, goatee, dressed like a college jock, Dockers, deck shoes, a teal Eddie Bauer sweater. He'd slapped his wife out of her chair in a Taco Bell. "Haven't you heard about Vic?"

"No. Has something come up with him?"

"You might say that," Cleveland said. "He got busted this afternoon. He, um, he murdered his old lady."

Dead silence. I had a quick flash of Linette Manetti, slender, girlish, dishwater blonde hair that hung to her waist. Retro-hippie paisley granny dress. Defiantly barefoot at her interview in my office, daring me to comment. I hadn't.

"He killed her?" Charlie Weeks echoed, straightening in his chair. "You mean that little blonde he showed us? What the hell happened?"

"The station caught the squeal off our police scanner," Cleveland said. "Neighbors reported a domestic dispute. The cop at the scene said the apartment was all smashed to hell, wouldn't let us film inside. They were bringing her body out when Vic showed. He tried some lame-ass alibi but they didn't buy it. He left in handcuffs. Story'll be on the eleven o'clock news, A-bag or maybe B. I got a nice goodbye shot of Vic through the prowl car window. He didn't look too happy."

"And so it goes," I said, hoping I looked less shaken than I felt. "Welcome to the wide world of domestic violence, guys. Let's get to work, beginning with the confidentiality pledge. Read it aloud with me please. *On my honor, whatever I see here, whatever we say here, stays here. I will discuss these sessions only with members of this group.*" Some of them mumbled the words at the top of their work sheets. Most didn't.

"The Bad Boyz Klub's now in session," Weeks added dryly. "Membership nine and shrinking fast."

I couldn't recall which joker named this particular therapy group the Bad Boyz Klub. Someone wisecracked about it in the first meeting and I found it scrawled on the slateboard after the coffee break, underlined, with a cartoon baseball bat for an exclamation point.

No problem. Domestic Violence Assailants Groups are edgy sessions. Anything that bonds the members to each other and hopefully to the therapeutic process is fine by me.

After Cleveland's bombshell, George Falkenburgh, a pudgy, earnest high school teacher related a domestic argument that didn't end in violence. He seemed proud of his new-found self-control. On the other hand, he'd been just as pleased when he'd described knocking his wife around at a family picnic. Family discipline, he'd called it. Right.

Still, it was better than silence. Sometimes in the first weeks domestic assailants are so resentful of court-ordered counseling that they scarcely talk. The Bad Boyz were surly and sarcastic, but at least some of them were talking.

And some weren't. Leroy Gant, a lanky, tousle-haired Tennessee import, hadn't said anything but his name so far. He might not. He'd stabbed his wife in a drunken quarrel and was facing prison time no matter what my counseling evaluation said.

The session fairly flew by, driven mostly by a discussion of Manetti's situation. Murder. An ugly word. I hoped someone would make a connection between Manetti's violence and their own, but I didn't point it out myself. Any chance for real change had to begin with them. So far, we were batting zero.

We closed the final hour with the pledge and they filed out. All but one.

Griswold, Oliver Daniel. He'd asked the group to call him Griz at the first meeting. No one argued. A six-foot, two-hundred-sixty pound biker, he'd trashed his ex-wife's car with a Louisville Slugger. There was no testimony he'd ever struck her, but one look at him was enough for the judge. Counseling or jail.

"Can I talk to you a minute, Doc?"

"A minute, but not much more," I cautioned. "What's up?"

"A simple question. Is that pledge we say for openers legal? I mean, are these meetin's really off the record? Or could some of this be used against us in court?"

"Anything you say here is protected by doctor-patient privilege unless it's an overt threat against someone. Why? Is there a problem?"

"I got no problem, Doc, but Vic Manetti does. He couldn't have killed his old lady this afternoon. He was with me all day."

I eyed him a moment. A joke? No, his body language said he was serious. "If that's true, shouldn't you talk to the police?"

"No way. Manetti's a dealer, you know? Coke, crack, weed, speed, whatever. He was pitchin' everybody in the john on the break at our first meeting. I happened to know some people who were lookin' to make a buy so I set up a meet. We were together all afternoon doin' a deal and a few lines of product. That's why he lied to the cops about where he was."

"But surely now that he's been arrested he'll explain."

"The cops won't believe him and the guys he did the deal with are serious people, outlaw Iron Hawgs, both of 'em. They aren't about to alibi Manetti even if he's crazy enough to rat 'em out. They'd waste him in a New York second and me with him."

"If you're not willing to help him, why are you telling me about this?"

"Because it's . . . wrong, that's all. Manetti ain't no choirboy but he didn't wax his wife. You're a Doc and Docs are supposed to fix things. Okay, how about fixin' this?"

"Without involving you, you mean?"

"Damn straight. It's tough about Vic but I ain't lookin' to get jammed up over it. Push comes to shove, Manetti's nothin' to me. You ain't either, for that matter."

"That almost sounds like a threat, Mr. Griswold."

"No, ma'am, I'm a little crazy but I ain't stupid. I never threaten ladies, especially not officers of the court." He rose, his beard split by a gap-toothed grin. He hesitated at the door. "You know, I got no beef with that affirmative action crap, but there's one big drawback to bein' a lady doctor."

"Such as?"

"You can't use the men's room and a lot of Bad Boyz Klub business goes down there. Last week,

Manetti wasn't only dealin' dope, he was tryin' to peddle his old lady's ass for two hundred a bang. Even showed pictures of her around. Beaver shots, you know? I think a couple guys mighta took him up on it. Manetti's scum and his old lady wasn't no better. You seem like a nice lady, passable lookin', educated and all. Why do you even bother about losers like them? I mean, what's the point?"

"I guess the point is that sometimes I can help. Sometimes things can get better."

"Even for trailer trash like Manetti?"

"Sometimes even for a guy like you, Mr. Griswold."

"You're gonna straighten me out, Doc?" He snorted. "You're a real dreamer, you know that?"

"Maybe I'm just an optimist. It comes with the territory. I'll, um, see what I can do about Manetti. See you next week?"

He stalked out without answering. In psychology there's a syndrome called the doorknob effect. A patient will often wait until his hand's on the doorknob to tell you what's really troubling him. Doorknob effect. Griz stayed to tell me about Manetti, but in the end he asked if there was any hope for Manetti. Or maybe for himself? Maybe, maybe not. As Freud said, sometimes a cigar is just a cigar.

"It's a scam, Colleen," Burris said, leaning back in his chair, lacing his fingers behind his head. "The guy's blowin' smoke at you tryin' to help out a buddy." Detective Gene Burris has thinning hair, stooped shoulders, and the gentlest brown eyes this side of a cocker spaniel. Deceptive eyes. His closure rate for homicide cases is one of the best on the force. And I'd stopped by his office to ask him to reopen one.

"I don't think he was lying," I said. "He had no reason to."

"People don't need reasons to lie, Doc. They do it to get over or because they're scared or just for the hell of it. Sometimes they lie when the truth would serve 'em better and you know it."

"Not this time," I said. "He had nothing to gain by telling me, and a lot to lose."

"He had nothing to lose. You're bound by doctor-patient confidentiality and he knows it."

"But he couldn't be sure I'd honor it. He took a chance."

"I'm telling you, Doc, we've got Manetti dead bang. He's got a history of violence toward his wife, he was stoked to the gills on crank and his alibi was a total crock."

"My . . . source said Manetti was doing drugs at the deal. He also said he'd been pimping for his wife. If she was earning for him, why would he kill her?"

"Who knows? Maybe he was too wrecked to know what he was doing. The M.O. even fit him to a tee, or maybe an AT&T. He beat her to death with a phone book."

"A phone book?"

"More or less. He used his fists for openers,

then finished her off with the book. According to his file he's used it on her before."

"He mentioned that," I nodded. "In the first session some members talked about why they were there. Manetti said he used a phone book to beat his wife because it didn't leave bruises."

"A prince of a guy."

"Okay, he's pond scum. So we just hang him on general principles whether he did it or not?"

He eyed me a moment, then slowly shook his head. "You know, if it was anybody but you, Doc, I'd write you off as a Froot Loop and forget it."

"But you won't."

"Not yet, anyway. I can't promise anything, but I'll keep the investigation active, see what we turn up. Deal?"

"Deal. I owe you one, Gene."

"Actually, I owe you one and we both know it," he said quietly. "Remember a few years ago when I was seeing you for post-traumatic stress after I . . . used my weapon on that kid."

I nodded.

"I recall coming to one session pretty loaded. I even talked about eating my gun. I've seen your post-treatment evaluation report on me. It didn't mention any of that."

"How did you get that report? They're confidential."

"Hey, I'm an ace detective, Doc, it's what I do. But my career would have been toast if you'd labeled me suicidal."

"I didn't think you were."

"Even so, you stepped over the line to give me a break, so I'll return the favor. Don't step over the line with this Bad Boyz Klub of yours. Dot every i, cross every t. Okay?"

"What are you saying?"

"I've already said more than I should have. Just be sure you do everything by the book with this bunch."

It was my turn to stare. "What's up, Gene? What's special about this group? Are you saying somebody's planted a ringer in it? A narc or something? Is that what you're telling me?"

"I didn't say that, Doc, and you'd better not say it either. In fact, we never had this conversation. Okay?"

"It's a damned good thing," I said, flushing. "Because if you'd actually told me that, I'd have to inform the court and go after somebody's butt."

"There's no need for that, Doc, it's got nothing to do with you. Just be careful is all. Please."

"I'll keep it in mind," I said, hesitating in the doorway. Doorknob effect? "One question, Gene. Was Vic Manetti the guy your undercover type was after?"

"It's always good to see you, Doc. Take care now, hear?"

"Damn it, I won't stand for it," I raged, pacing the worn carpeting. "It's illegal to say nothing of unethical."

"Unethical definitely," Mavis Dellums said placidly. "I'm not so sure about illegal." She was knitting at her desk behind a pile of paperwork, a massive, motherly brown woman with four kids, a fireman husband, and responsibility for the budget and personnel of a multimillion dollar mental health facility. My boss. My friend.

"But it's crazy, Mavis. They can't use anything they hear in court anyway, it's protected by privilege. But even so, our patients come here for therapy, not to be spied on."

"These particular patients didn't exactly crawl in on their own pleading for help," Mavis countered mildly. "They were sent here by a judge."

"All the more reason to be sure the process won't be used against them. It's just wrong."

"So is domestic violence, Colleen, but you deal with both sides of it every day. So how do you want to deal with this?"

"I'm not sure. Burris went out on a limb to warn me. If I kick up a fuss he could get burned. I don't want that."

"Then maybe you should just take his advice and be careful. Call me silly, but if I was working with a roomful of violent assailants, I think I could live with the idea that one of 'em was an undercover cop."

"Then what's next? Do we bug our offices? Turn over our files? No way. I won't have a police spy in my group. I want him gone. I'm just not sure how to go about it. Yet."

"Maybe your problem will solve itself. If this

undercover cop was after Manetti, he'll drop out of the group now that Manetti's in custody, right? End of problem."

"And if no one drops out?"

"Then I think you have more to worry about than one of your clients being a cop."

"What do you mean?"

"The thing is, I doubt the police would risk violating doctor-client confidentiality over a simple domestic abuse case. The guy they want must be into something a lot heavier. If I were you, girl, I'd be worrying less about your cop and more about the man he's after."

I opened my mouth to argue, then closed it. Because she was my boss, and my friend. And as usual, she was dead right.

No one dropped out. The following meeting had a full roster, nine clients. Damn.

"Gentlemen, welcome to the third session of—"

"The Bad Boyz Klub," Charlie Weeks interrupted.

"Minus one," someone added.

"I'm glad you mentioned it," I said. "Since it's on everyone's mind, let's spend this session discussing Mr. Manetti's problems."

"His big problem's life plus twenty years," Martin Cleveland said. "Can we cover that in two hours?"

"We can take up a collection," Jojo Lassiter cracked, giving Griz a nudge. "Send him a pizza with a file in it."

"Maybe you should save that file for yourself, Mr. Lassiter," I said. "Or are Manetti's problems so different from yours?"

"Vic made his own mess," Weeks said. "He was a loser, a degenerate who freaked out and killed his woman. It's got nothing to do with the rest of us."

"No? Let's consider a hypothetical situation a moment. Put yourselves in Manetti's situation, guys. Your wife, ex-wife, or significant other is murdered. Brutally. Whom do you think would be elected the number one suspect? Mr. Falkenburgh?"

The pudgy schoolteacher blinked, frowning. "Well, I suppose we'd be suspects, the husband always is, but —"

"But you're not an average husband, are you, Mr. Falkenburgh? According to your dossier, you slapped your wife around at a picnic in front of witnesses. How do you think the prosecuting attorney would react to that? Or a jury?"

"But it would never go that far," Falkenburgh said. "Maybe the police would suspect me at first, but they'd eventually find the real murderer."

"Wrong," Martin Cleveland said thoughtfully. "Cops quit looking when they think they've got the right guy. And we'd all be that guy, wouldn't we, Doc? That's what you're saying?"

"In Manetti's situation, with a record of violence and no alibi, you're right, Mr. Cleveland, you'd be the prime suspect. And so would every other man here."

"But this is all hypothetical crap," Earl Macklin said, the first time he'd spoken in the group. Macklin was a weasel-faced security guard who wore his uniform to meetings either because he was going to work or because he thought epaulets buffed up his skinny frame. "Manetti was an honest-to-God criminal. People in that life attract trouble. But most of us are just workin' slobs. Our wives aren't in danger."

"Mine is," Weeks cracked. "As soon as I get off probation."

"That's perfect, Charlie," I snapped. "You just threatened your wife in front of witnesses. And the fact is, every man in this room is capable of violence toward women. You're all members of the club. The Bad Boyz Klub."

"Hey, anybody wants a shot at my old lady, go for it," Charlie said. "My support payments are killing me." But for once no one laughed. They were still mulling over Manetti's problems. And their own. Good.

"All right, Mr. Macklin. Let's make our hypothetical case a bit more real. Suppose there was compelling evidence that Manetti did not kill his wife."

"Whoa, you're wandering off base, Doc," Martin Cleveland said. "The cops say the evidence fits Manetti like a glove."

"Like OJ.'s glove maybe," I said. "The police are convinced Vic did it because his wife was beaten with a phone book and Manetti'd used one on her before. But you all knew that, didn't you? He talked about it in the first session. He seemed rather proud of it, as I recall."

"So he used it again," Lassiter groused. "So what?"

"No," I said evenly. "Let's bring our problem totally into reality now. There actually *is* strong evidence that Vic did not kill his wife, that it must have been someone else."

A rustling through the room, shuffling feet, glances exchanged. "What kind of evidence?" Macklin asked.

"I'm sorry, I can't tell you that. But I can tell you the police haven't closed their investigation. It's ongoing."

"Then why's Manetti still in jail?" asked Charlie Weeks.

"Because, as Martin noted, the evidence fits him. And that's a problem, guys. Because if Manetti didn't do it but the evidence indicates he did, then that evidence must have been fabricated by someone who knew about his previous behavior."

"Like . . . one of us, you mean?" Cleveland said quietly.

"Not necessarily. Manetti mentioned the phone book here but he could have told others as well. But if you're looking for a pool of suspects with the proper knowledge and a history of violence toward women . . . ?"

"Welcome to the Bad Boyz Klub," Griz said darkly. "Jesus."

"You're serious about this Manetti business, aren't you?" Charlie Weeks asked. "This isn't just some schoolhouse game?"

"Most people take murder seriously, Mr. Weeks. Don't you?"

"But you're saying we could be in real trouble here, right?" Falkenburgh said. "Not only could the police suspect one of us of killing Manetti's wife, but if somebody else really did do it, it could happen again. He could stalk one of our wives knowing we'd be blamed for it."

"This is crazy," Jojo Lassiter said. "Nobody's gonna take a run at your old lady, Falkenburgh. Take a look around. We may have a few problems in this room but we ain't psycho killers."

"Looking's not enough, Mr. Lassiter," I said. "I've been a therapist nearly fifteen years. I've worked with troubled kids and hardtime cons, battered women and assailants, but if you put me on the stand and asked me to swear no one here's dysfunctional enough to commit murder, I couldn't do it. More than half of the killings in America stem from domestic violence and we definitely know you're all capable of that, don't we?"

"This ain't right," Cleon Tibbits, the other black in the group put in. A huge, alcoholic laborer, Tibbits' violence was usually triggered by booze, a resolvable problem. I had hopes for him. "The judge sends us here, now you're sayin' we could be jammed up for doin' what he said?"

"The court didn't put you here, Mr. Tibbits,

your behavior did. As for it not being fair, you're right. It might seem like poetic justice to some people, but it's definitely not fair."

"So life ain't fair," Macklin said. "Is this news to anybody? I sure as hell never caught a break and I'm not about to sit around waitin' for this crap to hit the fan either."

"No?" Weeks asked. "What have you got in mind, sport?"

"An alibi, for openers. From here on out I'm gonna make damned sure I'm around other people as much as possible. Mostly I'm covered because I'm at work or bowling or whatever."

"I never bowled in my life," Tibbits growled.

"Then maybe you'd better start, pal," Macklin shot back. "Unless you're lookin' to do natural life in a graybar motel room next to Manetti."

"Maybe we could work out a system," Falkenburgh put in. "If we all made up schedules, we could help cover each other. Meet for dinner instead of eating alone, maybe play cards or something."

"Turn into a real boys club, you mean?" Lassiter snorted, rising, glaring around. "This is a load of crap! It's bad enough I gotta listen to your whinin' about what a fuckup you are, Falkenburgh. I ain't interested in bein' your pal. Screw this, I'm outa here. How 'bout you, Griz?"

"No," Griswold said, shaking his massive head slowly. "I think I'm goin' along. If what the Doc says is true, we could be in somebody's sights already. The law or whoever. Makes sense to gang up, watch each other's backs."

"Like in the army," Tibbits said.

"Somethin' like that," Griswold said. "You in the army?"

"Eight years," Tibbits nodded. "Rangers. You?"

"Marines for five, last one in Leavenworth for sluggin' a captain."

"Hey, I'll buy you a beer behind that," Tibbits chuckled. "Thought about it real hard a few times myself."

"You see?" Falkenburgh said. "Maybe we've got more in common than we think. Maybe we can make it work."

"You're nuts, the lot of ya," Lassiter growled. But he didn't walk out. He eased back down in his chair.

"Okay, we can cover each other some," Weeks said, "but that's only half of it. Maybe we should do a little detective work of our own, check each other's alibis for the Manetti thing."

"Rat each other out, you mean?" Lassiter said. "This is gettin' better and better."

"We wouldn't burn anybody who didn't deserve it, which is more than you can say for what the cops might do to us," Weeks said. "Maybe Falkenburgh can make up a list of where everybody says he was and we can check it out."

"Who checks it out, Weeks?" Lassiter shot back. "You?"

"No, we do it in pairs, that way nobody can pull anything and like our pledge says, anything we find stays in the group. Except for the guy who actually did it. What do you say?"

Nods and a general murmur of assent.

"So how about it, Lassiter? Any reason why you don't want us to know where you were at the time?"

"It's nobody's business where I was. You ain't the law, Weeks. But I'll tell you what, if Griz here signs on, I'll go along." He glanced at Griswold, who nodded.

"Okay," Weeks nodded. "So let's get started. Who's first?"

The rest of the meeting was spent working out schedules and cross-referencing same. Technically it wasn't therapy, but since the toughest part of working with an assailants group is getting them to interact, I could live with it. Maybe they were only trying to save their miserable butts, but at least they were talking to each other.

I waited in the classroom after the session in case anyone wanted to see me. Like an undercover cop, perhaps. No such luck. But as I approached my car in the dimly lit underground ramp, a figure stepped out of the shadows. Lassiter, hardbitten and angry in a faded jeans jacket and a two-day stubble.

"Hi, Doc. I need to talk to you."

"Not here you don't, and if you take one more step, Mr. Lassiter, you'll get a faceful of pepper spray, industrial strength. Now back off before I call security."

"Chill out, Doc. I didn't mean to spook you."

"The hell you didn't."

"Okay, okay, maybe I did a little. Look, I need to show you something. It's in my vest pocket so don't shoot me or zap me or whatever." With one hand raised, he opened his jacket, lifted out a folder and flipped it open. A gold badge. "I'm a cop."

"Actually, that's a detective's badge," I said. "Who's the secretary of the patrolmen's union?"

"The union? Dan Postlewaite. Why?"

"Because anybody can buy a badge or steal one. Okay, so you're probably a real cop. So?"

"You don't seem surprised."

"Actually I've met enough cops that I don't get all wobbly-kneed when somebody flashes a badge at me, Detective Lassiter. Or isn't that your name?"

"My name's Jack Hutchinson. Hutch, to my friends."

"I'm not one of your friends. I'm more interested in what you're doing in a court-ordered therapy group using a false name."

"My job, just like you are."

"Wrong. I'm doing my job within ethical and legal limits. How do you think the judges who ordered these men into counseling would react to a cop infiltrating the group to spy on them?"

"I'm not here to spy, exactly. Look, Doc, I'll lay it out, straight up. The gang I'm working is super bad news, they're into guns, extortion, drugs, and probably murder. The last guy who tried to infiltrate them wound up dead in the road, hit and run. Almost looked like an accident, except he'd been run over five or six times by somebody who really enjoyed the work.

"He was a good cop and he was my friend and now my butt's on the line. The way you've got the Bad Boyz checking each other out one of those clowns might just stumble over my cover at which point I stand a real good chance of becoming a traffic fatality myself. Please, you've got to get them off this kick."

"I'm sorry, but I can't do that. Ethically, I'm bound to maintain the confidentiality of the group and you're compromising it just by being there."

"The *group?* The Bad Boyz Klub? For pete's sake, every one of them's a wife beater or worse. I don't understand how an intelligent woman can bear to be in the same room with them let alone try to help them. You don't really believe you're going to turn their heads around in fourteen weeks, do you?"

"Not all of them, no. Maybe one or two."

"One or two?" he echoed in disbelief. "And you're willing to blow a year's investigation and risk my life for that?"

"I'm not putting your life at risk, Detective, you are. I understand you're in a dangerous situation and I don't want to make things tougher for you, but I won't let you spy on my group and that's it."

"Or what? You publish my name in the paper?

How many court referrals do you think you'll get when word gets out that you let a cop killer walk so your little club could play detective?"

"Look, Lassiter, I'm not looking for a beef with you. Suppose we compromise? If you drop out now you can walk away with your cover intact. Make up any story you like. I won't lie for you but I won't contradict you either."

"And I'm supposed to bet my life you won't accidentally drop my name in the faculty lounge?"

"I've done counseling for the department and I have friends on the force who'll vouch for me. I can give a name or two."

"No thanks. After what happened to the last guy, the fewer people who know I'm here, the better."

"Then I guess you're stuck with my word, which is worth at least as much as yours, whatever you said your name was."

"Point taken," he conceded with a wry smile. A good smile. For a moment I glimpsed what he probably looked like minus the rock'n'roll hair and attitude.

"Okay, Doc, I walk away, you keep your mouth shut about me and we're even. Deal?"

"Not quite. I want to know if the man you're after —"

"I can't tell you anything about him."

"I'm not asking you to. I just want to know if he's a threat to the group?"

"Lady, being on the same planet with the guy

is risky, but your little club is in no more danger than anyone else."

"Fair enough. And Vic's wife? Could he have had anything to do with her death?"

Lassiter blinked, surprised by the question. "No, I don't see how. I keep pretty close tabs on him."

"All right," I said, beeping my car unlocked with the remote control. "Decide what you want me to say about your leaving, Detective, make a graceful exit and good luck. I hope things work out for you."

"Maybe I'll buy you a beer and tell you about it sometime."

"Sorry, I never socialize with clients," I said, sliding behind the wheel.

"But I'm not a client. You just fired me, didn't you? So how about a beer? Or dinner? Or something? Sometime?"

"Okay, maybe," I nodded, shaking my head at his persistence. "Sometime. Later." He grabbed the corner of the car door as I pulled it closed. "One last question, Doc. Why are you so sure Vic didn't kill his wife? Something he told you?"

"Good night, Detective." I closed the door and fired up the car.

"Psychic hotline?" Lassiter called after me, grinning as I backed out. "Or can you read minds?"

Halfway home, in both senses of the word. With luck, Lassiter/Hutchinson would drop out without a ripple, preferably without bad-mouthing me to the department. Which still left me with the second half of the problem. If the man he was hunting was as dangerous as he'd said, he didn't belong in a therapy group where the confidences shared by the participants could make them vulnerable to a predatory criminal. The Bad Boyz weren't angels, but they weren't beyond help either. Or at least, not all of them.

Lassiter's parting shot about being a mind reader stung a bit. Psychologist/mind reader/witch doctor. Synonyms. Arggh. And every shrink on TV is either a nebbish or a whiz kid who solves crimes by brilliantly interpreting a dream or a doodle.

I suppose it actually happens but people hit the lotto, too. I'm not one of them. The truth is simpler. The keys to effective clinical work are empathy, insight, and a nose for detail. Most breakthroughs take months, not minutes, and clients heal and reveal themselves in ordinary office interviews, not on ledges forty stories up.

I was so lost in thought I was nearly home before I realized I was being followed. Living in a quiet suburban neighborhood has its plusses. Strange cars stand out. The car was a new Cadillac Seville, burgundy with darkened windows. Lassiter? Unlikely. Cops don't drive Caddies, undercover or otherwise.

Perhaps it was the man he was after. I made a series of left turns in the village of Metcalf and thought I'd lost him, but as I crossed the

Genessee Bridge I spotted him again.

I pulled into my driveway, hurried into the house and waited beside the living room window. The Caddy cruised past, made a U-turn at the end of the block and parked across the street. No one got out.

I changed into sweats and tennis shoes, keeping a wary eye on the car the whole time. To hell with this. I slipped out the back door, skulked across a couple of lawns and came out behind the Caddy. I only wanted the plate number, but when I saw it I knew. It was a dealer plate. It figured.

Stepping into the street, I walked up to the Caddy and rapped on the window. It hummed open.

"What are you doing here, Mr. Weeks?"

"Hey, I'm just taking my therapy seriously, Doc, all that stuff about looking out for each other. I mean, suppose Falkenburgh's right and there's a serial killer around?"

"I see. So you're here to protect me?"

"Something like that. And I thought we could get to know each other better. Socially, I mean."

"And your wife? Isn't she part of your social life?"

"Libby's the understanding type, besides she'll never hear about it. Anything between us is privileged information, right, Colleen? C'mon, hop in. I'm sittin' in a forty-thousand dollar ride here. Let's live a little."

I took a deep breath, then rested my arms on

the window ledge, crowding him a little. "You want to know me better? Gee, where should I start? Four years ago I was attacked. I was between sessions at the institute and the husband of a woman I was counseling jumped me and dragged me into a utility room."

Weeks blinked rapidly. "What, um, what happened?"

"I got roughed up pretty badly. I'm not a wuss, I work out, I run, try to stay in shape —"

"I noticed that."

"Yeah, well it didn't matter. The guy outweighed me by a hundred pounds and he was wired on speed. I just couldn't handle him."

"So he — I mean, did he —"

"Rape me? Why? Would that bother you?"

"Well, no — I mean — I just —"

"Oh, don't be embarrassed. A lot of men have trouble dealing with women who've been victimized. Makes them feel inadequate or guilty about their own rape fantasies. I can understand that. I had trouble dealing with it myself."

"What did you do? See a shrink?" He chuckled uneasily.

"No. I bought a gun."

"A gun?"

"That's right. One of my cop friends picked it out. A derringer. Forty-five caliber. The kind Booth used to kill Lincoln only with better ammo. Very effective. I carry it all the time. I love the way it feels in my hand. *Hard,* you know? Freud thought guns were phallic substitutes.

What do you think?"

"I, um —"

"Personally, I think it's more like an un-phallic symbol. If guys think having a penis is power, well, mine's bigger than yours now and it's right here in my pocket. There's a danger to carrying a weapon, though. One I'm sure you can relate to."

"One I can — ?"

"Self-control. When somebody makes me angry I have real difficulty controlling my temper. I tend to blow up. The same way you do with your wife, Mr. Weeks. Of course, I'm not big enough to slap people around. But my little friend here is." I patted my pocket. "Do you understand what I'm saying to you, Charlie?"

"You, um, you want me to go, don't you?"

"I'll make it even plainer. If you ever follow me again or if I even see you in my neighborhood I'll rearrange your plumbing so you won't ever harass another woman. Because there'll be no . . . *point*, if you get my drift. Now take off."

"You're the one who needs a shrink," he muttered as he fired up his Cadillac and roared away. I watched him speed across the Genessee Bridge and disappear into the village, then took a .45 caliber roll of Life Savers out of my pocket and popped off the top one. Cherry. My favorite. I turned and trotted back to my cottage.

I spread the dossiers and interview notes files of the Bad Boyz Klub members on the kitchen table, made a cup of cinnamon tea, then settled down for some serious reading. For a change I wasn't looking for hints of repressed homosexuality or substance abuse. A simple connection would do.

As an undercover cop, Lassiter knew he wouldn't be able to use anything he heard in a therapy session in court. So why was he there? I was betting he'd joined the group simply to meet someone and get next to him. But would a domestic assault beef be enough common ground? Probably not. He'd need more.

I scanned Lassiter's records for the minutiae that make up a life, even a false one. Date and place of birth, where you went to high school, college if any, military service, employment record, prior convictions . . . and there it was.

According to the file, Lassiter had served two years for narcotics possession in Jackson Prison. I had no way of knowing which bio facts were false, but no way could a felon be a cop. The prison time had to be a lie, which could make it important.

I quickly scanned the files of the other Bad Boyz and got a hit almost immediately. Griswold had served time in prison too, and he was the only member of the group who had. It made sense. Lassiter said his target was dangerous and as an ex-con in an outlaw biker gang Griz definitely qualified. A prison record would give them a common bond.

Jackson's the biggest, toughest walled prison in the world with over six thousand hardcore inmates. Properly briefed and with a few yardbirds to vouch for him, Lassiter could make Griz believe he'd been there. As an ex-con he could be introduced to the Iron Hawgs without too many questions. It all fit.

There was no connection between Griswold and Linnette Manetti, but there didn't have to be. Vic had flashed her picture around so any of the Bad Boyz could have paid her a visit, as could anyone else he'd offered her to.

So what did I have? Apparently Griswold had important criminal connections or Lassiter wouldn't be after him. But did that mean I should bounce him out of my therapy group?

My professional experience with bikers has been mixed. Some are career felons, brain-damaged by the amphetamines they gobble like popcorn. Others are just outcasts who drift into the gang life looking for kindred spirits. But even the most sociopathic of them maintain a rudimentary sense of loyalty to their thug brotherhood, like wolves to their packs.

Griz had already demonstrated loyalty by trying to help Vic, and he'd put himself at risk by doing so. He might be a dangerous man, but so were the others. My gut told me he didn't pose a serious threat to the group. Still, I had a nagging feeling I was missing something about him, or someone. Some detail I'd seen in the records.

When in doubt, quit. Do something else, come back to the problem fresh. My Volvo was scheduled for maintenance so I drove over the bridge into Metcalf, parked the car at the dealership and dropped my keys through their mail slot. It was less than a mile home and the evening was warm so I didn't bother trying for a cab. I walked back instead, brooding all the way.

Metcalf is a small village of older homes on rolling hills, separated from Flint's urban sprawl by the Genessee Bridge over the murky Flint River. I paused in the middle of the bridge to stare down at the forty foot drop to the rocks below. The river's fifty yards wide but except for the narrow channel near the center, it's shallow as a freshman's fantasies.

The village lights were winking on and I could hear the roar of a crowd in the distance. Football game? No, not on a Tuesday. Soccer perhaps. Metcalf High had a first class . . . and that was it.

High school. Not Metcalf High, Flint Northern. They'd both gone to Flint Northern High and their birth dates were close enough that they could have been there at roughly the same time. That's the detail that had been bugging me.

I jogged the rest of the way across the bridge and down the narrow lane to my cottage. I burned into the kitchen, but even before I noticed that the files spread out on the table were disarranged I felt a chill, a subconscious warning that I wasn't alone. Someone was here. I froze, unsnapping my purse just as he stepped out of the shadows.

He was wearing a motorcycle helmet with the visor down and a denim vest blazoned with the

Iron Hawgs' emblem. It wasn't much of a disguise. To me anyway.

"How the hell did you get in here, Lassiter? What do you want?"

"The truth," he said, taking off the helmet, shaking his shaggy mane free. "Look, I'm really sorry for all this but not knowing could get me killed. You've got to tell me why you think Vic didn't kill his wife. Please."

"You must be awfully desperate to risk a burglary charge trying to find out, but I guess I can understand that. Okay, Detective, I'll tell you what you need to protect yourself but I want to know some things too, to make sure this situation never comes up again. Fair enough?"

"Deal, Doc, whatever you say."

"All right. From Vic's record of violence and drug use, he was certainly capable of killing his wife, in fact, since Linette was easily as violent as Vic, it's a wonder they hadn't killed one another long since. But he definitely didn't do it."

"Why not?"

"Your turn. How did you get in here and how much of the bio information in your dossier is accurate?"

He hesitated, then shrugged. "Older home, old locks, piece of cake. You need a new security system, Doc, and a dog, a big one. As for the bio info, most of it's true so I don't trip up on minor points. I was never in prison, though. After the army I went to Michigan State. Police Science major. If Vic had a history of violence, what makes you think he didn't just crank it up a notch and kill her?"

"He has an alibi," I said simply. "A witness was with Vic when it happened. Where were you at the time, by the way?"

"Me? I told you, on stakeout, watching my guy."

"And that's why you didn't want to tell the others where you were?"

"Exactly. So why hasn't this witness of yours come forward?"

"He can't without incriminating himself. He was doing a drug deal with Vic."

"One of the Bad Boyz?"

I nodded. "Is Griswold the man you're after?"

He hesitated, then smiled ruefully. "I asked around the department about you and they said you were sharp. They were right. Griz is an Iron Hawg, not the worst of them but bad enough. I'm hoping to work into the gang through him. I don't suppose you've got a cup of coffee handy?" His mood was easier now. Relaxed. Relieved?

"Sorry, but this hasn't turned into a social visit, Detective, at least not yet."

"No, I guess not. Okay, what you've got is a convicted felon who claims Vic's innocent of one crime because he was committing another one and won't testify to anything, is that about it?"

"Not quite. When Vic showed his wife's picture around in the men's room, you recognized her, didn't you?"

"Recognized her? I don't follow you." His face

was blandly immobile. Unreadable. He was good. But then he'd have to be.

"You and Linette were in high school together. If she remembered you she could have gotten you killed. Is that what happened? Did she recognize you?"

"Nothing happened, lady, because I have no idea what you're talking about. I was on stakeout the day she bought it and you're way off base. Look, I'd better go. I'm real sorry about busting in here and all. I won't bother you again." He shook back his hair and put on his helmet.

"Detective? Your story won't fly. Griz is Vic's alibi. They were together that day doing a drug deal. If you'd been watching him you'd know that. You should have known."

His visor was down so I couldn't see his reaction. He didn't move. He stood there, frozen.

"It's not too late to get past this," I continued quietly. "I interviewed Linette and I can testify that she was unstable and violent. But you've got to talk to me now. What the hell happened?"

"Sweet Jesus," he said, turning away. "After my partner was killed I spent months developing a cover identity that could get me access to the gang. Griswold's domestic violence beef gave me an opening, but when Vic flashed a picture of his wife in the john I felt like I'd been kicked in the belly. For all I knew she'd seen me already and ratted me out. I had to know." He turned away, shaking his head.

"So I, um, I went to see her. I offered her five

grand just to blow town until this was over. Figured the way Vic was treating her she'd jump at the chance. Instead she freaked out and attacked me. I couldn't believe it. Her old man beats her and sells her ass on the street and I hadn't done a thing to her. Nothing."

"She saw you as a threat to her family," I said simply.

"Family?"

"Or its equivalent. She was pathologically dependent on Vic, for drugs, sex, even violence. He was scum, but he was all she had. She was an emotional time bomb and you tripped her trigger. What happened when she attacked you?"

"I'm still not real clear on that. I've, um, I've been under a lot of pressure with this thing and I must've lost control for a minute. She tried to clobber me with a lamp and I decked her. I . . . hit her a lot harder than I meant to. She banged her head against a table, twisted her neck going down. I thought I'd just cold-cocked her but . . . She wasn't breathing. I tried mouth-to-mouth, seemed like forever. Nothing. She was gone. God." He sagged against the kitchen table, swallowing hard, covering his eyes with his fingertips. Then he steadied himself and took a deep breath.

"I should have called nine-one-one, but it happened so fast I wasn't thinking. Eight years on the force, I've never even drawn my weapon on anybody. I kept getting flashes of prison. Jackson. Like in my bio only for real. My God, Doc, do you know what happens to cops in jail? I thought if I could cover myself somehow . . . There was a little blood by her head so I dropped the phone book in it to make it look like Vic used it on her. I know that was wrong but all I could think about was getting clear. Vic's no loss, you said yourself it was a miracle he hadn't killed her before."

"But he didn't. Maybe he wouldn't have."

"That's kind of a moot point now. I'll be honest with you, Doc, I'm sorry as hell about this, but I'm not willing to throw myself away over it. I've spent my whole life trying to do the right thing. But if I'm in jail, there's no way I can ever make things right again. So the question is, what are you gonna do? Can you let this alone? Please. For God's sake, give me a break. I need a chance to redeem myself here. I'm begging you."

"Even if I was willing to go along, it wouldn't work, Hutch. I don't think you can live with this."

"And you're not willing to let me try, are you? Because it wouldn't be . . . ethical? A piece of crap like Vic Manetti gets priority, even if you have to bury me to do it, right? And I'm supposed to just lay down for it? Go to jail? Take it up the ass from bastards I've put away? Wrong, bitch! Wrong fucking answer!"

Without warning he lunged, swinging his helmet at my head like a flail. It bounced off my shoulder, slamming me against the counter and then he was on me, forcing me back, his hands on my throat, cutting off my air.

My spine was ablaze, ready to snap like a twig. My purse! I'd dropped it on the counter! Groping blindly as the room began to fade, I found the strap and dragged it to me.

Felt my car keys . . . the pepper spray on the key ring. Safety release? Couldn't remember how . . . something snapped off. I jammed the plunger down, spraying a full dose into Lassiter's eyes.

He roared, staggering backward into the table, knocking it over, going down. I reeled down the hall to the front door, stumbled down the steps, then I was off, shambling into an unsteady trot, instinctively heading for the lights of the village.

My lungs were on fire from the pepper spray I'd inhaled but gradually my legs fell into a jogging rhythm, pounding across the bridge, carrying me to safety. I was more than halfway across when I heard the motorcycle roar onto the bridge. Lassiter, his face hidden by his helmet shield, wearing the Iron Hawgs' vest. . . .

My God, he'd planned to kill me from the beginning. I'd die in a hit and run, Griswold would be blamed and Lassiter could swear his life away.

But not yet. He was coming at me full bore, seventy at least. No way I'd make it across the bridge. Jump? To the rocks forty feet below? No. I only had one chance.

Whirling, I sprinted back the way I'd come, heading directly for Lassiter and the center of the bridge. At the last second I veered off and made a desperate dash for the opposite railing.

Lassiter swerved to follow, so totally focused on running me down that he'd didn't realize the angle of his attack was wrong now. But I'd misjudged the distance too. He was too close, I couldn't wait.

I launched myself toward the railing, slammed into it and managed to scramble over, falling, hoping to God I'd come far enough, hearing the shriek of steel against concrete as Lassiter skidded into the wall behind me and the blast of an explosion —

The river hammered me like a fist, smashing the breath out of me. I gagged, sucking water, stunned, sinking, dying and knowing it, feeling the weeds and muck of the river bottom reaching up to gather me down. . . .

And somehow the slimy chill of the muck snapped me back to awareness, a guttering candle of will to live . . . and I made a last despairing thrust with my legs, vaulting myself upward, up toward the village lights glinting on the surface, up toward the air.

A smaller group filed in to take their seats. Somber, no joking. Each of them taking a silent head count, as I was. The Klub was three short now.

Vic was still in jail on drug charges, as was Griswold. Not for long though. Griz was going into witness protection in exchange for testimony about gang activities. It was the smart move, and in his wolfish way, Griz was a bright guy.

Lassiter? He lived for three days after the crash on the bridge. To their credit, the police hadn't tried to cover up his guilt in Linette Manetti's murder. Death and dishonor. A bad end. But one he'd earned.

I wasn't in much better shape. I'd broken my left arm at the bridge rail and the clumsy plastic cast was trussed in a sling. I was battered and bruised and weak as a road-killed rabbit. Still, working was better than brooding, so here I was.

"Gentlemen, I'm sure most of you have heard about what happened last week —"

"Be hard not to," Charlie Weeks interrupted. "You've been all over the news, Doc." Irrepressible. Mentally, I dropped him from my list of potential cures.

"Since you're all here by court order," I continued, "if anyone wants to transfer to another group I'll try to arrange it."

"Why bother?" Macklin snorted. "Way things are going the Bad Boyz Klub's gonna run out of members pretty quick anyway."

"I'm staying," Weeks said. "I haven't had this much fun since my first wife got hit by a train. In fact, I've made a few calls to see about getting on *Geraldo* or *Hard Copy* and —"

"Will you shut the fuck up, Weeks!" Cleon Tibbits stood up, a dark giant towering over the others in his grubby coveralls. "You don't get it, do ya? This ain't some fuckin' joke! It never was.

Vic's wife is dead, Lassiter's dead, Vic and Griz are in the slammer, and they got cells waitin' for the rest of us if we screw up one more time. What happened to Vic could have been any fuckin' one of us! Just because we're members of this stupid club.

"Well I'm sick of hearin' how the world's screwed ya'll over, sick of lookin' at your loser faces and seein' myself. I want out of this mess and anybody who can help, Doc or whoever, let's get to it. And any of you Bad Boyz who thinks I'm jokin' go ahead and laugh. But you'd best stand up first. How about you, Weeks? You think I'm funny?"

No one laughed. Not even Charlie Weeks. They eyed each other warily. Strangers again. I had no idea whether Tibbits' tirade made any impact at all, but I knew one speech couldn't change them. They'd spent their whole lives getting into this place. And overnight cures only happen in movies.

Still, it was an opening, a place to start, and we still had eleven weeks to try. Tibbits' rage would fade, men would show up drunk or high or just stop coming, and in the end I'd wind up reaching only one or two of them. As usual.

Or maybe the Bad Boyz really were as special as they pretended to be. Maybe I'd get lucky with them. Maybe this time I could actually reach three.

Doug Allyn is an accomplished author whose

short fiction regularly graces year's best collections. His work has appeared in *Once Upon a Crime* and *The Year's 25 Finest Crime and Mystery Stories*, volumes 3 and 4. His latest novel is *A Dance in Deep Water.* He lives in Michigan.

Image

John Lutz

"This is a car battery," Jack Olson said, "but sometimes it's used to get people started talking. Once they get running off at the mouth, they don't wanna stop."

He was a large man with a sad face and he was wearing a neat suit he wouldn't want to get messy. Nicko Doyle, standing just inside the shack's open door, was an even larger man but with the features of a malevolent leprechaun, complete with protruding, pointed ears. He was wearing old chinos and a sweatshirt. The man tied to the chair guessed Nicko, who'd carried the car battery inside, would do the work.

The shack was five miles outside of town, well back in the woods, and had no electricity. That was why they needed the car battery. They needed the shack because it was to hell and gone, and no one would disturb them

Vern, the driver who'd brought them here in the black Ford Bronco the battery had come out of, was somebody the man in the chair had never seen before that day. He was a wiry little guy who walked hunched over with his elbows tucked in and had an indignant expression in his watery blue eyes. He walked into the shack now and closed the door behind him. He was wearing old clothes, a rubberized white butcher's apron, and was carrying a metal tool box and some jumper cables with large alligator clamps. So he'd be the one, and not Nicko.

The man in the chair knew they'd figured out who he was — or more accurately who he *wasn't* — and they'd brought him to the isolated shack because they didn't want to gag or silence him in any way while they tortured him. The whole idea was that he'd be talkative when he wasn't screaming.

Sad-faced Olson ambled over to him and bent down so he could look him in the eye. "You lied to us for over a year," he said, "but you were only doing your job. It's a job I wouldn't have on a stick. You got a streak of character in you. We respect that. We're not animals and don't want you to suffer more'n you have to. We do want you to tell us what you know. The more you tell, the less you suffer."

"He'll tell everything," Vern said. He drew a hobby knife with a razor blade from his pocket and began cutting away the clothes of the man in the chair. "I'm better at my job than he was at his."

Within less than a minute the bound man was wearing only scraps of cloth, his wingtip shoes and black dress socks. He couldn't help it; he began to tremble and lost control of his bladder as Vern raised the lid on the tool box.

"You guys wanna stay and watch?" Vern asked, glancing up over his shoulder.

"No," Olson said. "It's hot in here and it already smells. I'll wait outside."

"I guess I'll stay," Nicko said.

Olson left the shack and used a white handkerchief to pat perspiration from his forehead. Then he walked down a narrow dirt path that he knew led to a small creek. When he was about out of earshot, he lit one of the thin, dark cigars he often smoked and watched a hawk or a buzzard circle in the eastern sky. The creek made a pleasant trickling sound, like time passing.

Twenty minutes of it passed before he saw Vern and Nicko making their way down the path toward where he was standing in bright sunlight. Vern was no longer wearing his butcher's apron.

"Get everything?" Olson asked, when they were closer.

"He admitted he was undercover FBI," Nicko said. "Real name was Frank Stokes."

"Can we be sure he was telling the truth?"

Vern smiled. "I'm like a priest in the confessional. Everyone tells me the truth."

"He knew damn near everything about our operation," Nicko said, "enough to put us away till the sun gets cold."

"So now we know where we stand," Olson said.

"Not quite, I'm afraid," Vern told him. "There's this." He held up Stokes' wallet, open to reveal a photograph of an attractive dark-haired woman in her twenties. She was smiling with her mouth open wide as if she'd just heard a good joke.

"Any other photos?" Olson asked Vern.

"No. They seldom carry photographs of people they love, but sometimes they can't resist. It's lonely work they do."

"And risky," Nicko said with a nasty grin and a glance back at the shack.

"So who is she?" Olson asked, nodding toward the photograph "His wife? Girlfriend?"

Vern looked embarrassed. "He refused to tell us."

"Some things you don't even tell your priest, I guess," Nicko said.

Olson stared at Vern. "You were brought in because you were the best in your profession."

"High muckety-fuckin'-muck," Nicko said.

Olson looked disgusted. "He was supposed to tell you everything."

"And he did — or would have if he hadn't died before I could get it out of him." Vern pointed at Nicko. "Your buddy wanted me to keep boosting the current in the jumper cables. It must have arced to his heart."

"Bastard didn't have a heart," Nicko said. He snatched the wallet away from Vern and stared at the photograph. "She's one fine lookin' piece, whoever she is."

"The kinda woman," Olson said, "who if she asked you at the right time, you'd tell her anything."

"She might know what Stokes knew," Nicko said uneasily.

"You want me to stay around town for a while after I clean up here?" Vern asked.

"For a while, anyway," Olson said. "Bayview's not that big a city, population maybe a hundred thousand."

Vern said, "Lots of my business is because of pillow talk."

Kate Adams unlocked the glass front doors of Speed-Stop Market and went inside. Since it was only a few minutes after sunrise, she switched on the overhead fluorescent fixtures. Then she dragged in the heavy stack of morning newspapers and cut the tight nylon band on them so people could get to them.

After the band had snapped free, she straightened up and held the scissors as if about to stab someone, a serious rather than enraged expression on her heart-shaped face. She stalked to her left then her right, now smiling sweetly but insanely, then threw back her head and laughed, pretending to stab herself in the chest with the scissors. She was twenty-two and had narrow hips and wide cheek bones and plenty of ambition. An acting career awaited her beyond Bayview. She was sure of it. She often used the store's surveillance video camera for what she considered cameo performances, but of course never when there were customers. In the evening, before leaving the store, she'd review the tape and try to iron bugs out of her technique — too much hand and arm movement, wider smile next time, improve posture, and for God's sake do something about that hair. She knew that to advance in her chosen career she'd have to find in herself the very best Kate Adams, her consistent image for screen and stage.

A gray pickup truck had pulled into the lot and parked near the door. Larry, a wallpaper hanger who came by every morning, climbed out of the truck and sauntered into the store. He was a tall, lanky man about thirty, with unruly black hair and bad teeth. "Super Slurp," he said, smiling at Kate.

"I don't know how you can drink these things so early in the morning," Kate said, working the machine to draw a large foam cup of the store's special carry-out beverage. She added a little more strawberry syrup to the carbonated water, the way she knew Larry liked it.

He used a plastic straw to sip. Smiled wider. "Any more luck landing acting jobs?" he asked.

"Sort of." She got a damp paper towel and wiped down the machine, which seemed always to be sticky.

"What's a 'sort of' acting job?" Larry asked.

"It was modeling work, really."

Larry showed his crooked teeth. "Kate, Kate . . ."

"Not that kind of modeling job," she said, wondering if he was really kidding her. "Photographs."

"Sure, for guys who pretend they have film in their cameras."

Kate found herself blushing, which wouldn't do for someone who planned on a major acting career. "Listen, Larry —"

"Don't get all mad and flushed," Larry said around his straw. "I know you meant for catalog pictures, something like that."

"It was for a picture frame distributor right here in Bayview," she said. "You know, like when you buy a frame there's always somebody's photo in it so it shows better."

"Yeah, glamor shots, like you'd want your wife or husband to really look. So when I go to the dollar store to buy a frame for my latest award, you might be in it."

"Might be," Kate said. "And not just new picture frames. New wallets, too."

Lois Stokes was an attractive blonde woman who seemed to have aged twenty years since yesterday. That was when she'd been informed her husband Frank was dead, and learned the way he had died. She was wearing a brave face today, but she had yesterday's eyes.

FBI Special Agent Willis Ames and Agent Ralph Camporini sat in the living room of her modest west side tract house, sipping the coffee she'd just brought them. Willis was a lean, hatchet-faced man from Maine, with touches of gray in his hair and bushy eyebrows. Camporini was a short, hefty man with a vertical scar on his right cheek that made him look remarkably like old newsreel images of Al Capone. Nobody in the Bureau called him Al Capone.

It was too warm in the living room, and the

smell of something left too long on the burner wafted in from the kitchen. It wasn't an appetizing scent. Lois sat across from the two agents, on the sofa, gripping her white ceramic coffee mug with both hands as if it was the thing most precious to her in the world. Willis found himself confused about whether he wished Agent Stokes had left children.

"It took you almost a week to find his body," Lois said dully of her husband, looking into the steaming mug instead of at Willis and Camporini.

"He was found by luck," Whys said. "If those campers hadn't decided to pitch their tent —"

"I know!" She cut him off, still staring into her coffee as if it were hemlock she was considering drinking. Then she raised her head and looked at Willis and he was startled by the change in her, the fierce light in her eyes. "I want Frank's killer found. What he did to him —" Words snagged in her throat, temporarily choking her. "I want the bastard found!"

"We think there was more than one," Camporini said in a soft voice.

"Did your husband give any indication of where he might be going the last time you saw him?" Willis asked, knowing the answer. Undercover agents did everything possible to keep their families out of their work, out of danger.

"Frank didn't share his work with me," Lois confirmed, staring back down at her coffee.

Willis thought she might be about to break

into uncontrollable sobbing again, as she had yesterday when they'd tried to question her. He and Camporini stood up and moved awkwardly to the door.

"If there's anything we can help you with . . ." Willis said.

"Find them!" Lois said.

"We will, Mrs. Stokes," Camporini assured her, before they went out.

Willis saw that Camporini's dark eyes were moist. He was the first agent to see Stokes' body after the campers had discovered it in its shallow grave.

"Find them!" they heard Lois Stokes say again in a tight voice, as the door swung shut on the hot, quiet house.

"I seen her," Nicko had said to Olson and Vern. "I went to this place for cigarettes and a Super Slurp, and there she was, grinnin' and sashayin' around like she was in a play or movie."

"You sure it was her?" Olson asked.

"If it wasn't her, it was her spittin' image. I watched her through the window for a while, till she noticed me. Then some customers went in. I waited a while and went inside so I could get a closer look at her. She was standin' there bigger'n shit, punchin' the cash register an' gabbin' with the customers, smilin' just like in her picture."

"You didn't do anything dumb, did you?" Vern

asked. "Anything that might make her suspicious?"

"Naw, I just asked if she was FBI Agent Frank Stokes' wife or girlfriend."

Vern stared at Nicko the way he'd stared at Stokes before starting in on his work. Nicko felt it all over his body.

"None of us are gonna do anything dumb," Olson said. "We got no room whatsoever for dumb."

"And no time," Vern added.

Olson said, "What the hell's a Super Slurp?"

Kate was behind the counter at Speed-Stop that night when the big man with the pointy ears came in. He'd been in before, she was sure. And even surer that the nattily dressed, sad-faced man she noticed waiting for him outside had been in before, only half an hour ago.

The big man grinned at her. "Got any *American Honey* magazines?" he asked "An' I don't mean somethin' for beekeepers to read. This is one of them kind with the clear plastic around them so you can't look at the pictures inside without buyin' it."

"I know," she said. She glanced at the teenage boy who'd been loitering in the store. He stood in a slouch and was reading a car magazine near the door.

"I've gotta go in back for that kind of magazine," she told the big man. "But I'm sure we've got them. Just a minute."

She was gone less than half a minute, not long enough to use the phone, even if there had been a phone back there.

She returned without the magazine — which the store never carried and shrugged apologetically. "Sorry, that one's sold out." She noticed that the teenage boy had left. The man waiting outside glanced into the store. Behind him, a black off-road vehicle had pulled up and stopped but didn't turn off its lights.

"It don't matter," the big man told her. "You come with me now."

Kate tucked in her chin and gave him her Lauren Bacall, from-down-under stare, figuring it might intimidate him. "I beg your pardon," she said archly.

He grabbed her by one arm and dragged her over the counter.

When she was crammed in the black Bronco with Vern and Olson, he returned to the store only for a minute to make sure there would be no trace of him having been there.

Then he got in his white Neon rental car and drove toward what Olson had called the rendezvous point.

"This woman," Willis said to Lois Stokes as he held up a photograph, "have you ever seen her?"

Lois looked briefly at the photo, then at him. "Yes. Her picture was in my husband's wallet."

Willis wasn't surprised. Undercover agents often carried photos of people other than their loved ones, not only to help establish fake identities, but to misdirect anyone who might harm them. Usually they were snapshots of strangers thousands of miles away who couldn't be traced.

"Who is she?" Willis asked.

"I have no idea. Neither did Frank. He bought a cheap little picture frame someplace and cut the photo that came in it down to wallet size. He figured she was some model off somewhere who nobody would recognize."

"He was half right," Camporini said. "She's a local model."

It took Lois a few seconds to realize what that might mean. "My God, you'd better —"

"It's too late," Willis said. "She was abducted last night from her work at Speed-Stop Market. A teenage boy saw a large man drag her from the store and force her into a vehicle containing two other men."

"When we learned she was a photographers' model," Camporini said, "and remembered we found your husband's wallet with no identification or photos in it, we thought we better check with you."

"That poor girl was taken by the men who tortured and killed Frank, and she can't tell them what they want to know."

"They'll only ask her some basic questions," Willis said, "to find out what your husband might have told her. How much he knew that he didn't tell them. Who else he might have told."

Lois didn't ask what would happen to Kate

Adams then. She'd identified her husband' body and she knew.

"We've had someone watching this house," Camporini told her in a gentle voice.

Lois didn't understand at first.

"One thing your husband didn't tell them was his address, or anything about you," Willis said. "If he had, they would have come for you and not Kate Adams." He didn't add that once Stokes' killers were sure Kate Adams wasn't his widow, they'd resume their efforts to find the real Mrs. Stokes. And in a city the size of Bayview, they would find her.

After leaving Lois Stokes, Willis and Camporini stopped at a service station and Willis used the phone. They were hoping to learn that Kate Adams' abduction was caught on the store's security camera videotape. But the lab informed him that the abductors had been too smart for that. The video camera was smashed, its cassette missing.

Kate watched the man she'd heard them call Vern enter the barn. The deserted farmhouse she'd noticed driving in was ready to collapse. The barn was in slightly better condition, but neither building would have electricity. She was sure that was the reason for the car battery Vern had taken from the Bronco then carried in and placed on the floor; it would be dusk soon, and they'd need light in the barn.

The big one who'd been in the store, Nicko,

walked around behind her and yanked the duct tape from her mouth so abruptly she yelped with pain.

"Don't take her lips off with the tape," Olson, the sad-faced one in the suit, said. "She's gotta use 'em to talk."

"I don't know anything about what you asked me," Kate told them. Her words were slurred because of the tingling pain in her lips.

Olson reached inside his suit coat and her heart almost stopped. Was his hand going to come out holding a gun?

But it wasn't a gun, it was her photograph, the one she'd posed for during her latest modeling job.

"That's you, isn't it?" Olson asked, holding the photo out so she could see it clearly.

Despite its lack of success so far, Kate tried to stay in her Lauren Bacall mode. Scared, but cool and a little defiant. "Sure, it's me. I told you I'm an actress-model. I posed for that photo so they could use it to help sell picture frames."

"It wasn't in no frame when we run across it," Nicko said.

"Somebody's cropped it. Look close and you can see the edges aren't evenly cut."

Olson held the photo toward the light filtering in through cracks between boards and studied it. "She's right about that," he said.

"So your husband or boyfriend trimmed it so it'd fit in his wallet," Vern said.

"I don't have a boyfriend!"

"That's hard to believe," Nicko said, stroking her hair.

"Those photos are all over the place," Kate told them, jerking her head to the side and making Nicko grin. "Look in any department store in town if you don't believe me."

Olson walked over to the barn door and stood in soft sunlight, his head bowed. Then he cursed and kicked at the plank wall. Barn swallows or maybe an owl fluttered overhead, startling everyone.

"Drive the Neon into town, Nicko," Olson said. "Shop for some picture frames."

Nicko looked at the Bronco battery, then at Kate. "You ain't really gonna believe her, are you?"

"No," Olson stud. "That's why you're driving into town."

"We won't start without you," Vern assured him.

That seemed to mollify Nicko.

Vern tossed him a ring of keys, and he stalked out.

They listened to the sound of the Neon starting and driving away.

"He won't be gone long," Vern said. As he spoke, he pressed the duct tape again over Kate's mouth, mashing hard to get adhesion and bruising the insides of her cheeks against her teeth. "A geek like him's got plenty of incentive to get back here."

And he was right. Less than ninety minutes

had passed before they heard the Neon drive up and park near the barn.

Its door slammed, and Kate heard footsteps outside.

Nicko came in carrying a cheap plastic picture frame about four by five inches.

"Same damned picture," he said, showing Olson and Vern what the frame held, "only she's sittin' next to a vase of flowers in this one that was cut out of the other."

The three men stared at Kate, at her image in the photograph, then went outside. She sat still and heard nothing for a few minutes, then heard them arguing. Their voices rose so they were yelling at times, but she couldn't figure out what they were saying.

Then Vern and Olson came back into the barn. Beyond them, she could see the big one, Nicko, standing near some trees. Even though night was falling, Kate could see that he had his hands stuffed in his pockets and was glaring at the barn with his head lowered, as if sulking.

"Won't need this, after all," Vern said, and picked up the car battery.

Kate was relieved. They believed her at last. Whatever good they thought she might do them, they knew better now and would release her.

His arms stretched straight and his shoulders hunched to support the heavy battery, Vern trudged toward the open barn door. It was getting dark outside fast now, and within seconds she could barely see him. She could no longer see Nicko at all, or even the trees he'd been standing near. She did notice it was going to be a bright, clear night, with a big half-moon and a wide scattering of stars.

Olson moved close to her. "I'm no damned animal," he said, almost in a whisper. "I got a daughter of my own somewhere." Then he smiled reassuringly and reached inside his suit coat again, and she thought he was going to withdraw her picture.

Instead he pulled out a gun.

"She wasn't tortured," Willis said, watching the medical examiner do a preliminary on Kate Adams' body where it had been discovered in the barn. "You know what that means?"

"Means they believed her story," Camporini said. "And we both know what *that* means."

Lois Stokes sat nervously on her living room sofa. Some of the coffee she'd been drinking had sloshed out of her cup onto the back of her hand. She barely felt the burn, instead becoming acutely aware that the hand was trembling. She knew what Willis and Camporini were going to ask her to do. She knew she'd say yes.

"The men who killed your husband also killed Kate Adams," Willis was saying. "They'll come for you. You can play it safe and leave —"

"Or I can stay here and be live bait," Lois said.

"We'll do everything possible to ensure your safety," Camporini told her.

"But it's true, you'll be bait," Willis confirmed.

Lois smiled at him, knowing he was at least leveling with her, knowing that the Bureau and the Bayview police couldn't possibly guarantee her safety.

"I'll stay here in Bayview," she said, "in this house. For as long as it takes."

She was no longer trembling, but she was still afraid.

Within a few days she was able to see them, at least some of them. When she walked outside to pick up the newspaper, a car would pass. The driver, always a man, never glanced at her, a still-attractive woman wearing a robe. When she went for groceries, she noticed some of the same shoppers in the supermarket, younger women without children and with an alertness about them, though they never acknowledged her presence.

She made sure her doors and windows were locked at night, as instructed, and though she never saw anything beyond darkened panes of glass, she knew they were out there, watching over her like guardian angels with guns.

And she knew if *she* was aware they were there, so might be whoever came for her.

What woke her at 3 A.M. on Wednesday of the second week was a faint clinking sound, like glass falling but not breaking.

By the time she'd come fully awake and sat up, she knew it was too late. The small taped section of window pane cut away to unlock the sash had fallen to the floor *after* the man had entered her bedroom.

He stood now at the foot of the bed, a gigantic figure that seemed to make the dark shapes of everything else in the room smaller and insignificant.

Lois reached over and switched on the bedside lamp.

He grinned down at her in the sudden light that hurt her eyes. He was wearing dark clothes, even a black or navy blue stocking cap. His teeth were bad and his ears were pointed. In his left hand was a role of silver duct tape. In his right was a large knife.

He raised the hand holding the tape and held a thick forefinger before his lips, signaling for her to be silent.

"Time for you to come along with me," he said.

"Why?" Playing for time, trying to control her fear.

"Because we wanna know what you know and who else you mighta told."

"Then?"

"Then we bring you straight back here. A little question an' answer session's all we're lookin' for."

The casual sincerity in his voice chilled her. She could almost believe him, this man who had killed or helped to kill her husband and Kate Adams.

He held the knife out and took a step toward the bed. "There's no need to shake like that," he told her. "Just walk with me out through the backyard to where we got a car waitin'."

Lois wondered where her protectors were. What had happened to her guardian angels? How had the man slipped past them? She tried to control her gaze so it wouldn't slide toward the door, tipping him off that she was waiting for help.

"What if I say no?" she asked.

The big man shrugged. "You're comin' one way or the other. It's no big deal either way for me. Don't have to be for you, either, if you come along nice. Get it over with, get back here, catch a few more hours sleep. This'll all seem like it was a dream. That'd be the easy way. The hard way, you don't wanna think about."

She emitted a quavering sigh that was almost a whine.

"All right," she said meekly.

She bent over stiffly from her sitting position on the bed and reached for her white fuzzy slippers. *Where was Willis? Camporini? Her husband's fellow agents who had let him down and were now failing his widow? She could not survive this alone! She knew it with a certainty that froze her heart.*

She slid her foot into her left slipper, unable to resist a glance at the door. *Where were they?*

The intruder was sharp. He saw her eye movement and his grin widened. "I might be big," he said, "but the Army taught me how to move around small, 'specially at night. And how to use this." He waved the knife. "I hate to see you covered up more'n you gotta be, but you can put on that robe and then we're leavin'. I always try to be a gentleman around ladies. You'll see that before the night's over."

"At least I'm glad of that," she said, leaning down for her right slipper. Through its toe she used her husband's Bureau issue Sig Sauer 9 mm handgun to shoot the gentleman.

Willis and Camporini entered the room in Bayview Police Headquarters where Nicholas (Nicko) Doyle sat with his attorney at a small oak table. Doyle's right arm was in a sling. Lois had shot him in the shoulder and the bullet had smashed his collar bone. He'd still been writhing on her bedroom floor when agents attracted by the shot had stormed into the room, seen the knife still in his hands and subdued and handcuffed him before realizing he'd been wounded. Nicko's attorney, a man named Gray, had indignantly pointed out that their actions had permanently disabled the shoulder.

"I want to know the specific charge against my client," Gray said. His head and pock-marked face looked too small for the shoulder pads of his chalk-striped blue suit. Like a mean little kid playing dress-up with his father's clothes.

"It's murder," Willis said bluntly.

Nicko and his attorney appeared confused.

"You told me it was *attempted* murder when

you read me my rights," Nicko said.

"It's changed."

"But I didn't kill that woman! She's still alive!" Nicko rose half out of his chair. "I only broke into that house to commit burglary! I used the knife to help pry open the window, that's all. I wasn't gonna kill nobody. Believe me, it ain't my style!"

Willis shrugged. "We're talking about two different women. You're being charged with the murder of Kate Adams. And I'm sure you'll cooperate to avoid also being charged with murdering Federal Agent Frank Stokes."

Nicko sat back and looked wary. Gray's posture changed slightly, but his face gave away nothing.

"A witness saw you leave the convenience store with Kate Adams in tow," Camporini said to Nicko.

Nicko and his attorney put their heads close together and conferred in whispers, then sat back.

"I read about the Adams case in the papers," Gray said. "You have a teenage boy who thinks he saw something from across the street. Any identification of my client would be highly suspect."

"We have more than that," Willis said.

Nicko rubbed his sore shoulder gingerly with his free hand but still appeared unworried. He was remembering how he'd removed the cassette from the store's security camera and taken it with him, but not before smashing the camera for good measure. He'd wiped the camera clean of prints and then stamped on it, and he'd been careful not to touch anything in the store other than the girl. He'd even wiped the door handle on the way out. He was positive he'd left no fingerprints.

"I don't think I need to talk to you about anything I don't wanna," he said with a confident smirk.

Willis nodded to Camporini, who walked across the room and removed a videocassette from his suit coat pocket.

"It's a bluff," Nicko assured his stone-faced attorney.

Gray looked off in the distance and said nothing.

Camporini switched on the small TV and VCR in the corner and inserted the cassette.

The screen flickered and a black and white security tape began to play. It was the kind that always showed the date and time in white letters at the bottom of the picture. There was Kate Adams, smiling and striking poses, walking slinkily with a hand on her hip, tucking in her chin and staring at the camera. A screen test, in case anyone was interested.

Then she was at the cash register, waiting on a series of customers.

Cut to Kate watching a slouchy teenage boy thumb through a magazine.

Then, unmistakably, Nicko Doyle entered the

store. He approached the counter and said something to Kate, who then excused herself and turned around, leaving the frame. A few seconds later the tape went blank.

"Kate Adams was a model and aspiring actress who used the store's security tape to perfect her technique," Willis said. Nicko and his attorney were staring hard at him now. Nicko had begun to perspire. "You must have come on too strong and frightened her, Mr. Doyle," Willis continued. "And maybe she knew you'd looked through the window and seen her mugging and posing for the security camera. Before she waited on you she went to the back room and removed the old cassette and replaced it with a blank. She knew you'd probably smash the camera and take the cassette if you were up to no good, so she hid the cassette she'd removed so there'd be a record of what happened up to that point."

Camporini pressed the rewind button, then the pause.

And there again in black and white, above the printed date and time of Kate's abduction, was the clear image of Nicko Doyle staring at her with an expression usually seen on wolves regarding sheep.

Willis sat down at the table, directly across from the shaken and perspiring Nicko. "Three things: You didn't kill Frank Stokes alone. You didn't kill Kate Adams alone. You can possibly escape death by lethal injection if you answer all our questions so you give us the others."

Nicko looked at Gray. Gray looked at Willis.

"We'll deal," the attorney said.

Willis nodded, not reminding anyone he'd said "possibly."

He hadn't actually lied. The Bureau had an image to maintain.

John Lutz is one of the most skilled mystery writers working today, with his most recent novels being *The Ex* and *Final Seconds*, co-authored with David August. A winner of the Mystery Writers of America's Edgar award for best short fiction, his work has appeared in dozens of anthologies and magazines. He lives in Webster Groves, Missouri.

Verdict

Nancy Pickard

"Ladies and gents, we'll take a recess."

The judge turned his jowly face toward the side of the room where the jury sat. On televisions across America, viewers saw light glint off the lenses of his eyeglasses. They heard him sniff once. Microphones caught the swish of his black sleeves moving across papers. From atop the podium from where he presided, the judge issued the same basic instructions which the people in his courtroom and the national television audience in their homes had heard him pronounce before every recess.

"You may go to the snack bar, or the restroom, or a bailiff will take you outside to smoke. Do not discuss anything about this trial with each other, or with anyone else. Do not read or watch or listen to any information about the case."

He jerked his left thumb toward a door to their left.

"Go now."

At the start of the trial, the members of the jury had been provided with notebooks, pens, and envelopes, and with instructions from the judge as to the proper time and way to take notes. Although the television audience was never permitted to see the jury, anyone could imagine that now, released to a recess, the jury members were placing the notebooks and pens into the envelopes, that they were leaving the envelopes on the seats of their chairs, and that they were then quietly filing out of the courtroom.

At home in her living room, Sandra Bennett also followed the judge's bidding with as much speed and efficiency as she could manage. She folded the cover down on her notebook, put the cap back on her ballpoint pen, and slipped them both into her envelope. Like the judge, she sniffed, smelling defeat for the prosecution. She struggled to push herself to a standing position, after which she dropped the envelope on the sofa cushion behind her.

She clicked the "mute" button on the remote control gadget for her television set so that she could not hear any legal experts analyze the previous testimony. Then she grabbed her crutches and hopped into her own snack room — her kitchen — to pop a frozen meal into her microwave. She estimated she might have twenty minutes to eat, go to the bathroom, and get back to the sofa for the next phase of the trial: closing arguments. Sandra loved closing arguments. She felt excited and eager as she selected a frozen spaghetti entree from the freezer compartment of her refrigerator. After she placed the cold package inside her microwave oven, she stood on one foot, her arms draped over the padding at the top of her crutches, and she watched the food go around and around as it cooked. She imagined there must be a microwave oven in the snack room at the courthouse, too.

It made her feel like a part of things.

Until she fell on ice and broke her left ankle in three places, Sandra Bennett had never even heard of Court TV. While the rest of the USA watched coverage of the O. J. Simpson trial, she was at work cleaning houses during the days and offices at night. In her limited spare time, all she had ever wanted to do was sleep.

Now, unable to return to work and with infinite hours of time on her hands, she lived and breathed the fascinating, hypnotizing channel that she had stumbled upon at the start of her convalescence. Every day there was live coverage of a trial in progress, from the moment the judge's gavel came down in the morning to the time it pounded again in the late afternoon to dismiss everybody for the night. In the mornings, she could hardly wait until 10 A.M. when the trials generally started, and in the evenings, she reviewed her notes of the day's testimony. Based on her notes, she tried to predict how the direct and cross examinations might proceed. She fell asleep seeing the principals in her mind's eye — the lawyers, the plaintiffs or victims, the defendants, and the judges — and imagining herself in the jury box, herself in the witness box, herself at one of the tables with the attorneys.

To relieve the tax liability for her employers, Sandra habitually carried her own tools and supplies from one job to another. One icy day in February, she had clutched the handle of her canister vacuum cleaner instead of a railing alongside some concrete steps. Her left foot had come down on ice, slipped out from under her, and she had crashed to the walkway, saving her precious vacuum, but cracking her left ankle beneath her.

No one was there to see her or to help her.

Alone, she struggled to her feet in tremendous pain, but unaware of how much damage she had done to herself. She only knew that she had to keep working; she couldn't afford to get sick or to be injured and disabled. At the age of forty-two, she lived alone and was her own sole support, as she almost always had been, and figured she probably always would be. When Sandra thought about herself, she thought of a heavy woman with a homely face with mismatched features — mouth too large for her eyes, nose too long for her chin, skin too pale to look healthy. She thought of herself as somebody people didn't notice. It worked out fine, she thought, that she only cleaned for people who were never home. But if she didn't work, her house rent wouldn't get paid, and she wouldn't be able to afford groceries, and she might as well die, she believed.

Somehow that day, managing at first by sliding down the employer's icy lawn on her bottom, Sandra got herself and her vacuum into her car. She didn't need her left foot to drive. She cleaned the next house on her hands and knees, dragging her wounded leg behind her like an injured pet on a leash.

At home that night, she constructed a homemade splint and she used a broom to support her when she walked. She managed like that for three weeks until finally she had to admit to herself that it wasn't healing.

"The problem," the doctor told her, "is that it *is* healing. Your bones are knitting, but they're doing it all wrong. Why in the world didn't you come in sooner? Now we're going to have to break it all over again and set it right so it can heal properly. Do you have insurance?"

"Yes," she lied, and wondered if he asked all of his patients that question, or if there was just something poor-looking about her. On the medical form she had filled out at the request of his receptionist, she had listed, not her own name, but that of one of her employers. Then she had written the name of an insurance company, and the policy number she had seen on a piece of paper in the employer's home. She did that only because she had heard that doctors wouldn't treat anyone without insurance. When she learned that she needed surgery, Sandra decided she would wait until after the operation to tell them the truth, and she would tell them she intended to pay for everything herself. They would come after her for the money, but at least she would already have her ankle fixed. And maybe, she might even be able to pay them a little, someday. Someday . . . like, when she won the lottery, or the Publisher's Clearing House Sweepstakes, or Donald Trump died and left her a million dollars.

Sandra kept an eye on the TV screen while she ate her spaghetti, but she made an honest attempt not to read anything into the expressions on the faces of the talking heads. She watched only because she needed to know when to resume her seat with the rest of the jury.

She'd already made up her mind about the verdict, and she wondered if they had, too. It was so obvious, to her, that the so-called victim was nothing but a little tramp, and the man she had accused of raping her was falsely accused. Sandra felt bad for him because he was having to endure this public embarrassment, not to mention that the poor guy had already sat in jail for nine months while he waited for his trial. But the agony would all be over soon for him. He was going to be acquitted. Sandra knew that, as sure as she was convinced that spring followed winter. She knew it would happen because she would cause it — will it — to happen.

She could do that, now that she had the power.

Sandra wished she had known about her special "power" during her own court case after the operation on her ankle. If she'd only known then that she had the inner power to sway juries and judges, she would have won that malpractice lawsuit. Instead, the doctor who had crippled her was adjudged not liable, while Sandra herself was commanded to pay his legal fees. As if she could! She, a cleaning woman with an annual income of all of $18,000 before the accident! Thank God, at least she didn't have to pay her own lawyer, who had worked on a contingency basis. They'd all seemed to be so angry at her — the doctor, the judge, the jury, and then her own lawyer — and she didn't really understand why. She hadn't put herself into surgery, and broken her own ankle again, and made it not heal! She was the victim, but they hadn't seen it that way.

"I can't afford to pay his legal fees," she'd told the judge.

"Find a way," he'd snapped at her. And then he had lectured her about nuisance suits. He had shaken his finger at her and warned her she might yet be charged with insurance fraud, for lying about insurance to the doctor and the hospital. That's why her own lawyer was mad at her, because she hadn't told him that part of the story, and he'd heard it first on cross examination. He said that's why they lost, because the jury couldn't believe her after that.

Sandra was hoping to appeal the verdict.

Now that she had the power.

The defendant of the current trial she was watching was so good-looking that Sandra fantasized about him when she wasn't viewing his trial, or writing letters to him in jail. The greatest thrill of her life was the day she got a letter back from him.

"Thank you for your support," he wrote. "You sound like you must be a very sensitive and beautiful human being."

She had written to him on the very first day of his trial. His letter came seven days later. Sandra immediately wrote back.

"I think if you get up on the stand and testify in your own behalf, the jury will believe you," she advised him, confident of her new ability to use legal words and phrases. She knew she had pretty handwriting, too. It had been a source of pride for her ever since elementary school. When she left notes for her employers — *"Please lock dog up next time"* or *"Got stain out of carpet in bedroom"* — they sometimes wrote back: *"You have beautiful handwriting! Please wash baseboards, okay?"* She thought that anybody who saw her handwriting would think she was a dainty, smart, feminine woman, maybe a teacher, or a business executive.

In her finest penmanship, she advised the defendant in the rape trial, "It will be your word against hers, and nobody in their right mind would ever believe *her*."

Closing arguments were about to begin.

Sandra hobbled back into her living room and sat down again. This time, however, she didn't prepare to take notes.

"Ladies and Gentlemen," the judge said, facing the invisible jury. "I advise you to listen very carefully to closing arguments, rather than taking notes. You already have all the testimony and evidence you're going to have." He nodded at the lead-off attorney, and said, "Proceed."

Sandra's heart was pounding. The palms of her hands were so sweaty with nervousness and anticipation that she couldn't have taken notes anyway without moistening and staining the precious pages of her notebook. She had eight such notebooks stacked on top of her television set. Eight trials. Eight verdicts she had accurately predicted, three of them she was positive she had actually controlled. They were the last three she had watched before this current trial. She felt that she had probably personally determined the outcome of the other five trials, too, but she hadn't realized she was doing it at the time. It was only after those five verdicts went the exact way she wanted them to go that she had the awakening: she was doing it. With her mind, her thoughts, her wishes, she was setting them free, or sending them to prison. She had the power.

As Sandra listened to the state's attorney make his final feeble attempt to win over the jury to the side of the so-called victim, her eyes narrowed and her mouth turned down in an expression of contempt.

"This case is simple," he began. "The evidence couldn't be clearer or more convincing. A woman drove alone in broad daylight to a library to check out some books to read. As she returned to her car with her arms loaded with her purse and books, this man —" He pointed in the direction of the defendant. "— was waiting in a van. He stepped out, grabbed her, pushed her into his van, threatened her with a knife if she didn't drive him where he told her to go, and then when they got there, he brutally raped and nearly killed her. She is lucky to have escaped with her life.

"Do not let him be lucky. Let his luck end here, today, in this courtroom."

Sandra listened as the lawyer summarized the physical evidence: DNA, fabric fibers, skin under a fingernail, the so-called victim's eyewitness testimony.

"Scientifically, it's an airtight case," the lawyer said. "You need have no fear you are convicting an innocent man. This isn't a case where a man is convicted by a mistaken eyewitness, only to be tragically proved innocent by DNA evidence thirty years later. No, we have the DNA evidence now, here, today. There is no mistake. There is no reasonable doubt. There is no doubt at all. The defendant was kidnapped by that man. She was horribly assaulted by him. She will suffer the trauma of that evil act for the rest of her life. And he did it. He did it. He did it!"

Overkill, thought Sandra, as she critiqued the state's final argument. Now she eagerly awaited the defense's turn. The defendant had testified in his own behalf, as she had counseled him to do in her letters. He had denied everything, and he had looked so handsome, so gentle, so innocent as he had done so. When confronted by the physical evidence, he had brought tears to Sandra's eyes when his voice cracked and he said, pleadingly, "Labs make mistakes."

Sandra believed him. She knew how innocent she had felt in her own trial, and nobody had believed her. She didn't want that to happen to him. To make sure the jury believed as she did, she closed her eyes and began to chant, "Not guilty, not guilty, not guilty." Over and over, intensely feeling his innocence inside herself, she chanted throughout the defense attorney's closing, the judges' instructions, and on through the day and into the night, while the jury deliberated, while they went home, while they slept. She imagined her words flying out from her head, through the dark streets and across the country to eight different bedrooms, working its way into the brains of the sleeping members of the jury.

The verdict came in quickly the next morning.

"Your Honor, we the jury find the defendant not guilty."

At home, on her couch, Sandra screamed with joy. She was exhausted, but her effort had been worth the hard work, the concentration, the sleepless night.

He was going free!

And she had done it with her special power. Only now did she allow herself to listen to the talking heads, the legal analysts:

"Are you surprised?" one of the regular hosts asked a lawyer guest.

"I'm never surprised by anything that juries do," he claimed.

"But the DNA —"

"Listen, after the O. J. Simpson trial, no jury will ever take anybody's word for anything. Juries know that labs do make mistakes. People screw up. It's always possible. And juries have learned that eyewitnesses are frequently, notoriously wrong. The defendant must have convinced the jury to believe him, and not her."

"You think it was his appearance on the stand that saved him?"

"Oh, yeah. It was a great performance."

At home, Sandra thought, "No! It was my power that did it."

The talking heads went on discussing a prosecution that hadn't been all it might have been, and a victim who hadn't presented herself in a sympathetic light, and an accused who had looked the picture of fresh, honest, clean-cut, handsome appeal.

Sandra basked in her victory, and his.

"Another day, another trial."

Sandra practically sang the thought as she awoke the next morning, so happy was she in her new life's mission.

Free the innocent.

Imprison the guilty.

It was to be her life's work, she saw that now.

The other parts of life were fading from her awareness: work, money to live on, her family in another city. Third notices from bills were piling up, but so far she had kept them all at bay with pleading, conciliatory phone calls. She didn't know how long that could continue; increasingly, she didn't care. She would do her job, perform her mission; God would provide.

Sandra dressed carefully the first day of any new trial. Like an actual jury member in the courtroom, she wanted to appear trustworthy, reliable, smart, reasonable, and fair. As she got ready on the morning after her latest victory, she imagined the handsome young defendant dressing, too. Was he already free?

"Thanks to me," she whispered, as she sank back down on the couch. She reached for the clicker, and settled back in for a new day, a new trial. A fresh notebook and her pen were ready at her side in case this new judge also gave permission to take notes. They all didn't.

When the doorbell rang right in the middle of opening statements, Sandra jumped as if the bell were directly wired into her spine.

Then she ignored it.

It couldn't be anybody important, she thought, feeling annoyed. She didn't know anybody important. It wouldn't be the water department coming to shut her off; she'd already talked to them on the phone and they'd given her another month to pay.

The doorbell rang again, then again. Whoever

it was wasn't going away. "Just a minute!" she yelled. "Hold your horses!" Angrily, she clambered to her feet.

She peered through the peephole.

"Oh, my God," she shrieked.

Happy, flustered, she opened the door.

There he stood, the defendant, on her own doorstep, looking even more handsome than he had on the stand! But she saw shock in his eyes — and then anger. She wasn't at all like her handwriting, that's what his face was telling her, before he had even opened his mouth.

"You gave me your address," he said, pushing past her and into her house. "So I'd know where you live, right? Well, here I am. This is what you wanted, right?" He laughed, but it sounded very angry. "You're not exactly what I wanted."

She was mortified, tongue-tied. Here he was! Come to thank her. She felt sorry she wasn't beautiful, so that he might love her as well as appreciate her.

He was looking at her crutch, her foam and aluminum cast.

"I broke my —"

He knocked her crutch away from her.

Sandra screamed, and reached for the edge of the front door, but he jerked it out of her fingers, and slammed it shut. He grabbed one of her arms and violently shook her back and forth on her one standing leg, as if her arm was a handle and she was a jug. She was strong, from years of hard, physical labor; her thick, muscular leg was like a post he couldn't knock down so easily.

"Why'd you write me that letter? You want me to do to you what I did to her? I can do anything I want. You saw it, I can get away with anything. I've got the power."

She was shocked to hear him say that. It was a lie. He didn't have the power. She did. She clung to him, refusing to fall, even as he was trying to push her to the floor.

"Wait, please wait," she pleaded. "What's the matter? I want to help you. Do you need some place to stay? Do you need a good meal? Listen, I'll cook something real good for you. Something really good. Please."

"You cook?"

He let her go so fast, she slammed up against the door.

He was a horrible person, she saw that now, he was brutal and cruel. With her power, she had mistakenly saved a rapist, a would-be murderer. He looked angry enough, disappointed enough, to kill her now.

"I'm a wonderful cook. Tell me what you like best. Come on into my kitchen. I'm so glad they let you go free." She was babbling, she knew, but the look on his face said he was enjoying her terror, her submission.

"From your letters, I expected a babe."

"I'm a beautiful cook."

"Surprise me. No, I want a steak — this big — and a baked potato with sour cream. You got that?"

"Sure, sure. I need my crutch."

He even picked it up for her, but then he thrust it painfully into her chest. She hobbled into her living room first. "I've got your whole trial on tape, you want to see the best part, the end, where they say you're not guilty?"

"Yeah, put it on."

Sandra put in the last tape of his trial, rewinding it back to just before the verdict. Inside her head, she began chanting, "I have the power. I have the power."

She screamed it silently inside her brain as the judge once again bade the jury foreman to stand up, as all eyes turned toward the jury, as the voice of the foreman said one more time, "Your Honor we find the defendant —"

"Guilty," Sandra screamed.

She turned just in time to see the look of shock on the defendant's face as she swung her crutch into his neck. Again and again she hit him, until he disappeared from her living room, as if he had never been.

She had the power.

On the TV, armed police officers ushered the defendant out of the courtroom.

Sandra limped over to her couch and cried. After a while, she dried her tears. The video tape had long since stopped running. It was surely time for Court TV to start again after the noon recess.

Sandra clicked it on.

Contentedly, she settled back. A murder trial

this time. Such a mean-looking defendant. Sandra could tell by looking at him that he was guilty.

Now that she had the power, everything would be all right. She could take the transcript of her own trial and just by concentrating, change the ending of it. She could find the video tapes of her childhood, and change herself into a rich and beautiful woman. She could be anything she wanted to be. Just by willing it to be so, she could evaporate the blood on her carpet, and she could erase the body that lay in her kitchen. But right now, she didn't want to think about that. She had a new trial to judge, and a new murderer to convict. This time, she wouldn't be fooled, this time she would get it right.

Sandra took up her pen and notebook, ready to follow any instructions the judge might give her.

Nancy Pickard's Jenny Cain mystery series has now reached 10 volumes, the latest being *No Body*. She has also recently turned her hand to editing again with the anthology *The First Lady Murders*, featuring various Presidential wives as detectives. Her short fiction has appeared in a wide variety of magazines and anthologies, including *Ellery Queen's Mystery Magazine*, *Funny Bones*, and *Cat Crimes at the Holidays*. She lives with her husband in Prairie Village, Kansas.

The Back Page

Faye Kellerman

He was always the first one there. Mr. Johnny-on-the-spot. Radar Robert Roadrunner. The Scoop. No matter how fast the other stringers moved, Biggy Hartley always managed to arrive before anyone else.

No one could figure it out.

Some of it made sense. Hartley worked for the *Chronicle* and the paper had the largest circulation. Stood to reason that it would have the most sources and the best resources. But even among his fellow reporters at the *Chronicle*, Hartley proved to be the early bird, finishing up when the others began, waiting with the proverbial worm in his mouth.

At first, it was annoying. Then it became irritating. Finally, it turned out to be downright frustrating. And Hartley played the part to the hilt. Chomping on a cigar like a cat-bird seated character out of a forties play. Arching his fat eyebrows and spitting bits of tobacco into the waste can.

When his colleagues expressed their consternation at his seemingly extraterrestrial sense of timing, Hartley answered evasively.

"I just get this feeling." Chomp. Spit. "Can't explain it. Like a buzz in my head."

"C'mon," they'd insist. "Who are you bribing?"

"You wish it was that simple." Hartley smoothed back thin, ash-colored hair and smiled widely with yellowed teeth. "It'd make you look better to the boss, wouldn't it. Nah, you can't rationalize away my success with money. Some people just got the knack. Can't help it. Just got the knack."

Hartley had grown up in San Diego. None of his co-workers could understand why he spoke with a Mid-Atlantic accent.

It wouldn't be *so* bad if the man had an ounce of humility. Instead, each success instilled Hartley with renewed arrogance. He boasted, bragged, and preened like a peacock, spending hours in front of the mirror practicing badass looks.

Narrow the eyes, wrinkle the nose . . . yeah, that's right. Now the sneer; raising the upper lip at the corner. Perfect.

Comical, except that Hartley got results. Which meant frequent raises and invitations to important functions. He would often arrive at the dinners in a rumpled suit with an open-necked shirt and scuffed shoes. His manner was abrasive. He flirted shamelessly with other men's wives. He had dirt underneath his fingernails.

"You can act anyway you want as long as you're number one!" he told fellow reporter, Carolyn Hislop. They were sitting in Hartley's office. As numero uno *ace* reporter, Hartley was the only investigative reporter on the paper who had a genuine room with walls and a door that closed. The rest of the plebeians, as he often called them, were stuck with cubicles.

"C'mon!" Carolyn answered. "Everyone knows you've got some kind of card up your sleeve. You're not a warlock. No one can be number one *all* the time."

"I can!" Hartley answered.

A distasteful expression swam across Carolyn's pretty face. For once, Hartley decided to pull back. He decided not to spit tobacco into his waste can. He decided not to brag or boast or talk in his mid-Atlantic accent. Because he liked Carolyn. She had big blue eyes and cleavage. He wanted to get into her pants.

"I can't explain it," he said, trying to act very sincere. "I get this feeling, Carolyn."

"What kind of feeling?"

"Like this buzz or this signal inside my brain." As Hartley talked about it, he realized he really couldn't *explain* it. He took a handful of nuts and popped them into his mouth. Chewing as he talked, he said, "I hear like a shortwave radio. Sometimes I even hear words . . . like the cops are talking to me." He paused. "Plus I sleep with the news station on. I hear lots of things in my sleep."

"C'mon!" she shot back, doing her best Lois Lane. "We all sleep with the news station on. We all hear the cops talking over the shortwave. We all hear the transmissions as they're going down. Why are you always first?"

"You hear the transmissions that come over

the public lines." Hartley took another fistful of goobers. "In my case, I hear the private TAC lines . . . the cops talking to each other before it even makes its way to the RTO. I just hear it in my brain — Ah *shit!*"

"What's wrong?"

"I bit into a piece of shell." Hartley spit into the waste can. Carolyn grimaced. He said, "Friggin' nut can. It says *shelled.* The nuts are supposed to be *shelled.* I'm gonna sue the bastards."

"You do that," Carolyn said. "Claim mental as well as physical distress. By the way, I think you're putting me on . . . all that crap about hearing it in your head."

"No!" Hartley protested. "I'm not putting you on. Why would I put you on? I'm trying to get into your pants."

Carolyn frowned. "Not a chance."

"Even if I shared my byline with you?"

She pondered the offer. "For how long?"

"A month —"

"Nope."

"A year?"

She nodded. "Maybe."

"Wait," Hartley backtracked. "A year's too long. Six months."

"Screw you."

"C'mon," Hartley said "I'll get you invited to all the parties. Drinks at Mais Oui, dinner at Pretensio's —"

"I don't need your smarmy deals. I can get invited on my own right."

"Yeah, so why haven't I seen you there?"

"Because I haven't made my move yet."

Meaning she hadn't shown enough skin to their lecherous boss. The man was a total sucker for a big pair of boobs.

"Besides," Carolyn went on, "I'd rather lay him than you anyway. Why eat hamburger when you can get steak?"

"Sometimes a hamburger can be very tasty."

"You're not even hamburger," she said. "You're headcheese."

"Headcheese?"

"Yeah, headcheese. The luncheon meat made from the ears and the eyelids of a pig. That's what you are, Hartley. You're a pig."

"You're just jealous."

"Damn right I'm jealous!"

She stalked off, shutting the door with force. The one bad thing about having a door. People were always slamming it in his face.

He had to be stopped, so they hired someone for the nasty task. He talked over ideas with Hartley's colleagues.

"I'll ice him when he pisses," he said to the others. "His back'll be to the door. He won't see a thing."

"Hartley uses the stalls."

"Even better. Then he definitely won't see anything. I'll shoot him through the door."

"You might miss him. Worse yet, you might hit the crapper. What a mess that would make."

The bathroom was out.
"I'll do it at his house."
So it was decided. At his house, using the old standby ruse. Plugging him with a thirty-two then masking the pop by tossing the house and making it look like a robbery.

That night, as Hartley turned his twenty-five-year-old red Datsun Z into his driveway, the hair on the back of his neck suddenly stood on end. Senses heightened, Hartley pulled the keys out of the ignition and tossed them back and forth between his hands.
There it was. The buzz in his brain.
What was it saying to him?
What was going on?
Listen to the buzz, Biggy.
Yeah, it was definitely there.
Buzz, buzz, buzz.
And it felt ominous although he wasn't sure why.
Figure it out, Biggy. You're the man with the plan.
Buzz, buzz, buzz.
And then he realized what it was.
It was the *music*.
The music from his house.
He couldn't hear it with his ears, but he could damn well hear it in his head.
Yep, it was in his head.
Weird.
Buzz, buzz, buzz.
And it was coming from *his* radio. Instead of

the news station, his damn radio was playing music. And *bad* music at that. Thrash metal. Some junked-up, long-haired pissy little moron in tight pants was screaming something. What was even more amazing was that some idiot thought it was worth recording.

The taste of today's kids.

Mind-boggling.

Of course, that really wasn't the main issue at hand. The main issue was why was thrash metal cacophony coming from his nightstand radio instead of the news station?

Maybe that *was* the news — a new thrash metal band.

He discarded that idea. More than likely, the bad music meant that someone had been inside his house and had changed his radio station.

That made Hartley nervous.

He approached the house with trepidation.

Slowly, slowly.

Come on, Biggy. Give 'im the old sneer.

What would Dick Tracy do in such a situation?

On tiptoes, he arrived at his front door. With great precision while crouching on the sidelines, Hartley deftly inserted the key into the lock.

Quietly, he turned the key.

With force, he pushed the door open while remaining in his hunkered-down position.

Immediately, the stillness broke into the rat-a-tat cadence of machine gun volley as bullets came flying through the open doorway. Hartley held his hands over his ears, his head bent down to his chest. Like some friggin' cornered cat. He prayed, waiting for the din to die down. It was loud — not as loud as the thrash metal music ringing in his ears — but loud enough to interfere with the buzz.

Then there was silence.

Hartley waited. He heard soft, muffled footsteps. Within moments, a man wearing all black, including a black hood over his face, came out of his door. Either Mr. Black was a hired assassin or the Ku Klux Klan had changed fashion consultants.

Hartley sprang, grabbing the man's legs, and bit him hard in the thigh. The man went down with a thud, landing on his head. The rest, as they say, was history.

And guess who got the scoop.

Once the TV cameras had been set up, Hartley conducted the interviews in his office. With a wheel of microphones surrounding him, Hartley told his story, "I felt that something was off. I *knew* something was off."

"How did you know, Hartley?" someone shouted. "How did you *know?*"

Hartley downed a mouthful of nuts. "I just knew. Just like I know all the breaking action. That's me. Mr. Johnny-on-the-spot. Radar Robert Roadrunner. The Scoop. I hear all the action in my brain."

More questions as Hartley gobbled more nuts.

"No, I can't explain. It's just like this buzz — ah *shit!*"

"What?" asked a group of anxious reporters. "What is it? A bomb? A disaster? A mass murder? Another political sex scandal?"

Hartley replied, "I just bit down on a shell. I'm going to sue those bastards!"

The networks bleeped out the cusswords. MTV left them in.

Sitting in the dentist chair, his mouth numbed and filled with cotton, Hartley breathed in lungful after lungful of laughing gas.

Friggin' nutshells.

It had started out slowly as a dull ache. Within a week, his right jaw had swollen to twice its size until the pain had become unbearable. Without recourse to quell the agony, he finally summoned up the nerve to see the dentist.

"Cracked down the middle," the oral surgeon reported. "The tooth can't be saved. It'll have to come out."

Hartley figured the toothache was penance for all his bragging about his good luck. Well, if this was the worst — although it was pretty bad — he could live with it.

If it didn't happen again.

The gas took the edge off the anxiety, but Hartley's heart still raced when the surgeon entered the operatory.

"How're we doing?" the doctor asked.

Hartley thought, *I'm sure you're doing well, but*

I'm doing shitty. Unfortunately, he was too crocked out to say anything.

"Open up," the surgeon said. "It'll only take a minute."

Hartley managed to open his mouth.

With practiced skill the dentist placed the forceps around the crown of the back molar. He gripped the handles, then paused. "What's that?" he asked.

"Ahhhhh," Hartley responded.

"I hear something." Another beat. "Do you hear something?"

"Ahhhhhh," was Hartley's answer. But he *did* hear something. The buzz in his brain. The *voices* as always. But how could the dentist hear it?

"Ahhhhhhhhh," Hartley responded, trying to talk louder.

"Can't understand a word you're saying." With care, the surgeon rotated the forceps. Up and down, up and down, back and forth, back and forth until he could feel the ligaments holding the tooth to the gum breaking. "Ah well."

Hartley heard the cracking of tooth matter along with the voice. Again, he tried to talk, but the gas . . .

"There it is again," the surgeon said. "Like someone's playing a radio inside your head."

"Ahhhhhhhhhhhh," Hartley tried to scream.

"Now calm down," the surgeon insisted as he turned up the nitrous portion of the nitrous oxide. "You were doing okay. Just hang in there. It's almost over."

Hartley felt his voice box weaken . . . just couldn't move. But he could damn well hear.

The surgeon chuckled, "You know, you read about funny things in the dental journals . . . about radio transmissions that come through dental fillings. I never believed the stories. But maybe that's what I'm hearing. Has that ever happened to you?"

Hartley couldn't talk.

"There!" the surgeon said triumphantly. He held a bloody tooth aloft. "Got it." Slowly, he turned down the nitrous. "Done. Hartley, I've got you breathing more oxygen now. You should come around in about a minute or two. I'll just let you relax."

The door closed. Again, Hartley said nothing. Worse than that, he *heard* nothing.

Absolutely nothing.

No buzz, no voices, no sound.

All of it gone, gone, gone!

Damn those nutshells. He should have sued the bastards.

But what was the point now? Gone!

No more Mr. Johnny-on-the-spot.

No more Radar Robert Roadrunner.

No more the Scoop.

No more parties and special invitations.

No more press conferences.

No more office with a door.

Gone, gone, gone.

So what was left for him? Just a life as an ordinary reporter. As these thoughts came into his brain, Hartley became increasingly depressed. As soon as he was physically able, he reached over to the gas tanks, lowered the oxygen tap to almost nil and turned the nitrous knob on full blast.

Good old nitrous.

He always wanted to die laughing.

Faye Kellerman combines the excitement and taut plotting of police procedurals with an in-depth look at the Orthodox Judaism religion into a series of acclaimed novels that is still going strong. Her first book in the series, *The Ritual Bath*, featuring LAPD detective Peter Decker and widow Rina Lazarus, won the Macavity award for best novel. She lives in California with her husband, novelist Jonathan Kellerman, and her family.

Hero

Jeremiah Healy

I

Frank Rossi sat in his swivel chair by the telephone table at the gallery end of the jury box, watching the "real cop" testify from the witness stand. As a court officer, Frank was by statute entitled to police powers himself, like the right to carry the Glock 17 on his right hip. And he went to the firing range every Friday to make sure he could hit what he aimed at. Because that same statute also said a bailiff could arrest a perp if he saw something illegal go down on the street. Only problem was, any time Frank'd be on the street, he'd be wearing civvies instead of his uniform, and fat chance Angela Rossi's only son would risk his life to bring in some scumbag.

You can picture yourself as Sylvester Stallone playing Rambo, or even Rocky, but when you're more like Sly as the fat sheriff in *Copland*, who'd you be kidding, huh?

Frank liked being a court officer well enough, though, despite the low pay. After all, it was an eight-to-four job with plenty of dead space in it, and no cameras in the courtroom to catch a poor civil servant on the doze. Most of the dead space came from a trial being less like your slick, bang-bang movie and more like a theater play the actors and all were still rehearsing, with lots of stops and delays in the action. If endless testimony and truckloads of documents counted as "action." But Frank thought the different people he got to see made up for all the bullshit.

Take this trial, for instance. *Commonwealth vs. Dennis Doyle.* Or Dennis "the Menace," which was Doyle's mob nickname. Frank actually enjoyed seeing the Irish Mafia get roasted for a change. Doyle himself was a big guy, kind of role you'd give Brian Dennehy with the broad shoulders, beefy face, and wavy hair. Every tooth in his head perfect from birth or dentistry, Doyle had to be in his sixties trying real hard not to look a day past fifty, and pulling it off. Of course, he pulled off a lot of things, running most of the rackets on the South Shore, but according to the prosecution, the Menace had made the mistake of whacking somebody by his own hand in Frank's county. Doyle claimed he was framed, which was par for the course, given that somebody had to have pumped three slugs into the victim. Frank had seen the crime-scene photos of the body when they were put into evidence and passed around the jury. Not pretty pictures, either, and even Dennis the Menace with all his money got denied bail on the charge back at his arraignment.

Which was about all the poor prosecutor had won, far as Frank could tell. Assistant D.A. Ellen Duchesne was short and fat, with a whiny voice that made her seem not exactly up to the task at hand. You'd cast her as Rhoda's sister from that old sitcom, feeling sorry for her every time she opened her mouth.

Mainly, though, you'd feel sorry for her because of the tap dance the defense attorney was doing on the prosecution's evidence. Frank had to admit, he ever got in felony trouble himself, be nice to afford Aaron Weinberg on the mound pitching for him. Medium height with a beard, the guy was kind of a bald Al Pacino. Sharp dresser, yeah, but sharp as a tack, too. And genuinely "courtly" to everybody, not like those assholes on O.J.'s "dream team."

Weinberg managed to look noble even when he was talking with Doyle's number-two guy, one of those thirtyish, executive types with a quarterback's build that every mob seemed to be bringing up as the next generation. Edward was his name, but Frank thought of him as just "Eddie," account of the guy reminded him of Eddie Haskell from the old *Leave It to Beaver* show. Doyle's Eddie would sit in the first row of the gallery, directly behind the defense table, though he was gone from the courtroom a lot, probably running errands for his boss. Eddie had the good fortune not to be indicted for this particular homicide, as he was driving Mrs. Doyle home from some kind of charity function at the time.

Which brought Frank to the most interesting part of the case, at least from his standpoint. Mrs. Lisa Doyle. About five-six in sensible heels, but with great legs that seemed to vibrate as she walked down the center aisle of the courtroom. She always took the gallery bench right behind Weinberg, so the Menace could see her by turning only halfway in the defendant's chair. And so the loving couple could kind of clasp hands briefly over the bar enclosure rail whenever the two other bailiffs brought Doyle to or from the defense table. Maybe thirty or so, Lisa didn't dress to show off the rest of what Frank figured to be a dynamite figure under the clothes, but she couldn't do much to hide that face, even when she was bringing a dark hankie up to it — just so — to dab at her eyes from time to time. Eyes that hung back a little above cheekbones like Michelle Pfeiffer's, only with longish black hair, like Michelle wore hers in *Married to the Mob.* Which made Frank laugh a little, he had to admit.

Here Lisa Doyle reminds you of your favorite actress in that movie, and the poor broad actually *is* married to the mob.

Then Frank Rossi caught himself staring at her because he suddenly realized she was sending him a smile. Kind of a warm, dreamy one, which Frank held on to almost too long. Almost long enough for her husband to maybe turn sideways a little and notice. Which thank Christ he didn't, especially since, with Aaron Weinberg earning his money, Dennis the Menace was probably gonna walk out of the courtroom a free man.

II

In the bailiffs' locker room, Frank changed from his uniform to a flannel shirt and blue jeans. The jeans were loose enough at the waist to let him stick the Glock over his right hip under the shirt, which his late mother always thought looked sloppy but which made Frank feel a lot more secure. After he was done changing clothes, Frank left the courthouse through the employee's entrance, thankfully spared the "anti-terrorist" arch of metal detector that visitors had to go through on the other side of the building.

Hitting the open-air parking lot, he got into the old wreck of a Buick that had been his mom's and started the usual ritual. Drive to a bar, have a few pops while catching part of a ballgame on the tube, Monday Night Football that October evening. Then stop off at the video store to return last night's selection and pick up a new one to watch later in his apartment. From bed, fantasizing the VCR was letting him pull back the sheets for the best-looking woman in the flick. Frank saw a lot of guys renting the hard-core porn tapes, but half the bimbos in them were stone-ugly, and the other half were dense as a fucking post, the way they talked, if the director let them talk at all.

No, Frank preferred the real thing, somebody with a genuine personality. Kathleen Turner in *Body Heat* or Sharon Stone in *Basic Instinct*, if he was into flashy and dangerous. Sandra Bullock for good fun, Winona Ryder for sensitive —

Whoa, boy. Pay attention to the traffic. Plenty of time to make up your mind after you're on the corner stool a while.

And it was a while, sitting on that corner stool at the bar, before Frank noticed the blonde over in the booth, all by herself. She was wearing tinted glasses and a bulky turtleneck. He watched two guys try their luck, neither getting as far as sliding onto the bench across from her. Hard to tell much about the broad with the shades and sweater, but there was something about the way she was holding her head that rang a bell. She even looked over at him, more than a couple times, almost like that —

Hey, who you kidding now? You got Doyle's wife on the brain. Go back to your ballgame.

Which Frank did, for one more beer before leaving the change on the bartop and going out the door.

He didn't recognize the voice behind him because he'd never heard her yell before.

"Frank, you want to wait up?"

He stopped and turned. The blonde, with a walk he did recognize.

Frank looked around the block nervously. "The hell you think you're doing?"

"Trying to talk with you." Lisa was less than an arm's length away now, her tone conversational. "Okay?"

Frank didn't think it was, but he couldn't tell her so.

She said, "I've been watching you in that courtroom for a week now. Found out your name, put on this wig and glasses, and followed you to that bar back there."

"Why?" was all Frank could manage.

"My husband. Aaron thinks he's going to get off on this murder charge."

Frank thought, "Aaron," not "my husband's lawyer."

Lisa said, "And I think he's right."

So did Frank, but what did that matter?

She leaned a little closer. "I can't stand being married to Dennis anymore, Frank."

He began to turn away. "You want a divorce, find your own lawyer."

Lisa touched his arm. Didn't grab it or even the shirt. Just a touch, nails long and pink. Frank felt something like electricity ripple through him.

All the way through him.

Lisa said, "I don't want to get divorced, Frank. I want to be widowed."

"You're talking crazy now."

"I'm not crazy, but I will be if I have to spend another night with Dennis. He's a pig, Frank. And I need somebody to take him out of my life."

"I don't do murder." Frank turned away. Partly to get away, sure, but partly — mostly — to see if Lisa Doyle would touch him again.

She did, and it stopped him because she picked a slightly different spot on his arm for her fingers.

Same feeling though.

Lisa said, "I can offer you money, Frank. And lots of it, once Dennis is dead."

"Okay, that's crazy just as it stands," Frank said, thinking he was sounding perfectly reasonable. "You expect me to kill a guy — a goddamned mobster — without being paid for it up front?"

That dreamy, Michelle Pfeiffer smile from the courtroom. "I've come up with a way to make it worth your while. I'm going to be staying at our beach house on the shore tomorrow night." Suddenly she was tucking a folded piece of paper into his shirt pocket. "That's the address, with my little diagram for parking at a shopping center five blocks away, so nobody'll notice your car. This time of year, none of our neighbors use their houses during the week."

Frank said the first thing that popped into his head. "What about your security?"

"Security?"

"That Eddie guy or his goons?"

The dreamy smile. "You watch too many movies, Frank."

Lisa Doyle walked away. Frank stood where she'd left him, following her with his eyes until she got into a silver Mercedes sports coupe and drove out of sight.

That's when he said to himself that he'd think about it. Just think about it.

But before heading north to his apartment, Frank Rossi stopped at the video store and rented a copy of *Married to the Mob.*

III

That next Tuesday, in the courtroom, Frank sat in his chair at the end of the jury box and watched Lisa Doyle. When he realized he had to stop watching her, he turned toward the witness stand and thought about watching her.

Absently, Frank felt sorry for Ellen Duchesne, her whiny voice botching the direct examination of a crime lab techie who'd run some tests on fibers found at the homicide scene. Just as Aaron Weinberg began slicing and dicing the techie on cross-examination, Eddie the number-two guy came in the courtroom, waiting until the morning recess to confer with Dennis the Menace. The two mobsters leaned toward each other above the bar enclosure like a couple of suburbanites chatting over a picket fence.

Once, when Frank turned back to Lisa, she was staring at him, mouthing the word "tonight."

That's when he turned away again, he thought for good. By the clock on the courtroom wall though, barely three minutes had passed before his eyes strayed over again. And again.

Frank Rossi found himself looking up at the clock often, thinking the hands must be moving backwards, it still seemed so long till four o'clock and quitting time.

After changing in the locker room, Frank tried to follow his usual routine. Walk to the car, drive to the bar, early hockey game on the TV over the top shelf. Midway through the first period and only one beer, though, he found himself going through the door. At the video store, Frank returned *Married to the Mob* and came out onto the sidewalk, breathing hard. Before he was behind the wheel again, Frank knew which way he was going to turn.

South. Toward the shore.

Frank did a drive-by of Lisa Doyle's address at normal speed, nothing to call attention to himself.

It was a saltbox cape with weathered shingles, backing right onto the ocean. Her silver Mercedes coupe, snugged up against a garage door, glittered like a piece of jewelry. Frank could see a couple of lights in the cape, one downstairs, one up. The windows of the surrounding houses stood dark, though, and there were no cars in front of them.

Continuing along the street, Frank found the little shopping center right where Lisa's diagram put it. If nobody else was using the shore houses, enough other folks must be year-rounders, because the lot seemed nearly full, and his Buick could kind of hide in the crowd.

Frank turned off the ignition and sat for a while. Sat until he thought a guy alone in an old wreck might look suspicious.

Then realized that wasn't the reason he wanted to get out of his car.

Frank opened the driver's side door and heaved himself to his feet. After locking up, he started walking the five blocks back toward the house. Started huffing, too, and consciously slowed down.

Hey, you don't want to faint on her stoop, right?

At the cape, Frank moved up the path, the Mercedes to his right now catching some moonlight, the same moonlight that twinkled the ocean water beyond. He was about to push the button on the jamb when the door itself swung open.

A table lamp deeper in the house turned her into a silhouette, the sheer body stocking the kind he'd seen only on women in mail-order catalogs.

"I've been waiting for you, Frank," said Lisa Doyle in a voice from one of his dreams.

IV

Wednesday morning, Frank Rossi couldn't believe how he felt, even just sitting in his bailiff's chair. Tingling all over, the way a real movie star must feel after a night with a starlet.

Only Lisa Doyle wasn't any kid, and she knew how to do everything perfectly. Not like the porn films he'd rented before growing tired of them, the bimbos looking like they were bored or faking or so obviously coked up it amounted to the same thing. No, Lisa was a . . . a sorceress, taking him to the top once, twice, and even

Frank didn't believe the third time.

By the same token, there was no bullshit about her. He was going to enjoy her body and talents only until she got the money to pay him for killing her husband.

And Lisa Doyle had even come up with the perfect way to do that, Frank had to admit.

"So," she said as soon as he arrived for the second night, "let's run through it again."

Lisa had rearranged the dining room chairs in her living room, just like she'd shown him the prior evening. Four of the chairs outlined the courtroom's bar enclosure on either side of its center-aisle gate. One of the chairs represented the first gallery bench, where Lisa had sat throughout the trial, dabbing her eyes with that black hankie.

Now, in the beach house, she pointed to the small revolver she'd laid in Frank's hand. "Let's practice you passing it to me again."

He turned the gun over. "You sure the serial numbers are wiped off?"

"Positive. Dennis always said, 'You need a clean piece, this is the one you use.' "

Frank didn't think he wanted to know why Dennis the Menace would believe his wife might need a "clean piece."

Lisa said, "You've smuggled that through the employee entrance in the morning, where there's no metal detector and you're not searched. In the locker room, when nobody's watching, you put the gun in the side pocket of your uniform pants with the black hankie around it. Now, go ahead."

"Go ahead what?"

Lisa took a small breath before smiling. "Put the gun in the hankie and everything in your right pocket. Good. Now, make like it's just before court starts. You walk around the chairs like they're that bar fence, and I'll turn away from the gate."

As he had the night before, Frank felt a little silly, but he moved along the two chairs as though they were actually the bar enclosure. Using his left hand, he pushed on the imaginary "gate" stepping into the "center aisle."

Over her shoulder, Lisa said, "That's when I'll turn back around and bump into you, so the gun already has to be in the black hankie and in your hand for me."

"What if I slip up and put a fingerprint on the gun by accident?"

"While it's in your pocket?"

"Or while I'm pulling it out."

"Then just be sure you're the first one to Dennis."

Frank pictured what she meant.

Lisa frowned. "You okay?"

"I'm okay."

"You look kind of —"

"I'm okay, all right? Now what?"

Lisa smiled again, that dreamy . . . "Just like we did last night."

Frank shook his head, but he moved through

the living room as though he were walking down the center aisle. After six strides, he said, "Judge'll be out in a minute" to an imaginary person before turning and walking back.

Lisa frowned a little. "You'll look more natural in the real courtroom, I think."

Frank "opened" the gate again and approached his usual "swivel chair" at the gallery end of the jury box.

"And besides," she waved at the surrounding walls, "there won't be any cameras to catch it anyway."

In the Doyles' living room, Frank sat down in the chair that was supposed to be his own.

"After that," said Lisa, "all we have to do is wait till the morning break, and —"

"Recess."

"What?"

"The morning recess, the judge calls it."

"Fine." That smile. "When she says it's time for the morning recess, you say 'All rise' like any other day. Then I lean over the bar rail to Dennis, and I push the gun into his hand."

"What if that Eddie guy is there?"

"Half the time he isn't."

"He might see you, though."

"Don't worry about it."

"Or Weinberg. He'll be right there, too."

"Frank," a little impatience maybe creeping through the smile. "I'll pass the thing so nobody sees me."

"But without leaving any prints on it."

"What the hankie's for, remember?" Lisa closed her eyes a moment. "That's when I scream, 'Dennis, no!' "

"And I yell 'Gun, gun, gun!' "

Lisa stopped, a hand rubbing the ear closest to Frank. "That's how you're going to do it, three times like that?"

"It's the way they trained us."

"Fine, so that's what you'll do. And then . . . ?"

"Then . . ." Frank hesitated until the dreamiest smile yet about melted him. "Then I pull my Glock and shoot him."

"Just 'shoot' him?"

Another hesitation. "Kill him."

"Say it again."

Frank cleared his throat. "I kill him."

"Try it three times, loud, like when you yell about the gun."

"I kill him, I kill him, I kill him!"

A different smile. "Now you've got the idea."

Afterward, in bed, Lisa said, "You probably should leave soon."

Frank spoke to the ceiling, the sheets still caked to him all over. "When?"

"Say ten minutes. You want to shower, it's —"

"No." Frank shifted a little, but didn't get any more comfortable. "I mean, when do you think we'll do it?"

"Pretty soon. Aaron says he doesn't see that whiny prosecutor having much more to throw at Dennis."

What Frank heard was the "Aaron" part again. "You trust him?"

"Who?"

"Your husband's lawyer."

A sigh. "You've probably seen him in action more than I have, but yeah, I trust his judgment on the trial stuff."

Frank couldn't bring himself to ask anything more about Weinberg.

"Frank?"

"Yeah?"

"Don't worry. You'll be a hero. Believe me, Dennis really killed that guy. Not to mention a dozen others."

Right then, Frank Rossi was thinking less about the people Dennis the Menace Doyle had shot and more about the ones Frank himself hadn't.

V

Thursday morning before court, Frank noticed that Eddie wasn't in the gallery. Doyle himself almost lounged in his chair at the defense table, joking with Aaron Weinberg like a salesman knowing he was going to close a big deal. At the first recess, Frank did a dry-run with Lisa, not actually bumping her in the center aisle, but feeling out the distances and timing.

When the trial resumed, Weinberg started hammering at a Commonwealth "earwitness," as Frank liked to call people who heard something about a crime but didn't actually see the thing go down. By the time Doyle's attorney was done, the witness looked battered, and dumpy Ellen Duchesne looked beaten.

Lisa, on the other hand, looked beautiful. Just before lunch, she acted like she had something in her eye, using the hankie to hide her giving Frank a wink.

And that's when he knew for sure he was going to do it. All the doubts he'd felt — qualms, his late mother would have called them — just seemed to slide away inside his chest, and Frank genuinely relaxed in the swivel chair.

He was going to do it. Less for the money and more for Lisa, to get her free of that arrogant pig.

In fact, you look at it the right way, you're kind of her hero, solving this problem she has.

Thursday night, when Lisa opened the front door of the beach house for Frank, she had on a dress instead of lingerie, but it was a different kind of dress than the quiet business ones she wore to court for her husband's trial. This was kind of skimpy, plain black and a little shiny, too. Like silk, maybe.

When Frank stepped into the foyer, he could see the dining room chairs arranged again in the living room. "We gonna do another rehearsal?"

"Passing the gun, you mean?"

"Yeah."

"Later."

"Later?"

"After we go upstairs. I have a treat for you."

Frank could actually feel his knees shaking from excitement as he climbed the steps behind her.

Once in the bedroom, Lisa turned to him. The sheets were already pulled down, the lights muted. Frank kind of liked that she'd dimmed the lights because he knew he didn't have the greatest physique in the world, nothing like a male version of the body on her.

Lisa gave him the dreamy smile, her teeth the brightest things in the room. "Tear off my dress."

That stopped him, but excited him, too. "What?"

"Tear off my dress."

"I . . . I don't get . . ."

"Frank," reaching for his hand, "you've been a good guy through this so far, and I want you to have something special out of it tonight." She brought his hand up to her neckline. "I want you to tear this thing off me, get to see what I'm wearing underneath."

Frank could feel the silky material, could feel himself swelling below his belt buckle, bigger than he'd ever —

"Come on, Frank. I want you to."

And suddenly, irresistibly, he wanted to as well. He ripped the dress down the side of her body, then across, like a huge letter "L" with the foot kind of diagonal instead of straight.

Which was when he could see that what she was wearing underneath was nothing at all.

"It's tomorrow, right?"

After Frank had spoken the words to the ceiling, he turned away from Lisa and stared at her torn dress on the bedroom carpet.

"How did you know?" she said.

He turned back to the ceiling. "Because after it happens, we don't see each other again except for you giving me the money, and tonight felt kind of like . . ."

"A going-away present?"

Lisa's voice sounded thick to Frank, almost as if she was going to cry.

He said, "Something like that, yeah."

Her voice steadied. "Aaron told us today he doesn't think he has to put on much of a defense case, and for sure not call Dennis to the stand as a witness himself."

"So, if we don't do it at the morning recess —"

"We may not get another chance."

Frank could see it, feel it. Lisa was right.

In an even steadier voice, she said, "Tomorrow you're going to be a hero, Frank. And a week later, you'll be rich to boot."

Frank Rossi was conscious of hearing both things Lisa Doyle told him, but he realized it was only the first part that he cared about.

VI

At five minutes to the morning recess, Eddie the number-two guy still hadn't shown up in the courtroom, and Frank let himself breathe a little easier in his swivel chair. It'd been a piece of cake getting the snubbie revolver wrapped in Lisa's handkerchief through the employee's entrance and, at his locker, into the side pocket of his uniform pants. And Frank had passed it to Lisa at the center aisle so smoothly, he'd felt like a feather as he floated down the aisle, exchanged a stupid crack with another bailiff at the rear of the room, and then walked back to his chair.

When the judge announced the morning recess, Frank stood quickly. Calling out, "All rise," he was aware of everybody else getting to their feet. But then the rest of it played out in a kind of slow motion, like one of those shoot-'em-up scenes from a spaghetti western.

Lisa, her hankie between her hands, leaning over the gallery rail to Dennis Doyle, like she always did. Him taking both of her hands in his, again like always.

Then Lisa jumping back as the two bailiffs casually approached the defendant, her mouth opening, her words splitting the air.

Somewhere between "Dennis" and "no!," Frank was bringing the Glock out of his holster, the two bailiffs jumping back themselves from Lisa's scream. Frank bellowed the magic word "Gun!" three times as he opened fire, the shots making his ears ring.

The first slug struck Dennis Doyle square in the chest, just as the man was looking down at the revolver in his own hand. The second caught him near the left shoulder, knocking the mobster off-center. The third bullet punched Doyle in the throat, carrying him back over his chair and onto the defense table. By now, everybody in the room except for Frank had dropped to their haunches, yelling like they were real excited about looking for a contact lens on the floor.

And then there was nothing but the smell of cordite hanging heavy around him, every living eye staring up at the hero near the gallery end of the jury box.

Funny, the thing you think will be the worst part turns out to be the easiest.

Passing that revolver to Lisa without fumbling it out of the hankie or putting a fingerprint on the frame was what had occupied Frank the most, but the thing he'd really worried about was the shooting itself. With a real human being in his sights, would he be able to pull the trigger?

But, turned out, everything felt exactly the way it did on the firing range. Frank had found himself not so much aiming as just pointing and squeezing off the rounds, seeing the little puffs of cloth and blood come up as the slugs impacted their target. There was no video of the scene to play back, of course, except the one in his head, which improved slightly each time Frank revisited it during his week's paid leave of absence from the job.

He'd also worried some about the Shoot Team interrogation, but that proved to be so routine he was almost embarrassed to answer their questions. The guys who really drew the heat were the two bailiffs who supposedly checked the defendant carefully each time they brought him into the courtroom, because — after all — that little snubbie had to come from *some*where.

Frank was less concerned about Aaron Weinberg. The defense attorney immediately told the press that there was "absolutely no reason" Dennis Doyle would have thought he needed to shoot his way out of the charge against him, especially given Weinberg's confidence "in the jury's eventual verdict." Obviously, Lisa had done a nice job of shielding the gun from her husband's lawyer.

In fact, as things unfolded, the biggest pain in the ass for Frank was all the fuss the media made over him. He stopped clipping the newspaper headlines — or even taping the broadcast stuff with his VCR — by the end of the second day. The fucking jackals, they camped outside his apartment around the clock, just waiting for him to go buy a loaf of bread or a sixpack of beer to pump him for "additional comments" or "aftershock feelings" on the incident which had made him "The Dirty-Harry Hero."

At least, Frank conceded, they'd gone with a movie he liked.

In the end, though, it wasn't till the fifth day — when two state troopers brought down a drive-by shooter after a high-speed chase that the media picked up stakes and moved their circus

to somebody else's front yard. Frank telep
his superior, saying he figured he could
back in to work then, but still was told to
until after the weekend.

Which washed fine with Frank. Given the d
he'd had with the media — not to mention t
nights with Lisa before that — he could use tl
rest. He began to spend his time more normall
going out for a few beers, the hero stuff still there
but starting to slack off in the bars. The way
Frank saw it, he was getting his life back on
track.

But what had happened in Lisa's bedroom and the courtroom had been a part of his life, too. And, starting up the old Buick to drive to her house for his money, Frank Rossi realized that he had no regrets about having lived those parts and having been her hero — for real.

"It's open," was Lisa Doyle's muffled answer to his knock on the front door.

Frank entered the foyer, noticing that all the furniture from the dining room had been moved back to where it belonged.

"I'm upstairs."

He climbed the steps, thinking how differently he'd felt every other time he'd done so.

"My bedroom, Frank," in the dreamy voice.

The tantalizing thought of a "bonus" went through his head, and he walked a little faster to the open door of the room Frank associated with the best hours he'd ever lived.

Before what he saw stopped him dead.

"God, Frank, don't be shy now."

On the bed, a briefcase lay open like a clamshell, cash stacked inside it. Lisa stood next to the bed, fanning a pack of greenbacks with her left thumb, the hand behind her, like she was pregnant and resting it on her butt.

But Lisa wore the silky black dress from their last night together. The torn one, only with a bra and panties clearly visible underneath.

Frank said, "I don't . . ."

"I thought it might be kind of fun to do it one last time." She gestured with the cash in her left hand. "On the bed, but with your money spread all around us."

Frank just stared.

Lisa took two steps toward him. "Come on, what do you say?"

He couldn't say anything, truth to tell, but he swallowed hard and began walking toward her.

When Frank was about an arm's length away — like they'd been that first time after she'd yelled to him on the street — Lisa Doyle brought her right hand out from behind her back and fired the gun in it three times.

Frank thought somebody had hit him in the chest with a sledgehammer. Then the walls and ceiling began to switch places. He felt the back of his head bounce off the floor, but somehow it didn't hurt.

Which seemed kind of funny, you know?

Stretched out flat, staring at the ceiling from a

different perspective than he'd gotten those nights from her bed, Frank heard other footsteps and saw two faces superimpose themselves on the ceiling, looking down at him now. Lisa's, right side up and . . .

Eddie's, upside down?

Sure, thought Frank. Because he's standing behind you.

"I didn't kill him?" from Lisa's face.

"The fucking whale's got to bleed out," from Eddie's. "Way it's going, shouldn't take too long."

Your eyes and ears still work, but so hard to . . . breathe.

Lisa's face said, "Should I shoot him again?"

"No. Lab stuff from the cops wouldn't look right, the sex crazed hero gets shot on the floor after you already popped him for tearing your dress off to rape you."

Frank wanted to say something, but could only burble out some . . . spit?

She turned away. "Jesus, he's trying to talk."

"I'll give you this, Lise," said Eddie. "The fucking guy never knew we were setting him up."

Coming from a new direction, Lisa's voice sounded bitter. "We wouldn't have had to, you'd done the frame on Dennis right from the start."

"Yeah, well, I didn't," said Eddie's face, grinning down at Frank. "Every day of that trial, the boss had me hustling my ass all over the fucking place, trying to find out who'd fingered him. But, once Weinberg got Dennis off in court, the boss would have figured why I was coming up empty."

"And figured us," from Lisa.

"Hey." Eddie looked away now. "Make sure you don't smear the whale's fingerprints on that fucking dress."

Lisa Doyle's face loomed back into Frank's vision, and he tried to muster a smile to thank her for the sight.

She spoke with those eyes as well as her mouth. "Sorry, Frank, but I needed you to make this thing work. Do you understand?"

Frank Rossi tried to remember which movie that reminded him of, but there wasn't quite . . . enough time . . . to . . .

Jeremiah Healy's street smart detective John Francis Cuddy has appeared in thirteen novels, most recently *Spiral.* He's also made several appearances in anthologies as well, including *Legal Briefs*, *Cat Crimes II*, and several of *The Year's 25 Finest Crime and Mystery* volumes. A former president of the Private Eye Writers of America, he has spoken extensively about mystery writing around the world, including the Smithsonian Institution's Literature series.

Therapy

Jonathan Kellerman

Dr. Tinker thought it might be therapeutic, so she videotaped the morning news.

No problem capturing the three-minute segment, every station was playing nearly identical footage. But she suspected it wouldn't make the evening broadcast. The victim wasn't important enough and, in this city, there was never any shortage of that kind of thing.

She wasn't sure she'd use the tape with Amber; one could never predict the way patients reacted.

Just a guess, but a creative one. She prided herself on her creativity. That was precisely what appealed to her about being a therapist: the work was a perfectly seasoned stew of science and art. And humans were so wonderfully variable: the same old, predictable reactions co-existing with those terrible flashpoints of crisis that gave no warning.

Her patients loved her. One of the reasons the Survivor's Center placed her at the top of the referral list.

The cases they sent her were wrenching horrors, but satisfying; she knew she was doing good work. Often the patients couldn't pay even a small fraction of her fee, but she still had enough private long-terms to keep her income at a steady level. With the HMO's coming in, who knew . . . but that was another issue, a self-centered distraction.

And distractions were fatal to the work; the key was to focus exclusively on the person sitting in the other comfy chair.

You could have the best paper credentials, every sub-specialty certification and academic honor, but if you couldn't crawl into someone else's head, go beyond empathy to *sensation,* you were useless.

To Karen Tinker, being a good therapist meant becoming a non-person, a psychic shadow, tossing one's ego into the closet for forty-five minute stretches. Seven stretches a day, six days a week.

Fifty-one weeks a year. From August 23 through the 30th, she booked herself a first-class flight to an obscure tropical island, checked into a clean but middling resort hotel, and spent the entire time reading by some pool, wearing dark sunglasses and avoiding men's admiring glances.

She was thirty-six years old, looked a bit younger, had been licensed for a little over six years. Nearly ten thousand little chunks of non-personhood. Not counting her internship, her post-doc, all the other things she'd done to get here.

Classroom lessons.

The nightmare lessons — stop, in the closet, Ego.

The waiting room bell sounded. Amber Browning right on time, as always.

Dr. Tinker put her coffee cup down on the

desk and walked across the cozy office to a wall of bookshelves where the TV and the VCR sat, electronic interlopers, among the textbooks and the neatly-labeled cases of scientific journals. Rewinding and cueing the tape, she placed the remote control atop the mahogany drum table that flanked her comfy chair. Like her desktop, the table was nearly clear. Just a cut-crystal tissue box she'd seen in a catalogue and thought perfect. It emptied several times a week.

Everything in place. She threw back her shoulders, straightened her back, put on her best reassuring smile, and strode smoothly to the door.

Amber was talking before she sat down.

How was that for progress! For the first few months, nothing. Then, hesitant spurts. Recently, a flood.

No tears, yet, but that was fine.

She said, "I don't know if you saw the news, but . . ."

She stopped, lip quivering, eyes fixed on the carpet. Dr. Tinker came over and placed a hand on her shoulder. The girl looked up. Not having to complete the sentence seemed to comfort her.

She unbuttoned her cardigan and lowered herself into the other chair.

Girl, not woman. Twenty-one, but a long way from adulthood.

Like Dr. Tinker, she looked younger than her age.

Other similarities . . . focus, Karen.

Dr. Tinker sat, too, crossing her legs and placing her hand over the remote control.

"So."

Amber shrugged.

So small. Finely-boned, pale, definitely the waif.

The only child of two loving people who'd done all they could to help her, but it hadn't been enough.

A pretty girl, if you got past the sunken eyes and the small, downturned mouth. Dark eyes receding like fugitives, shadowed by black lashes that she no longer mascaraed.

A good student, French Club, girl's softball, Red Cross volunteer, nothing more traumatic for most of the eighteen years than an infrequent C on a test. Accepted by a college halfway across the country, she'd planned to leave home for the first time.

Change in plans.

Because of him.

Black lashes but blonde hair. He went for blondes, had an eighteen-year history of predation of blondes. Small-boned, fair-haired girls, between sixteen and twenty-four.

Dr. Tinker had obtained a look at his file.

Six arrests in eighteen years. The data said he'd most likely committed seven to ten times as many crimes, more if you included the juvey offenses that stayed sealed. Six arrests, five plea bargains and reductions of charges, finally a conviction for attempted sexual assault, fifteen years in the state prison.

Automatic good-time brought that down to seven years, four months, and his avoidance of overt violence while behind bars shaved *that* to thirty-nine months.

And then he was out. Assigned to a parole officer with 344 other active cases and required to submit to random drug tests.

Which was fine with him. Drugs weren't his thing.

He handled the streets well enough, living quietly in a halfway house filled with other felons, everyone trying to figure the angles, do their habitual thing without getting caught again.

He found a job on a roofing crew.

Amber Browning's bad luck. He'd been nailing shingles to the eaves of her parents' pretty colonial house, seen her drive up in her little graduation-gift car, bounce happily to the front door and open it, calling out, "I'm home!"

Suzy Sweetie; right out of a TV show. Watching from atop the roof, he'd gotten that old feeling.

The roofing gig lasted a week, ample time to find out which bedroom was hers, to get a fix on the family's habits, learn there was no alarm, no dog, the rear bathroom window could be jimmied by a blind moron.

For the next two weeks, he returned to the neighborhood at night, driving slowly. On the fourteenth night, the parents went out for the evening. Dressed fancy, meaning something that would keep them busy for a while.

Lithe blonde only-child home alone.

The rest was easy.

Then bad luck: on the way home, two uniforms spotted his broken taillight — how could he have missed that? — and pulled him over. He was sure he'd maintained perfectly, citizen's smile, no sweating or coming on too strong, *yes, officer; no officer.* But they'd sensed something, cuffed him and popped the trunk.

Inside was his kit: ski mask, gloves, masking tape, his cuffs, condoms because with the new tests you couldn't leave anything behind, the novelty shop revolver, totally bogus but effective with waifs. The knife that was real.

Bummer.

Then the game shifted again and along came this public defender, generally you couldn't expect much out of them, but this one was smart. Wanting to actually try the case, not plead.

Pointing out that the police hadn't obtained permission to search his trunk, a busted light wasn't even on the same planet as probable cause.

Case dismissed.

Yes!

"No!" Amber's mother had screamed.

Amber said nothing.

That worried Mr. and Mrs. Browning the most. They loved their baby more than anything, could have handled hysteria, howling, sleepless nights, agonized shrieks evoking memories of infant fevers.

But the dry eyes, the padlocked mouth, the refusal to surrender to pain. The smile — *that* smile.

"It's not that she never talks about it," Mrs. Browning confided to Karen during the intake, Amber out in the waiting room, wearing a too old-for-her cardigan and reading a magazine. "She does — not often, but sometimes. But the way she does it — such a . . . casual tone of voice — I know this sounds strange, but she almost seems blasé, doctor. She's always been shy — maybe it's my fault. I was shy, too, at her age. Maybe I didn't set the best example."

"There's only one person at fault," Karen Tinker told her, with gentle forcefulness, "and it's not you. Cecille, what you're describing is normal." She repeated the word, very softly. "I've seen it so many times."

"All right," said the woman, not looking convinced at all. "I suppose I have to put her in your hands, now."

"So you watched it," said Amber.

"I did."

"Weird."

Dr. Tinker said nothing. Part of the art was you played the silences.

Amber said, "I mean — like having your wish come true. My wish. I guess I should feel fantastic. Like justice has been done. But I —"

The girl shook her head. Her long yellow hair was cropped very short, had been for a while, and nothing swirled. Dr. Tinker wondered if she'd ever want to swirl it again.

She said, "There's no right way to feel, Amber."

"I guess — maybe it's too early. I'm still freaked out by it — there I was, eating breakfast and watching TV and — the first thing I felt was shock. I'd always thought of him as invincible — the devil, Satan, Freddy Krueger, whatever. Like he could do whatever he . . . do damage to everyone else but never get damaged himself."

She sighed. "I should feel relieved — and I guess I do. In terms of him. I mean one thing's for certain, he can't . . . bother me again."

"Not ever," said Dr. Tinker. "Never."

Amber looked the other way. "The thing is — let's face it, there are so many others just like him. It could be anyone — some perfectly normal-looking guy you pass on the street, some guy you go out with, thinking he's a gentleman."

She laughed. "Are there any gentlemen? Any gentle men?"

It took a second for Dr. Tinker to be certain her voice would be steady. "Yes. Of course."

Amber's dark eyes misted. "I don't know — I don't know if I'll ever believe that. Not intellectually. In here." She patted her belly.

Dr. Tinker remained silent.

"I know, I know," said the girl. "All in due time."

"In due time means *your* time, Amber."

"My time . . . as if I own time."

"You don't think you do?"

"I guess . . . sometimes time seems to be slipping by — I do have to admit, it wasn't bad at all. Hearing about it. Especially the part about it being a knife. That was perfect — pretty bloodthirsty, huh?"

"I think you can be forgiven a certain amount of bloodthirstiness, Amber."

Amber gave the smile that troubled her parents. "What I mean by the knife is the parallel. A perfect match, eye for an eye. And the way he was hit from the back. Just like . . ." The eyes seemed to come forward, out of the shadows. "What do you think actually happened?"

"We may never know," said Dr. Tinker. "But psychopaths tend to hang out with other psychopaths and they all have low impulse control. He could have gotten someone angry — said the wrong thing at the wrong time."

"Something trivial?" said Amber. "I like that. It dehumanizes him . . . live by the knife, inherit the knife." Now the girl was grinning. "Yes, I definitely like that."

Dr. Tinker smiled. Amber stared at her. Then she laughed. Then she cried.

It was their best session ever.

Alone in her office again, Dr. Tinker poured herself a cup of coffee and sank down in her desk chair. Thirteen minutes until the next appointment.

Her chest hurt. Probably tensed up the whole

time, listening to Amber sob and rage.

She put the cup down and sat back, eyes closed, forcing herself to breathe slowly and deeply, progressively relaxing each muscle, the routine she used for her tensest patients, the frozen ones.

Amber, thawing nicely. The prognosis was good. Excellent.

And she hadn't even needed to play the tape.

Out in the parking lot, Cecille Browning noticed the difference right away. The old bouncy walk, a smile on her baby's lips, but a real one, not *that* one.

She got out of the station wagon and jingled the keys. "Want to drive, honey?" Thinking maybe. Finally.

"No thanks, Mom."

"You're sure?"

"Yes, Mom." Amber kissed her mother's cheek and Cecille was careful to hide her disappointment.

Progress was being made. Slowly, but . . . Dr. Tinker, wonderful Karen Tinker. What a name for a therapist! But she did feel Amber was being repaired.

The time Karen had given Cecille had been helpful, too. Building up her own confidence.

She and Amber got in the wagon and Cecille began driving home.

"Any plans for today, sweetheart?"

"I dunno — I think I'm going to rest."

"Sure, honey. I have a few errands to run — want to keep me company?"

"Um, I don't think so, Mom — is that okay?"

"Of course, sweetheart."

The wagon merged into traffic and the two of them sank into one of their silences. Amber thinking about getting under the covers and just blacking things out, the three-quarter hour had made her so, so tired.

Her mother composing a list of things to do.

Pick up the dry cleaning.

Buy steaks and salad greens for dinner.

Call the pool man because the water was clouding up, even though he'd just replaced parts in the filter and charged a fortune.

Clean the knife. She'd washed it last night, but hastily, and some rusty stains lingered along the cutting edge.

So scrub it really good. Stare at it for a while, then get rid of it.

Bake a cake. Maybe angel food, because she wanted to take off a few pounds.

Where to get rid of the knife . . . the lake. Perfect.

She felt her hands tense on the steering wheel, felt the urge to do something, anything.

Therapy was great, but sometimes you needed to *do* something.

Jonathan Kellerman's Alex Delaware series has been critically lauded since the first title, *When the Bough Breaks*, which won the Mystery

Writers of America's Edgar award and the Anthony Boucher award, both for best first novel. Since then his novels, the latest being *Survival of the Fittest*, have continued to garner bestselling success. A Clinical Professor at the University of Southern California School of Medicine, he is married to novelist Faye Kellerman.

Natural Death, Inc.

Max Allan Collins

She'd been pretty, once. She was still sexy, in a slutty way, if you'd had enough beers and it was just before closing time.

Kathleen O'Meara, who ran the dingy dive that sported her last name, would have been a well-preserved fifty, if she hadn't been forty. But I knew from the background materials I'd been provided that she was born in 1899, here in the dirt-poor Irish neighborhood of Cleveland known as the Angles, a scattering of brick and frame dwellings and businesses at the north end of 25th Street in the industrial flats.

Kathleen O'Meara's husband, Frank, had been dead barely a month now, but Katie wasn't wearing black: her blouse was white with red polka dots, a low-cut peasant affair out of which spiked well-powdered, bowling ball-size breasts. Her mouth was a heavily red-rouged chasm within which gleamed white storebought choppers; her eyes were lovely, within their pouches, long lashed and money green.

"What's your pleasure, handsome?" she asked, her soprano voice musical in a calliope sort of way, a hint of Irish lilt in it.

I guess I was handsome, for this crowd anyway — six feet, one-hundred-eighty pounds poured into threadbare mismatched suitcoat and pants, a wilted excuse for a fedora snugged low over my reddish brown hair, chin and cheeks stubbled with two days growth — looking back at myself in the streaked smudgy mirror behind the bar. A chilly March afternoon had driven better than a dozen men inside the shabby walls of O'Meara's, where a churning exhaust fan did little to stave off the bouquet of stale smoke and beer-soaked sawdust.

"Suds is all I can afford," I said.

"There's worse ways to die," she said, eyes sparkling.

"Ain't been reduced to canned heat yet," I admitted.

At least half of the clientele around me couldn't have made that claim; while those standing at the bar, with a foot on the rail, like me, wore the sweatstained workclothes that branded them employed, the men hunkered at tables and booths wore the tattered rags of the derelict. A skinny dark-haired dead-eyed sunken-cheeked barmaid in an off-white waitress uniform was collecting empty mugs and replacing them with foaming new ones.

The bosomy saloonkeeper set a sloshing mug before me. "Railroad worker?"

I sipped; it was warm and bitter. "Steel mill. Pretty lean in Gary; heard they was hiring at Republic."

"That was last month."

"Yeah. Found that out in a hurry."

She extended a pudgy hand. "Kathleen O'Meara, at your service."

"William O'Hara," I said. Nathan Heller, actually. The Jewish last name came from my father, but the Irish mug that was fooling the saloonkeeper was courtesy of my mother.

"Two O's, that's us," she grinned; that mouth must have been something, once. "My pals call me Katie. Feel free."

"Well, thanks, Katie. And my pals call me Bill." Nate.

"Got a place to stay, Bill?"

"No. Thought I'd hop a freight tonight. See what's shakin' up at Flint."

"They ain't hiring up there, neither."

"Well, I dunno, then."

"I got rooms upstairs, Bill."

"Couldn't afford it, Katie."

"Another mug?"

"Couldn't afford that, either."

She winked. "Handsome, you got me wrapped around your little pinkie, ain't ya noticed?"

She fetched me a second beer, then attended to the rest of her customers at the bar. I watched her, feeling both attracted and repulsed; what is it about a beautiful woman run to fat, gone to seed, that can still summon the male in a man?

I was nursing the second beer, knowing that if I had enough of these I might do something I'd regret in the morning, when she trundled back over and leaned on the bar with both elbows.

"A room just opened up. Yours, if you want it."

"I told ya, Katie, I'm flat-busted."

"But I'm not," she said with a lecherous smile,

and I couldn't be sure whether she meant money or her billowing powdered bosoms. "I could use a helpin' hand around here. . . . I'm a widow lady, Bill, runnin' this big old place by her lonesome."

"You mean sweep up and do dishes and the like."

Her cute nose wrinkled as if a bad smell had caught its attention; a little late for that in this joint. "My daughter does most of the drudgery." She nodded toward the barmaid, who was moving through the room like a zombie with a beer tray. "Wouldn't insult ya with woman's work, Bill. . . . But there's things only a man can do."

She said "things" like "tings."

"What kind of things?"

Her eyes had a twinkle, like broken glass. "Things. . . . Interested?"

"Sure, Katie."

And it was just that easy.

Three days earlier, I had been seated at a conference table in the spacious dark-wood and pebbled-glass office of the public safety director in Cleveland's city hall.

"It's going to be necessary to swear you in as a part of my staff," Eliot Ness said.

I had known Eliot since we were both teenagers at the University of Chicago. I'd dropped out, finished up at a community college and gone into law enforcement; Eliot had graduated and became a private investigator, often working for insurance companies. Somewhere along the way, we'd swapped jobs.

His dark brown hair brushed with gray at the temples, Eliot's faintly freckled, boyish good looks were going puffy on him, gray eyes pouchy and marked by crow's feet. But even in his late thirties, the former Treasury agent who had been instrumental in Al Capone's fall was the youngest public safety director in the nation.

When I was on the Chicago P.D., I had been one of the few cops Eliot could trust for information; and when I opened up the one-man A-1 Detective Agency, Eliot had returned the favor as my only trustworthy source within the law enforcement community. I had remained in Chicago and he had gone on to more government crimebusting in various corners of the midwest, winding up with this high profile job as Cleveland's "top cop"; since 1935, he had made national headlines cleaning up the police department, busting crooked labor unions, and curtailing the numbers racket.

Eliot was perched on the edge of the table, a casual posture at odds with his three-piece suit and tie. "Just a formality," he explained. "I caught a little heat recently from the city council for hiring outside investigators."

I'd been brought in on several other cases over the past five or six years.

"It's an undercover assignment?"

He nodded. "Yes, and I'd love to tackle it myself, but I'm afraid at this point, even in the Angles, this puss of mine is too well-known."

Eliot, a boyhood Sherlock Holmes fan, was not one to stay behind his desk; even as public safety director, he was known to lead raids wielding an ax, and go undercover in disguise.

I said, "You've never been shy about staying out of the papers."

I was one of the few people who could make a crack like that and not get a rebuke; in fact, I got a little smile out of the stone face.

"Well, I don't like what's been in the papers lately," he admitted, brushing the stray comma of hair off his forehead, for what good it did him. "You know I've made traffic safety a priority."

"Sure. Can't jaywalk in this burg without getting a ticket."

When Eliot came into office, Cleveland was ranked the second unsafest city in America, after Los Angeles. By 1938, Cleveland was ranked the safest big city, and by 1939 the safest city, period. This reflected Eliot instituting a public safety campaign through education and "warning" tickets, and reorganizing the traffic division, putting in two-way radios in patrol cars and creating a fleet of motorcycle cops.

"Well, we're in no danger of receiving any safest city honors this year," he said, dryly. He settled into the wooden chair next to mine, folded his hands prayerfully. "We've already had thirty-two traffic fatalities this year. That's more than double where we stood this time last year."

"What's the reason for it?"

"We thought it had to do with increased industrial activity."

"You mean, companies are hiring again, and more people are driving to work."

"Right. We've had employers insert 'drive carefully' cards in pay envelopes, we've made elaborate safety presentations. . . . There's also an increase in teenage drivers, you know, kids driving to high school."

"More parents working, more kids with cars. Follows."

"Yes. And we stepped up educational efforts at schools, accordingly. Plus, we've cracked down on traffic violators of all stripes — four times as many speeding arrests; traffic violations arrests up twenty-five percent, intoxication arrests almost double."

"What sort of results are you having?"

"In these specific areas — industrial drivers, teenage drivers — very positive. These are efforts that went into effect around the middle of last year — and yet this year, the statistics are far worse."

"You wouldn't be sending me undercover if you didn't have the problem pinpointed."

He nodded. "My traffic analysis bureau came up with several interesting stats: seventy-two percent of our traffic fatalities this year are age forty-five or older. But only twenty percent of our population falls in that category. And thirty-six percent of those fatalities are sixty-five or up . . . a category that comprises only four percent of Cleveland's population."

"So more older people are getting hit by cars than younger people," I said with a shrug. "Is that a surprise? The elderly don't have the reflexes of young bucks like us."

"Forty-five isn't elderly," Eliot said, "as we'll both find out sooner than we'd like."

The intercom on Eliot's nearby rolltop desk buzzed, and he rose and responded to it. His secretary's voice informed us that Dr. Jeffers was here to see him.

"Send her in," Eliot said.

The woman who entered was small and wore a white shirt and matching trousers, baggy oversize apparel that gave little hint of any shape beneath; though her heart-shaped face was attractive, she wore no make-up and her dark hair was cut mannishly short, clunky thick-lensed tortoise-shell glasses distorting dark almond-shaped eyes.

"Alice, thank you for coming," Eliot said, rising, shaking her hand. "Nate Heller, this is Dr. Alice Jeffers, assistant county coroner."

"A pleasure, Dr. Jeffers," I said, rising, shaking her cool, dry hand, as she twitched me a smile.

Eliot pulled out a chair for her opposite me at the conference table, telling her, "I've been filling Nate in. I'm just up to your part in this investigation."

With no further prompting, Dr. Jeffers said, "I was alerted by a morgue attendant, actually. It seemed we'd had an unusual number of hit-and-skip fatalities in the last six months, particularly in January, from a certain part of the city, and a certain part of the community."

"Alice is referring to a part of Cleveland called the Angles," Eliot explained, "which is just across the Detroit Bridge, opposite the factory and warehouse district."

"I've been there," I said. The Angles was a classic waterfront area, where bars and whorehouses and cheap rooming houses serviced a clientele of workingmen and longshoremen. It was also an area rife with derelicts, particularly since Eliot burned out the Hoovervilles nestling in Kingsbury Run and under various bridges.

"These hit-and-skip victims were vagrants," Dr. Jeffers said, her eyes unblinking and intelligent behind the thick lenses, "and tended to be in their fifties or sixties, though they looked much older."

"Rummies," I said.

"Yes. With Director Ness' blessing, and Coroner Gerber's permission, I conducted several autopsies, and encountered individuals in advanced stages of alcoholism. Cirrhosis of the liver, kidney disease, general debilitation. Had they not been struck by cars, they would surely have died within a matter of years or possibly months or even weeks."

"Walking dead men."

"Poetic but apt. My contact at the morgue began keeping me alerted when vagrant 'customers' came through, and I soon realized that automobile fatalities were only part of the story."

"How so?" I asked.

"We had several fatal falls-down-stairs, and a surprising number of fatalities by exposure to the cold weather, death by freezing, by pneumonia. Again, I performed autopsies where normally we would not. These victims were invariably intoxicated at the times of their deaths, and in advanced stages of acute alcoholism."

I was thoroughly confused. "What's the percentage in bumping off bums? You got another psychopath at large, Eliot? Or is the Butcher back, changing his style?"

I was referring to the so-called Mad Butcher of Kingsbury Run, who had cut up a number of indigents here in Cleveland, Jack the Ripper style; but the killings had stopped, long ago.

"This isn't the Butcher," Eliot said confidently. "And it isn't psychosis . . . it's commerce."

"There's money in killing bums?"

"If they're insured there is."

"Okay, okay," I said, nodding, getting it, or starting to. "But if you overinsure some worthless derelict, surely it's going to attract the attention of the adjusters for the insurance company."

"This is more subtle than that," Eliot said. "When Alice informed me of this, I contacted the State Insurance Division. Their chief investigator, Gaspar Corso — who we'll meet with later this afternoon, Nate — dug through our 'drunk cards' on file at the Central Police Station, some 20,000 of them. He came up with information that corroborated Alice's, and confirmed suspicions of mine."

Corso had an office in the Standard Building — no name on the door, no listing in the building directory. Eliot, Dr. Jeffers, and I met with Corso in the latter's small, spare office, wooden chairs pulled up around a wooden desk that faced the wall, so that Corso was swung around facing us.

He was small and compactly muscular — a former high school football star, according to Eliot — bald with calm blue eyes under black beetle eyebrows. A gold watch chain crossed the vest of his three-piece tweed.

"A majority of the drunks dying either by accident or 'natural causes,' " he said in a mellow baritone, "come from the West Side — the Angles."

"And they were overinsured?" I asked.

"Yes, but not in the way you might expect. Do you know what industrial insurance is, Mr. Heller?"

"You mean, burial insurance?"

"That's right. Small policies designed to pay funeral expenses and the like."

"Is that what these bums are being bumped off for? Pennies?"

A tiny half smile formed on the impassive investigator's thin lips. "Hardly. Multiple policies have been taken out on these individuals, dozens in some cases . . . each small policy with a different insurance company."

"No wonder no alarms went off," I said. "Each company got hit for peanuts."

"Some of these policies are for two-hundred-and-fifty dollars, never higher than a thousand. But I have one victim here —" He turned to his desk, riffled tough some papers. "— who I determined, by crosschecking with various companies, racked up a twenty-four-thousand-dollar payout."

"Christ. Who was the beneficiary?"

"A Kathleen O'Meara," Eliot said. "She runs a saloon in the Angles, with a rooming house upstairs."

"Her husband died last month," Dr. Jeffers said. "I performed the autopsy myself. He was intoxicated at the time of his death, and was in an advanced stage of cirrhosis of the liver. Hit by a car. But there was one difference."

"Yes?"

"He was fairly well-dressed, and was definitely not malnourished."

O'Meara's did not serve food, but a greasy spoon down the block did, and that's where Katie took me for supper around seven, leaving the running of the saloon to her sullen skinny daughter, Maggie.

"Maggie doesn't say much," I said, over a plate of meat loaf and mashed potatoes and gravy. Like Katie, it was surprisingly appetizing, particularly if you didn't look too closely and were half-bombed.

We were in a booth by a window that showed no evidence of ever having been cleaned. Cold March wind rattled it and leached through.

"I spoiled her," Katie admitted. "But, to be fair, she's still grieving over her papa. She was the apple of his eye."

"You miss your old man?"

"I miss the help. He took care of the books. I got a head for business, but not for figures. Thing is, he got greedy."

"Really?"

"Yeah, caught him featherin' his own nest. Skimmin'. He had a bank account of his own he never told me about."

"You fight over that?"

"Naw. Forgive and forget, I always say." Katie was having the same thing as me, and she was shoveling meat loaf into her mouth like coal into a boiler.

"I'm, uh, pretty good with figures," I said.

Her licentious smile was part lip rouge, part gravy. "I'll just bet you are. . . . Ever do time, Bill?"

"Some. I'm not no thief, though. I wouldn't steal a partner's money."

"What were you in for?"

"Manslaughter."

"Kill somebody, did you?"

"Sort of."

She giggled. "How do you 'sort of' kill somebody, Bill?"

"I beat a guy to death with my fists. I was drunk."

"Why?"

"I've always drunk too much."

"No, why'd you beat him to death? With your fists."

I shrugged, chewed meat loaf. "He insulted a woman I was with. I don't like a man that don't respect a woman."

She sighed. Shook her head. "You're a real gent, Bill. Here I thought chivalry was dead."

Three evenings before, I'd been in a yellow leather booth by a blue mirrored wall in the Vogue Room of the Hollenden Hotel. Clean-shaven and in my best brown suit, I was in the company of Eliot and his recent bride, the former Ev McMillan, a fashion illustrator who worked for Higbee's department store.

Ev, an almond-eyed slender attractive brunette, wore a simple cobalt blue evening dress with pearls. Eliot was in the three-piece suit he'd worn to work. We'd had prime rib and were enjoying after-dinner drinks; Eliot was on his second, and he'd had two before dinner, as well. Martinis. Ev was only one drink behind him.

Personal chit-chat had lapsed back into talking business.

"It's goddamn ghoulish," Eliot said. He was quietly soused, as evidenced by his use of the word *goddamn* — for a tough cop, he usually had a Boy Scout's vocabulary.

"It's coldblooded, all right," I said.

"How does the racket work?" Ev asked.

"I shouldn't have brought it up," Eliot said. "It

doesn't make for pleasant after-dinner conversation."

"No, I'm interested," she said. She was a keenly intelligent young woman. "You compared it to a lottery. . . . How so?"

"Well," I said, "as it's been explained to me, speculators 'invest' in dozens of small insurance policies on vagrants who were already drinking themselves to imminent graves — malnourished men crushed by dope and/or drink, sleeping in parks and in doorways in all kinds of weather."

"Men likely to meet an early death by so-called natural causes," Eliot said. "That's how we came to nickname the racket 'Natural Death, Inc.' "

"Getting hit by a car isn't exactly a natural death," Ev pointed out.

Eliot sipped his martini. "At first, the speculators were just helping nature along by plying their investments with free, large quantities of drink — hastening their death by alcoholism or just making them more prone to stumble in front of a car."

"Now it looks like these insured derelicts are being shoved in front of cars," I said.

"Or the drivers of the cars are purposely running them down," Eliot said. "Dear, this really is unpleasant conversation; I apologize for getting into it —"

"Nonsense," she said. "Who *are* these speculators?"

"Women, mostly," he said. "Harridans running West Side beer parlors and rooming houses. They exchange information, but they aren't exactly an organized ring or anything, which makes our work difficult. I'm siccing Nate here on the worst offender, the closest thing there is to a ringleader — a woman we've confirmed is holding fifty policies on various 'risks.' "

Ev frowned. "How do these women get their victims to go along with them? I mean, aren't the insured's signatures required on the policies?"

"There's been some forgery going on," Eliot said. "But mostly these poor bastards are willingly trading their signatures for free booze."

Ev twitched a non-smile above the rim of her martini glass. "Life in slum areas breeds such tragedy."

The subject changed to local politics — I'd heard rumors of Eliot running for mayor, which he unconvincingly pooh-poohed — and, a few drinks later, Eliot spotted some reporter friends of his, Clayton Fritchey and Sam Wild, and excused himself to go over and speak to them.

"If I'm not being out of line," I said to Mrs. Ness, "Eliot's hitting the sauce pretty hard himself. Hope you don't have any extra policies out on him."

She managed a wry little smile. "I do my best to keep up with him, but it's difficult. Ironic, isn't it? The nation's most famous prohibition agent, with a drinking problem."

"*Is* it a problem?"

"Eliot doesn't think so. He says he just has to relax. It's a stressful job."

"It is at that. But, Ev — I've been around Eliot during stressful times before . . . like when the entire Capone gang was gunning for him. And he never put it away like that, then."

She studied the olive in her martini. "You were part of that case, weren't you?"

"What case? Capone?"

"No — the Butcher."

I nodded. I'd been part of the capture of the lunatic responsible for those brutal slayings of vagrants; and was one of the handful who knew that Eliot had been forced to make a deal with his influential political backers to allow the son of a bitch — who had a society pedigree — to avoid arrest, and instead be voluntarily committed to a madhouse.

"It bothers him, huh?" I said, and grunted a laugh. "Mr. Squeaky Clean, the 'Untouchable' Eliot Ness having to cut a deal like that."

"I think so," she admitted. "He never says. You know how quiet he can be."

"Well, I think he should grow up. For Christ's sake, for somebody from Chicago, somebody who's seen every kind of crime and corruption, he can be as naive as a schoolgirl."

"An alcoholic schoolgirl," Ev said with a smirk, and a martini sip.

"You want me to talk to him?"

"I don't know. Maybe. . . . I think this case, these poor homeless men being victimized again, got memories stirred up."

"Of the Butcher case, you mean."

"Yes . . . and, Nate, we've been getting post-cards from that crazy man."

"What crazy man? Capone?"

"No! The Butcher . . . threatening postcards postmarked the town where that asylum is."

"Is there any chance Watterson can get out?"

Lloyd Watterson: the Butcher.

"Eliot says no," Ev said. "He's been assured of that."

"Well, these killings aren't the work of a madman. This is murder for profit, plain and simple. Good old-fashioned garden variety evil."

"Help him clear this up," she said, and an edge of desperation was in her voice. "I think it would — might — make a difference."

Then Eliot was back, and sat down with a fresh martini in hand.

"I hope I didn't miss anything good," he said.

My room was small but seemed larger due to the sparseness of the furnishings: metallic, institutional-gray clothes cabinet, a chair, and a metal cot. A bare bulb bulged from the wall near the door, as if it had blossomed from the faded, fraying floral-print wallpaper. The wooden floor had a greasy, grimy look.

Katie was saying, "Hope it will do."

"You still haven't said what my duties are."

"I'll think of something. Now, if you need anything, I'm down the hall. Let me show you."

I followed her to a doorway at the end of the narrow gloomy hallway. She unlocked the door with a key extracted from between her massive breasts, and ushered me into another world.

The living room of her apartment held a showroom-like suite of walnut furniture with carved arms, feet, and base rails, the chairs and davenport sporting matching green mohair cushions, assembled on a green and blue wall-to-wall Axminster carpet. Pale yellow wallpaper with gold and pink highlights created a tapestry effect, while floral satin damask draperies dressed up the windows, venetian blinds keeping out prying eyes. Surprisingly tasteful, the room didn't look very lived in.

"Posh digs," I said, genuinely impressed.

"Came into some money recently. Spruced the joint up a little. Now, if you need me after hours, be sure to knock good and loud." She swayed over to a doorless doorway and nodded for me to come to her. "I'm a heavy sleeper."

The bedroom was similarly decked out with new furnishings — a walnut-veneer double bed, dresser, and nightstand, and three-mirror vanity with modern lines and zebrawood design panels — against ladylike pink-and-white floral wallpaper. The vanity top was neatly arranged with perfumes and face powder and the like, their combined scents lending the room a feminine bouquet. Framed prints of airbrushed flowers hung here and there, a large one over the bed, where sheets and blankets were neatly folded back, as if by a maid, below lush overstuffed feather pillows.

"I had this room redone, too," she said. "My late husband, rest his soul, was a slob."

Indeed it was hard to imagine a man sharing this room with her. There was a daintiness that didn't match up with its inhabitant. The only signs that anybody lived here were the movie magazines on the bedstand in the glow of the only light, a creamy glazed pottery-base lamp whose gold parchment shade gave the room a glow.

The only person more out of place in this tidy, feminine suite than me in my tattered second-hand-store suit, was my blowsy hostess in her polka-dot peasant blouse and flowing dark skirt. She was excited and proud, showing off her fancy living quarters, bobbing up and down like an eager kid; it was cute and a little sickening.

Or maybe that was the cheap beer. I wasn't drunk but I'd had three glasses of it.

"You okay, Bill?" she asked.

"Demon meatloaf," I said.

"Sit, sit."

And I was sitting on the edge of the bed. She stood before me, looming over me, frightening and oddly comely, with her massive bosom spilling from the blouse, her red-rouged mouth, her half-lidded long-lashed green eyes, mother/goddess/whore.

"It's been lonely, Bill," she said, "without my man."

"Suh . . . sorry for your loss."

"I could use a man around here, Bill."

"Try to help."

"It could be sweet for you."

She tugged the peasant blouse down over the full, round, white-powdered melons that were her bosom, and pulled my head between them. Their suffocation was pleasant, even heady, and I was wondering whether I'd lost count of those beers when I fished in my trousers for my wallet for the lambskin.

I wasn't *that* far gone.

I had never been with a woman as overweight as Kathleen O'Meara before, and I don't believe I ever was again. Many a man might dismiss her as fat. But the sheer womanliness of her was overwhelming, there was so much of her, and she smelled so good, particularly for a saloonkeeper, her skin so smooth, her breasts and behind as firm as they were large and round, that the three nights I spent in her bed remain bittersweet memories. I didn't love her, obviously, nor did she me — we were using each other, in our various nasty ways.

But it's odd, how many times, over the years, the memory of carnality in Katie's bed pops unbidden into my mind. On more than one occasion, in bed with a slender young girlish thing, the image of womanly, obscenely voluptuous Katie would taunt me, as if saying, *Now I was a* real *woman!*

Katie was also a real monster. She waited

until the second night, when I lay next to her in the recently purchased bed, in her luxuriant remodeled suite of rooms in a waterfront rooming house where her pitiful clientele slept on pancake-flat piss-scented mattresses, to invite me to be her accomplice.

"Someday I'll move from here," she said in the golden glow of the parchment lamp and the volcanic sex we'd just had. She was on her back, the sheet only half-covering the globes of her bosom; she was smoking, staring at the ceiling.

I was on my back, too — I wasn't smoking, cigarettes being one filthy habit I didn't partake of. "But, Katie — this place is hunky-dory."

"These rooms are nice, love. But little Katie was meant for a better life than the Angles can provide."

"You got a good business here."

She chuckled. "Better than you know."

"What do you mean?"

She leaned on one elbow and the sheet fell away from her large, lovely bosom. "Don't you wonder why I'm so good to these stumble-bums?"

"You give a lot of free beer away, I noticed."

"Why do you suppose Katie does that?"

" 'Cause you're a good Christian woman?"

She roared with laughter, globes shimmering like Jell-O. "Don't be a child! Have you heard of burial insurance, love?"

And she filled me in on the scheme — the lottery portion of it, at least, taking out policies on men who were good bets for quick rides to potter's field. But she didn't mention anything about helping speed the insured to even quicker, surer deaths.

"You disappointed in Katie?" she asked. "That I'm not such a good Christian woman?"

I grinned at her. "I'm tickled pink to find out how smart you are, baby. Was your old man in on this?"

"He was. But he wasn't trustworthy."

"Lucky for you he croaked."

"Lucky."

"Hey . . . I didn't mean to be coldhearted, baby. I know you miss him."

Her plump pretty face was as blank as a bisque baby's. "He disappointed me."

"How'd he die?"

"Got drunk and stepped in front of a car."

"Sorry."

"Don't pay for a dipso to run a bar, too much helpin' himself. . . . I notice you don't hit the sauce so hard. You don't drink too much, and you hold what you do drink."

"Thanks."

"You're just a good joe down on his luck. Could use a break."

"Who couldn't?"

"And I can use a man. I can use a partner."

"What do I have to do?"

"Just be friendly to these rummies. Get 'em on your good side, get 'em to sign up. Usually all it takes is a friendly ear and a pint of rotgut."

"And when they finally drink themselves into a grave, we get a nice payday."

"Yup. And enough nice paydays, we can leave the Angles behind. Retire rich while we're still young and pretty."

His name was Harold Wilson. He looked at least sixty but when we filled out the application, he managed to remember he was forty-three.

He and I sat in a booth at O'Meara's and I plied him with cheap beers, which Katie's hollow-eyed daughter dutifully delivered, while Harold told me, in bits and pieces, the sad story that had brought him to the Angles.

Hunkered over the beer, he seemed small, but he'd been of stature once, physically and otherwise. In a face that was both withered and puffy, bloodshot powder-blue eyes peered from pouches, by turns rheumy and teary.

He had been a stock broker. When the Crash came, he chose to jump a freight rather than out a window, leaving behind a well-bred wife and two young daughters.

"I meant to go back," Harold said in a baritone voice whose dignity had been sandpapered away, leaving scratchiness and quaver behind. "For years, I did menial jobs — seasonal work, janitorial work, chopping firewood, shoveling walks, mowing grass — and I'd save. But the money never grew. I'd either get jackrolled or spend it on . . ."

He finished the sentence by grabbing the latest

foamy mug of warm beer from Maggie O'Meara and guzzling it.

I listened to Harold's sad story all afternoon and into the evening; he repeated himself a lot, and he signed three burial policies, one for $450, another for $750 and finally the jackpot, $1000. Death would probably be a merciful way out for the poor bastard, but even at this stage of his life, Harold Wilson deserved a better legacy than helping provide for Katie O'Meara's retirement.

Late in the evening, he said, "Did go back, once . . . to Elmhurst. . . . Tha's Chicago."

"Yeah, I know, Harold."

"Thomas Wolfe said, 'Can't go home again.' Shouldn't go home again's more like it."

"Did you talk to them?"

"No! No. It was Chrissmuss. Sad story, huh? Looked in the window. Didn't expect to see 'em, my family; figured they'd lose the house."

"But they didn't? How'd they manage that?"

"Mary, that's my wife, her family had some money. Must not've got hurt as bad as me in the Crash. Figure they musta bought the house for her."

"I see."

"Sure wasn't her new husband. I recognized him. Fella I went to high school with. A postman."

"A mail carrier?"

"Yeah. 'Fore the Crash, Mary, she woulda looked down on a lowly civil servant like that. But in Depression times, that's a hell of a good job."

"True enough."

The eyes were distant and runny. "My girls was grown. College age. Blonde and pretty, with boyfriends, holdin' hands. . . . The place hadn't changed. Same furniture. Chrissmuss tree where we always put it, in the front window — we'd move the couch out of the way and . . . anyway. Nothing different. Except in the middle of it, no me. A mailman took my place."

For a moment I thought he'd said "male man."

O'Meara's closed at 2 A.M. I helped Maggie clean up, even though Katie hadn't asked me to. Katie was upstairs, waiting for me in her bedroom. Frankly. I didn't feel like doing my duty tonight, pleasant though it admittedly was. On the one hand, I was using Katie, banging this broad I was undercover, and undercovers, to get the goods on, which made me a louse; and on the other hand, spending the day with her next victim, Harold Wilson, brought home what an enormous louse she was.

I was helping daughter Maggie put chairs on tables; she hadn't said a word to me yet. She had her mother's pretty green eyes and she might have been pretty herself if her scarecrow thin frame and narrow, hatchet face had a little meat on them.

The room was tidied when she said, "Nightcap?"

Surprised, I said, "Sure."

"I got a pot of coffee on, if you're sick of warm beer."

The kitchen in back was small and neat and Maggie's living quarters were back there, as well. She and her mother did not live together. In fact, they rarely spoke, other than Katie issuing commands.

I sat at a wooden table in the midst of the small cupboard-lined kitchen and sipped the coffee Maggie provided in a chipped cup. In her white waitress uniform, she looked like a wilted nurse.

"That suit you're wearing," she said.

Katie had given me clothes to wear; I was in a brown suit and a yellow-and-brown tie, nothing fancy but a step or two up from the threadbare duds "Bill O'Hara" had worn into O'Meara's.

"What about 'em?"

"Those were my father's." Maggie sipped her coffee. "You're about his size."

I'd guessed as much. "I didn't know. I don't mean to be a scavenger, Miss O'Meara, but life can do that to you. The Angles ain't high society."

"You were talking to that man all afternoon."

"Harold Wilson. Sure. Nice fella."

"Ma's signing up policies on him."

"That's right. You know about that, do you?"

"I know more than you know. If you knew what I knew, you wouldn't be so eager to sleep with that cow."

"Now, let's not be disrespectful —"

"To you or the cow? Mr. O'Hara, you seem like a decent enough sort. Careful what you get yourself into. Remember how my papa died."

"No one ever told me," I lied.

"He got run down by a car. I think he got pushed."

"Really? Who'd do a thing like that?"

The voice behind us said, "This is cozy."

She was in the doorway, Katie, in a red kimono with yellow flowers on it; you could've rigged out a sailboat with all that cloth.

"Mr. O'Hara helped me tidy up," Maggie said coldly. No fear in her voice. "I offered him coffee."

"Just don't offer him anything else," Katie snapped. The green eyes were hard as jade.

Maggie blushed, and rose, taking her empty cup and mine and depositing them awkwardly, clatteringly, in the sink.

In bed, Katie said, "Good job today with our investment, Bill."

"Thanks."

"Know what Harold Wilson's worth now?"

"No."

"Ten thousand. . . . Poor sad soul. Terrible to see him suffering like that. Like it's terrible for us to have to wait and wait, before we can leave all this behind."

"What are you sayin', love?"

"I'm sayin', were somebody to put that poor man out of his misery, they'd be doin' him a favor, is all I'm sayin'."

"You're probably right, at that. Poor bastard."

"You know how cars'll come up over the hill, Twenty-fifth Street, headin' for the bridge? Movin' quick through this here bad part of town?"

"Yeah, what about 'em?"

"If someone were to shove some poor soul out in front of a car, just as it was coming up and over, there'd be no time for stoppin'."

I pretended to digest that, then said, "That'd be murder, Katie."

"Would it?"

"Still . . . you might be doin' the poor bastard a favor, at that."

"And make ourselves ten thousand dollars richer."

"You ever do this before, Katie?"

She pressed a hand to her generous bare bosom. "No! No. But I never had a man I could trust before."

Late the next morning, I met with Eliot in a back booth at Mickey's, a dimly lit hole-in-the-wall saloon a stone's throw from city hall. He was having a late breakfast — a Bloody Mary — and I had coffee.

"How'd you get away from Kathleen O'Meara?" he wondered. He looked businesslike in his usual three-piece suit; I was wearing a blue number from the Frank O'Meara collection.

"She sleeps till noon. I told her daughter I was taking a walk."

"Long walk."

"The taxi'll be on my expense account. Eliot, I don't know how much more of this I can stand. She sent the forms in and paid the premiums on

Harold Wilson, and she's talking murder all right, but if you want to catch her in the act, she's plannin' to wait at least a month before we give Harold a friendly push."

"That's a long time for you to stay undercover," Eliot admitted, stirring his Bloody Mary with its celery stalk. "But it's in my budget."

I sighed. "I never knew being a city employee could be so exhausting."

"I take it you and Katie are friendly."

"She's a ride, all right. I've never been so disgusted with myself in my life."

"It's that distasteful?"

"Hell, no, I'm having a whale of time, so to speak. It's just shredding what little's left of my self-respect and shabby little code of ethics, is all. Banging a big fat murdering bitch and liking it." I shuddered.

"This woman is an ogre, no question, and I'm not talking about her looks. Nate, if we can stop her, and expose what's she done, it'll pave the way for prosecuting the other women in the Natural Death, Inc., racket, or at the very least scaring them out of it."

That evening Katie and I were walking up the hill. No streetlights in this part of town, and no moon to light the way. Lights in the frame and brick houses we passed, and the headlights of cars heading toward the bridge, threw yellow light on the cracked sidewalk we trundled up, arm in arm, Katie and me. She wore a yellow peasant blouse, always pleased to show off her treasure chest, and a full green skirt.

"Any second thoughts, handsome?"

"Just one."

She stopped. We were near the rise of the hill and the lights of cars came up and over and fell like prison searchlights seeking us out. "Which is?"

"I'm willing to do a dirty deed for a tidy dollar, don't get me wrong, love. It's just . . . didn't your husband die this same way?"

"He did."

"Heavily insured and pushed in front of his oncoming destiny?"

There was no shame, no denial; if anything, her expression — chin high, eyes cool and hard — spoke pride. "He did. And I pushed him."

"Did you, now? That gives a new accomplice pause."

"I guess it would. But I told you he cheated me. He salted money away. And he was seeing other women. I won't put up with disloyalty in a man."

"Obviously not."

"I'm the most loyal steadfast woman in the world 'less you cross me. Frank O'Meara's loss is your gain — if you have the stomach for the work that needs doing."

A truck came rumbling up over the rise, gears shifting into low gear, and for a detective, I'm ashamed to admit I didn't know we'd been shadowed, but we had. We'd been followed, or anticipated. To this day I'm not sure whether she came from the bushes or behind us, whether fate had helped her or it was careful planning and knowledge of her mother's ways. Whatever the case, Maggie O'Meara came flying out of somewhere, hurling her skinny stick-like arms forward, shoving the much bigger woman into the path of the truck.

Katie had time to scream, and to look back at the wild-eyed smiling face of her daughter washed in the yellow headlights. The big rig's big tires rolled over her, her girth presenting no problem, bones popping like twigs, blood streaming like water.

The trucker was no hit-and-skip guy. He came to a squealing stop and hopped out and trotted back and looked at the squashed shapeless shape, yellow and green clothing stained crimson, limbs, legs, turned to pulp, head cracked like a melon, oozing.

I had a twinge of sorrow for Katie O'Meara, that beautiful horror, that horrible beauty; but it passed.

"She just jumped right out in front of me!" the trucker blurted. He was a small, wiry man with a moustache, and his eyes were wild.

I glanced at Maggie; she looked blankly back at me.

"I know," I said. "We saw it, her daughter and I . . . poor woman's been despondent."

I told the uniform cops the same story about

Katie, depressed over the loss of her dear husband, leaping in front of the truck. Before long, Eliot arrived himself, topcoat flapping in the breeze as he stepped from the sedan that bore his special EN-1 license plate.

"I'm afraid I added a statistic to your fatalities," I admitted.

"What's the real story?" he asked me, getting me to one side. "None of this suicide nonsense."

I told Eliot that Katie had been demonstrating to me how she wanted me to push Harold Wilson, lost her footing and stumbled to an ironic death. He didn't believe me, of course, and I think he figured that I'd pushed her myself.

He didn't mind because I produced such a great witness for him. Maggie O'Meara had the goods on the Natural Death, Inc., racket, knew the names of every woman in her mother's ring, and in May was the star of eighty witnesses in the Grand Jury inquiry. Harold Wilson and many others of the "unwitting pawns in the death-gambling insurance racket" (as reporter Clayton Fritchey put it) were among those witnesses. So were Dr. Alice Jeffers, investigator Gaspar Corso, and me.

That night, the night of Katie O'Meara's "suicide," after the police were through with us, Maggie had wept at her kitchen table while I fixed coffee for her, though her tears were not for her mother or out of guilt, but for her murdered father. Maggie never seemed to put together that her dad had been an accomplice in the insurance scheme, or anyway never allowed herself to admit it.

Finally, she asked, "Are you . . . are you really going to cover for me?"

That was when I told her she was going to testify.

She came out of it fine. She inherited a lot of money from her late mother — the various insurance companies did not contest previous payouts — and I understand she sold O'Meara's and moved on, with a considerable nest egg. I have no idea what became of her after that.

Busting the Natural Death, Inc., racket was Eliot's last major triumph in Cleveland law enforcement. The following March, after a night of dining, dancing, and drinking at the Vogue Room, Eliot and Ev Ness were in an automobile accident, Eliot sliding into another driver's car. With Ev minorly hurt, Eliot — after checking the other driver and finding him dazed but all right — rushed her to a hospital and became a hit-and-run driver. He made some efforts to cover up and, even when he finally fessed up in a press conference, claimed he'd not been intoxicated behind that wheel. His political enemies crucified him, and a month later Eliot resigned as public safety director.

During the war, Eliot headed up the government's efforts to control venereal disease on military bases; but he never held a law enforcement position again. He and Ev divorced in 1945. He married a third time in 1946, and ran, unsuccessfully, for mayor of Cleveland in 1947, spending the rest of his life trying, without luck, to make it in the world of business, often playing on his reputation as a famed gangbuster.

In May, 1957, Eliot Ness collapsed in his kitchen shortly after he had arrived home from the liquor store where he had bought a bottle of Scotch.

He died with less than a thousand dollars to his name — I kicked in several hundred bucks on the funeral, wishing his wife had taken out some damn burial insurance on him.

AUTHOR'S NOTE: Facts, speculation, and fiction are freely mixed within this story, which is based on an actual case in the career of Eliot Ness. My thanks to George Hagenauer for his research assistance.

Max Allan Collins is a two-time winner of the Shamus award for Best novel for his historical mysteries *True Detective* and *Stolen Away*, both featuring Chicago private detective Nate Heller. He is also an accomplished editor, having compiled the anthologies *Murder Is My Business*, *Vengeance Is Hers*, and *Private Eyes*, all with Mickey Spillane. He lives with his wife, author Barbara Collins, and their son in Muscatine, Iowa.

The Oath

Marilyn Wallace

A quicksilver streak rippled the water, tossing back an image of a fat moon pushing its way out of deep water. Joyce Golden cleared the condensation from her side mirror with a single deft swipe of her index finger and then flicked off the radio. The regular roll and crash of the surf drowned out her sigh.

"Your hair almost dry?" Gerry Lamb caught up the tangle of dark hair that covered the back of her neck and brought his mouth down to hers. His lips lingered sweetly on hers. When he broke away from the kiss, he said, "Not quite. Sorry. Guess we can't leave yet."

"You were the one who said we shouldn't leave until we had a last swim, alone on the nighttime beach." She rummaged in her backpack, found her comb, yelped when she hit the first knot.

"But you were the one who bargained for an extra twenty minutes. After your hair was dry. You said you'd turn the key and turn our privileged lives back toward the city then." He took the comb from her and began to gently work through the biggest tangle.

"Ah, the talent in a sculptor's hands. This was a perfect week, Gerry. So perfect I almost don't mind the thought that I'll be in my office by eight tomorrow morning."

Waking to the brilliant painted sky over the Montauk waters had eased the knot she'd tied in her shoulder muscles during all those hours hunched over Mrs. Tokarian's medical records until she'd found the key: the buzzing in the woman's ear had been the result of a combination of drugs prescribed by two different doctors. Reading the collected work of Thomas Hardy in the midday heat in a canvas chair, fingers trailing in the warm sand, had dissolved the chronic lump in her chest where she stored her anger at the new system that didn't allow doctors and patients to make decisions based on human needs but rather on the requirements of the insurance companies. Eating lobsters four nights out of seven, butter running down their arms, savoring the taste later as they lay in the center of the moonlit bed had been payback for the eighteen-hour days, the six-day weeks, the twenty-eight months since she'd taken more than two days in a row to herself.

On cue, her cellular phone shrilled at her.

"You're still on vacation, remember? Someone's covering for you." Gerry tugged the comb through the last knot and reached for the phone. "I'll tell them you've disappeared."

"Don't." She grabbed the phone from him, said, "Yes?"

"Dr. Golden? This is Maria at the service. I know you're not due back until tomorrow, but it's Mrs. Canelli. Her water broke. She's really scared. I told her Dr. Bracken was covering and he'd meet her at the hospital but the poor thing sounded so frightened, I promised to see if I could find you."

Mrs. Canelli was forty-three, her first baby was probably going to weigh in at about nine pounds, and she'd spent her entire third trimester terrified, despite the classes, a supportive husband, tests that showed everything pointed to a normal delivery.

"Call Mrs. Canelli. Tell her I'm about three hours from the city and I'll meet her at the hospital as soon as I can. Tell her that if I were pregnant, Dr. Bracken would be the person I'd want with me. But assure her I'll be there as fast as I can."

Gerry tossed the comb into the backpack. "At least she had the courtesy to wait until the last minutes of the last day. Look at that fog. You ever see anything roll in so fast?"

"At least she didn't wait until I pulled the car into the garage, trudged the two blocks to my apartment, shucked my clothes, and crawled into bed." The moon was lost behind the cloud enveloping the car, shrouding the trees on the far side of the road. The drive back might take ten, twenty, even forty minutes longer, depending on visibility.

It was time to go, time to return to her practice on the Upper West Side of Manhattan. Her vacation was over, the perfectly restorative respite nearly at an end.

Perfectly restorative. Except, when Joyce Golden started up the Taurus, flicked on the lights, imagined the foamy breakers rolling onto the sand, she saw Paco Morales' face as he lay writhing on the examining table in her office. As she had every night for the past ten months, she blinked back the sight of him, so young, so puzzled, so very broken inside.

Twelve years old. Brown hair not yet tracing the sideburns his older brother sported. Skin still a child's pink under the café au lait. Nose still powdered white from the heroin that had been shoved into his nasal cavity, the heroin that had killed him, that she had been powerless to counteract because Jorge, his older brother, hadn't found him in time.

Get over it, she told herself, but she knew it might take a lifetime. She looked over her shoulder and backed out of the clearing, pulled onto the deserted road, slipped a Tracy Chapman tape into the deck and turned up the volume. Trees loomed out of the fog along the edge of the road, dark soldiers guarding the houses on the ocean side. Through breaks in the heavy clouds, the moon's round belly gleamed, white and full.

Mrs. Canelli had waited. Family practice was everything Joyce Golden had dreamed, everything she wanted when she turned down the chance to work with Downstate's leading endocrinologist. It was corny, but she liked being part of the grander cycle, liked the idea that she'd be helping a new life take its place in the teeming, pulsing throng of humanity.

Maybe Baby Canelli would carry some of Paco Morales' spirit back into the world. That would be too neat, but the thought comforted her.

She took her foot off the gas as she approached the curve in the road. This was the place the papers called Dead Man's Hairpin. Five crashes, two deaths since 1994. Almost all of them people who had lifted too many drinks in the beach magic of the Long Island summer, or snorted too many chemicals in the bathroom of some local pub. She never passed this spot without a shiver. But the road was clear and she drove on.

"Now I know why you wanted to leave after eleven. It's not that you were trying to prolong your time with me. It's the road, even in the fog. Free sailing. Does this last all the way to the Long Island Expressway?"

She grinned. "Hey, you know it won't. People drive into the-city-that-never-sleeps at all hours. When we get near Manhattan, we'd get slowed down, even if it's three in the morning. I hope Baby Canelli isn't too anxious to make his appearance. I really do want to be on hand to greet him." She reached for another tape, gasped as her headlights lit up the road.

"Holy shit." Gerry clutched the dashboard, his eyes wide in a suddenly ashen face. "Pull over. Holy shit."

Beyond the tall weeds, what was left of a small red convertible was folded around the upright of a signpost, like a piece of gum some kid had stuck on the bottom of a chair leg. White smoke rose from the hood, mingling with the fog and casting a hellish aura over the scene.

Joyce Golden lifted her foot from the accelerator, braked to a stop. "Wait here. You just wait here. This looks like it could be messy." She yanked open the door and scrambled across the road.

Some poor driver had managed the Hairpin and then . . . what? Perhaps a small creature, a rabbit who forgot to be scared, had startled the driver into an overreaction. The stink of rubber on blacktop hung in the air. This accident had just happened, seconds before she arrived. She ran toward the car, heard a low, mournful moan, pushed through the brambles along the edge of the road. The smell of gasoline grew stronger.

The front door lay open. The driver, pinned by the mangled steering wheel, had managed to work one leg free. "Help me," he whispered, and she played the flashlight beam down the length of his body.

The smell of blood, metallic and rich, assaulted her as she knelt at the open door. Red and thick, the blood covered the man's thigh, his chest, his head. She pulled a tissue from her pocket, dabbed at his face, fell backward in shock.

Anthony Pharsis.

He sits in the courtroom as though he's a pasha watching a parade of his subjects, arm flung nonchalantly across the back of the chair, head tilted. It is his eyes that make her angry, the cool detachment that cuts through her heart and delivers the message that he will prevail, that her bleeding heart testimony will evaporate like summer fog in the sunshine even before the words leave her lips, that his lawyer has a plan.

And, unbelievably, he is right.

Four people, including a New York City cop, testify that Tony Pharsis was at an apartment on West 81st Street across from the Hayden Planetarium at their regular Fourth Tuesday poker game the night someone jammed heroin up Paco's nose. That carries more weight with the jury than the testimony of Tony's second-in-command, a beefy Bronx thug named John Fiola, who swears he held Paco down while Tony filled the boy's nostrils with heroin to teach his brother Jorge a lesson. Jorge owed Tony twenty-three thousand dollars, and Tony didn't want word to get out that he let people run up lines of credit. Jorge missed three chances to pay up, John says, and then Tony sent the warning. Pay tomorrow or he'd have to teach him a lesson.

John Fiola claims he was so stricken by an attack of conscience that he carried the hundred-ten-pound boy six blocks to Doc Golden's office as soon as Tony left.

The jury listens, blank-faced, as she describes Paco's condition. Contusions on both sides of his face where strong fingers held his head in a tight grip. They watch her point to the shape and position of the bruises on the drawing the D.A.'s office has provided. They seem to grasp her explanation that all her ob-

servations point to the involvement of two people in the murder of Paco Morales: One person held him down. Another person pushed a lethal dose of heroin into his nose.

And then the jury hears from Tony's attorney about the deal the D.A. made with John Fiola. Reduced charges in return for testifying against his former boss.

The jury takes three days and six hours to come back and when the verdict is announced, she feels numb. When Tony Pharsis finishes hugging his lawyer and sidles through the crowd, he leans close enough for her to smell the oil slicking his hair, and to hear his whisper when he passes her. "Hey, Doc, you want to suck my dick? Make both of us feel better, don't you think?"

What began as a low moan turned to a scream of pain as she tried to move his arm. She pushed her head into the car, saw the million glinting lights of shattered windshield lying on the seat, saw the dagger of glass that pierced his chest between two ribs on the right side, low enough so that it had probably missed his heart, high enough to puncture a lung.

"Don't touch me," he rasped. "Just get medical help. Call a doctor."

How many lives had been ruined because Anthony Pharsis had sold heroin in quantities large enough to keep whole cities nodding out for weeks? Not that she could blame him for all the problems of society. Not that she could say with any certainty that Tony the Bone should have been any better than the rest of the world at interpreting the messages about making money by any means. But even if she gave him all that leeway, he had killed a twelve-year-old boy and then thumbed his nose at the justice system.

He had done it once. Once that everyone knew about. Because Tony Pharsis didn't suffer any ill consequences of his behavior, he surely felt immune from punishment, free to strut around and order up new lessons on what happens when things don't go his way. Exactly as he had in all his thirty-four wretched years on this earth.

"Shit, if you don't do something, I'm gonna fucking bleed to death. I need a doctor." His hand, slick with blood, fumbled for her but she was beyond his reach.

The look of contempt on his face as she digs into her pocket for a handkerchief. She has promised herself she won't dissolve on the witness stand, that it will do Paco no good for her to indulge in a messy display of emotions. But the image of the boy lying on that paper-covered table, his eyes rolled back in his head, is too fresh. Involuntarily, she pictures his mother, three years earlier. Trembling with fear, pointing to Paco's hand. He had nicked his fingernail with a linoleum knife in art class and then wrapped his hand in paper towels so he could finish the printmaking project. He was so proud of the cards. His family sent them that Christmas.

The only sound she heard was the hissing of steam still pouring from the radiator. The driver opened his eyes again, looked at her, his face contorted in agony. "Oh, shit, it's you. Ain't I lucky, Doc? You gotta help me. I have money. Lots of money. You want a million dollars? I'll give you a million dollars. Help me, Doc."

"I'm remembering what I learned in medical school, Tony. Funny, I never had to think about this before. It's part of what you promise when you become a doctor, and I never understood why it was worded that way. I mean, why don't doctors just promise to do the best they can, the best they know how to do, under all circumstances? But that's not what you swear to. You ever hear of the Hippocratic oath, Tony?" Gently, she brushed the hair out of his eyes. "Look at me, Tony. I asked you a question. Did you ever hear of the Hippocratic oath?"

Anthony Pharsis frowned, his body clenching like a fist as another wave of pain and confusion swept through him. "You keep playing with me like this, Doc, I'm not gonna make it. Get an ambulance. You don't want to touch slime like me, fine. Just call it in. You're a doctor. You have to help me."

She stood up, brushed the prickers off her shirt, looked down at the twisted body and the uncomprehending face. "Okay, I guess you don't know about the oath doctors take when they start practice. Too bad. It would help you understand."

Joyce Golden turned her back on the car and walked away, pushing though the brambles, half running across the road. Cigarette in hand,

Gerry leaned against the Taurus, eyes squinting against the stream of blue smoke that curled in the night air. "Everything okay?"

"Let's go, all right? It's pretty grim. Everything is not okay. I couldn't help him." She chose her words carefully, to protect him.

Gerry tossed the cigarette onto the blacktop, ground the glowing coal with his heel, bent to shred the remaining tobacco until it drifted into the fog and disappeared. "Shouldn't you call the cops, at least? I was going to do that, but I figured you're the doc, you know what you're doing."

"Get in, okay? I want to get going."

He shrugged, climbed into the passenger side. "We have to call. Somebody's got to clear away the wreckage, transport the body, take care of notifying the poor bastard's family." He reached for her cell phone.

"Don't!" She spoke more sharply than she'd intended. "I'm sorry, I didn't mean to snap at you. But if you call from this phone, they'll capture my number in their emergency system, and they might make us hang around while they ask questions and fill out forms in triplicate and generally hold us up, and I promised Mrs. Canelli I'd meet her at the hospital and I already made a five minute detour. So, when we pass a pay phone, you can jump out and call nine-one-one, and then we'll just be on our way."

She pulled onto the road. No cars coming from either direction. She would not miss Baby Canelli's first appearance into this odd and unpredictable world. That wouldn't be fair, not after she promised Mrs. Canelli she'd be there. She squinted at the road sign looming out of the fog: Long Island Expressway West. One mile.

"Here," she said when she saw a phone lit like a Hopper painting at the rear of a deserted gas station. She pointed the car between two white buckets that had been planted with geraniums and pulled to a stop ten feet from the phone booth. "You can call from here."

Frowning, Gerry climbed out of the car and stood with his back to her as he lifted the receiver, dialed, nodded, and waved as he spoke.

Gerry Lamb probably didn't know the Hippocratic oath, either. And if he did, he might not agree that she'd lived by the promise she'd made when she became a doctor. But Joyce Golden was absolutely certain that by choosing to keep her commitment to Mrs. Canelli, she had acted in the spirit of those famous words: First, do no harm.

Marilyn Wallace was the editor for the five volumes of the *Sisters in Crime* short story anthology series, and also teamed up with Robert J. Randisi to edit the anthology *Deadly Allies*. Her award-winning mystery series features Jay Goldstein and Carlos Cruz, two homicide detectives in Oakland, California. Other novels include the Taconic Hills series, including *So Shall You Reap* and *Lost Angel*.

Backwater

Michael Z. Lewin

Sunday night Janice Downs was unhappy. Steve knew that she couldn't do the dishes until he cleared the trap and unblocked the sink but it was like he was glued to the couch. Was he staying in front of the TV on purpose to annoy her?

Even if he wasn't, nothing was easy with him since he got out. If she asked him again he'd put it off even longer. Janice wondered if maybe she'd asked him the wrong way in the first place. There'd been stuff on some of the shows about how you should say "would you?" to men instead of "could you?". Or was it the other way around? Janice gave her head a quick shake. She didn't know what to do. Then the telephone rang.

Her first impulse was to let Steve get it. It would unglue him from the couch. But as it rang he sat staring at the screen without a blink. "Phone's ringing," he said at last.

With a sigh Janice went to the telephone stand in the little hallway between the kitchen and the living room. "Hello?"

A man's voice asked, "Is that the Paradise Star?"

"The what?" Janice asked.

"Paradise Star. Chinese takeout."

"You got the wrong number."

"I'm very sorry," the man said.

"That's all right," Janice said.

"No, really, I am sorry," the man said. "I hate it when people do that to me. It's inconsiderate."

"Yeah," Janice said. "You're right." The guy talked funny, but it was sort of nice.

"I really am sorry to have disturbed you."

"No problem, hon," Janice said and she hung up.

From the couch Steve said, "Who you calling 'hon'?"

"Nobody," Janice said.

"Had to be somebody. Or are you talking to yourself now?"

"Just a wrong number, all right?" Janice said. "It was just some plumber asking if I had any little jobs that needed doing, like unblocking sinks. But I said, naw, my husband was going to do it as soon as he got fed up with watching TV, unless he died first."

"I said I'd do it, and I will," Steve said. He waved a wrench. "See this?"

"What do you want me to do? Bring the sink in here?"

"Shut up," Steve said. " 'Cause this show's just getting to the good part. The bad guy is about to kill the bitch. I wouldn't want to miss that, would I?"

"Wouldn't you?" Janice wondered. Or couldn't you?

On Monday morning Adele Buffington made a point of getting to work before eight, little as she wanted to. As it turned out, everyone else had the same idea. For once an allocation meeting would start on time.

Only Francis Twilly among the seven social workers remained standing. He was an odd-looking man, with tiny ears on a large head. And he wore a Brooks Brothers suit, and a tie. But the most striking thing about his appearance at the moment was how pleased he was with himself.

"It's my pleasure and privilege," Francis said, "to welcome you to the first allocation meeting of the combined and expanded Indianapolis Family Care Agency. It's a thrill and an honor for me to be taking charge of IFCA. And I want to promise you, here and now, that I will dedicate myself to being the very best IFCA director that I can."

Great, Adele thought sourly. But then she thought, I must not let myself get sour about this.

Tina, across the table, caught Adele's eyes. Tina looked to the heavens in despair. That made it all right. To be sour in company was better than to be sour alone. Good old Tina, the only survivor apart from herself from the old agency.

Francis said, "Although I am still almost a stranger to you all, and an outsider, I am aware that one of you at this table applied for the job of director too. But I want to say now, Adele, I certainly won't hold grudges if you won't."

"Of course not, Francis," Adele said. "After all, you didn't choose you in preference to me."

"Exactly!" Francis said. "It was not me who rejected you. And I have every confidence that we — all of us — will work together as one big happy team."

Adele wondered if he had seen her exchange of looks with Tina. Aloud she said, "I'm sure we will."

"Grand," Francis said. "So, let us begin."

"I've prepared a referral list," Adele said. "It's in the folder on the table."

"Thank you, Adele," Francis said. "Everybody has told me how very good you are." He smiled at her.

If I'm so damn good, Adele thought. Oh well. She smiled back.

Francis took the top sheet from the folder. "The first item is a call received from a Mrs. Claudia Preston on Talbot Street, just north of Twenty-fifth Street. Mrs. Preston says there is a homeless girl who seems very young who is always around the back of her house and near Fall Creek. Now, who's got caseload space to look into it?"

The telephone on Homer Proffitt's desk rang but the first hand to get it belonged to Genghis Gordon. "Go to Muncie for me this afternoon?" Genghis asked.

"I don't think so," Homer said. He reached for the phone but Genghis pushed his hand away.

"I've got a date," Genghis said, "and she won't wait if I am late."

"Don't her daddy let her out after dark?" Homer said.

"Fun-ny," Genghis said. "Of course he does, as long as she's done her homework."

Homer shrugged. "All right. I'll go to Muncie."

"Thanks, man," Genghis said. "I owe you one, I really do." He picked up the phone and handed it to Homer. Then he blew a kiss.

"Detective Sergeant Proffitt," Homer said.

"Homer, it's Adele. It's about dinner tomorrow . . ."

"I sure do love a woman who is eager," Homer said.

"Old as you are, you can't tell the difference between hunger and eager?"

"Just don't say you're canceling on me, ma'am."

"No, but I do want to change where we're going. La Parisienne is just too refined, too social worky, for the way I'll be feeling."

"You're not having a bad day by any chance are you, ma'am?"

"I do so love a perspicacious man," Adele said.

"You going to tell me about it, ma'am? Or do I have to sit up and beg?"

"You know that guy they gave the job I wanted to?"

"I do recall something along those lines," Homer said.

"Well, he's sucking every drop of 'good and gracious loser' out of me. By tomorrow night what I'm going to need is some real cop food. Big pieces of red meat. Side order of blood."

Janice's telephone rang. This time she was in the kitchen doing the dishes from dinner. She wasn't expecting a call, so she just wiped her rubber gloves on a towel. "Hello?"

A man said, "Paradise Star Chinese takeout?"

"No, not here," Janice said.

"Oh, I haven't done it again, have I?" the man said. "I am so sorry. I even wrote the number on my hand."

"And couldn't read your own *hand*-writing?"

"I must say," the man said, "your voice is a lot nicer than any of the takeouts I've called. It's very musical."

"Who are you?" Janice asked.

And then Steve put his hands around her neck.

"Oh, Jesus!" she said. "You scared me to death!"

"I'm sorry," the man on the phone said, "I never meant —"

"Not you," Janice said, and she hung up the phone.

"Who the hell you talking to?" Steve asked.

"Nobody," Janice said. "It was just a wrong number."

"You think I'm stupid, don't you?"

"He just wanted a takeout, that's all."

"You're not a takeout," Steve said. "Or are you?"

Janice turned to face him. She put her rubber-gloved hands around his waist. "You're just not happy with anything since you got out, are you, hon?"

"Look, I'm trying," Steve said. "I'm trying."

"I know," Janice said.

"Just don't give me a hard time, all right?"

Tuesday morning Adele went to Talbot Street. The house closest to Fall Creek did not have a visible street number, but Adele made her way through the weeds that overgrew the front path. Voices answered her knock immediately, but they were canine voices. Adele knocked again. The dogs barked louder but this time a woman called, "Go away."

"Mrs. Preston?" Adele called back. "Mrs. Claudia Preston?"

"I've got a bat," the woman inside said. "I'm not afraid to use it."

"Are you Mrs. Claudia Preston?"

"I've paid my real estate tax."

"I'm a social worker, Mrs. Preston. You called about a girl?"

After a moment, Adele heard locks being undone. She stepped back in case the dogs flew out the door once it was open. But only a tall but slightly stooped woman emerged. She was in her seventies and wore a black shawl around her shoulders. She said, "And there's been a strange man."

"With the girl?"

"No," Mrs. Preston said. "But he hangs

around. And he uses the phone over there. I've seen him."

Adele looked across the street. Sure enough there was a booth. "It works?" she said.

"Yes," Mrs. Preston said. "I called you, didn't I?"

A public phone could mean a drug dealer, Adele thought. But she asked, "Has this man been disturbing you?"

"And he stands by the creek," Mrs. Preston said.

"If you're worried about him I can —"

"Oh, I'm not worried, young woman."

"All right," Adele said. "Then why don't you tell me more about this young girl."

"And I'll deal with her too, if I catch her."

"How young is she?" Adele asked.

"She gets in the bins and takes things," Mrs. Preston said. "And she begs for food. All summer long I've seen her. But now she's started stealing carrots. My boy, Gerald, planted those carrots. I water them every day. The dogs are going out at night from now on. You see if they don't."

"Mrs. Preston," Adele said with as much force as she could muster, "how old is this girl?"

"Young."

"Ten? Thirteen? Sixteen?"

Mrs. Preston nodded.

Adele gave up on age. "Where does the girl sleep? Do you know?"

"In an empty house, I expect," Mrs. Preston

said. “There’s lots empty round here. And if I catch her, I’ll see to her. I will.” From inside the house a dog growled. Mrs. Preston reacted as if to a spoken instruction. She turned her back on Adele and went inside. As Adele stood outside the door she heard locks being turned.

In the late afternoon Janice’s telephone rang. “Hello?”

“Paradise Star?”

“It’s you again. I thought it might be. I don’t usually get calls this time of day.”

“This time,” the man said, “I dialed your number on purpose.”

“Why’d you do that?”

“To see if I’d get the Paradise Star.”

In spite of herself Janice chuckled. “That makes a kind of sense, I guess.”

“But I still got you. And I’m glad because it’s much nicer to talk to you than to a Chinese takeout.”

“For all you know,” Janice said, “I’m ninety-five and have great-grandchildren.”

“No, you’re not,” the man said. “You’re, what? Twenty-eight?”

Janice stood stunned. “How’d you know that?”

“Just a lucky guess.”

“No, it wasn’t. Not the way you said it. Are you a mind reader or something?”

“That’s it,” the man on the phone said. “A mind reader.”

But Janice didn’t know what to think, and at

that instant the door slammed. Steve was back. Quietly she said, "I've got to go now, but I want to know."

Steve marched into the house. Loudly Janice said, "Sorry, but you got the wrong number." And she hung up.

"You're getting a lot of wrong numbers all of a sudden," Steve said.

"Well, I can't help that, can I?"

"Hot for you is he?"

"What's that supposed to mean?"

"He'd better look out. I'll take him out. I'm not so stupid that I can't see what's happening in my own house."

"Whose house?" Janice asked.

"Yeah. Well," Steve said. "But that guy needs someone to fix his wrong numbers for him, once and for all."

"I'll see to him," Janice said. She felt tired.

"That's what I'm afraid of."

"That's not what I meant," Janice said, "as you damn well know."

"So you say."

"But at least he talks nice to me," Janice said, "which is more than my husband ever does, for all he's been away three years."

Steve shuffled where he stood. "I . . . I try," he said.

For the girl who lived in an empty house by Fall Creek it was a lucky evening. She found two black plastic bags behind a Chinese restaurant and the discarded food near the top one of the bags was still warm.

When she examined her find half a block down the alley, there was enough that was still edible among the waste to feed her for two days or more. She made a new bag from one of the ones she'd torn open. She packed it, and headed back toward her house. But on the way she stopped beside a bush at the edge of the creek. The bush was entwined in the fence of a large back yard.

The girl could smell Chinese food on her hands. She'd wash them when she got home. That was why it was better to do the other thing now. It saved a trip and it saved a washing. Besides, Auntie Vi used to say that birds cleaned themselves in dirt. The dirt picked up the bad stuff on their feathers. So that was another reason it would be a good thing to dig in the dirt now. There was light in the sky, but there was nobody around.

"Is that steak rare enough for you, ma'am?" Homer asked.

"What will you do if I say it isn't?" Adele said.

"Take it back to the kitchen and have them cut a fresh hunk off the cow, of course."

"And here's me hoping my big, strong policeman would cut the hunk himself."

"Sorry, ma'am," Homer said. "That might get the suit dirty."

"I'd expect Twilly to say something like that. Not you, Homer. But I suppose it's what I get for going out to dinner with a policeman. Social workers and policemen don't mix. Everybody knows that. Speak different languages."

"Some more wine, ma'am?" Homer said.

"Sure," Adele said. She pushed her glass forward.

As Homer poured he said, "Just who is this Twilly I'm being compared to again?"

"Francis Sharp Suit Twilly, the new director of IFCA."

"And this fella likes to keep his suit clean? What a bummer."

"He likes everything clean," Adele said. "I bet he dips his wife in disinfectant before he . . ."

"Before he what, ma'am?"

Adele took a drink. "Before he eats off her," she said. "Can we order another bottle?"

The girl waited until everything looked quiet. Then she put her bag down and slipped over the low fence. Stepping carefully, she made her way to the garden. There she stooped at the nearest row of carrots and began to pull some.

The girl had only freed four large carrots when she heard a shout. "Get off!" Mrs. Preston shouted from an open door. "My boy, Gerald, planted those carrots."

"Damn," the girl said to herself. She stood up.

"I told social workers about you. I'm letting the dogs out."

The girl heard a canine yelp. This was new and she didn't like it. She sprinted for the fence. She scrambled over and ran for her house which was on the remains of an old road that paralleled the creek bank.

She only rested once she was inside, having thrown herself through the side window she used as a way in and out of the house. At first she was pleased because she was safe and still had the four carrots. But in the next moment she was angry because she had left her bag of Chinese food behind.

The telephone at Janice's house rang. Before she answered it Janice looked out the back window. Steve was under the car, doing something in the fading light. "Hello?"

"Hello," the man said.

"It's you again."

"Yes."

"What do you want tonight? Chicken and bamboo shoots? Or are you on the chow main?"

"I . . ."

Janice smiled because the man seemed uncertain of himself. She said, "You must really love Chinese food to call the takeout so often."

"I want to take you out to eat," he said.

"To eat? Me?"

"But if you don't like Chinese it could be something else."

"I like Chinese, but if you think you can just call here and —"

"Please, Janice," he said.

"How do you know my name?"

"I . . . guessed."

"You don't guess a name," Janice said.

"You must've said it."

"No, I didn't. No more than you said yours."

"I'm Paul."

"So how do you know my name, Paul? And how did you know how old I am?"

"I . . . I just feel I know you."

"Like hell," Janice said. "I think I better get the law on to you."

"Please, don't do that."

"Then tell me how come you know about me."

"I . . . If you meet me for dinner or a drink, then I'll tell you. I will. Honest."

Janice considered the offer. She said, "Yeah, okay."

"You will?"

"You'll tell me, right?"

"Right."

"Well, why not. It's been a long time since I had a laugh."

"You'll come out tonight?"

"OK."

"That's great," Paul said.

"Just for a drink. Do you understand? A drink, nothing else."

"Sure," Paul said. "Look, you live on Talbot Street, right?"

"I'm not even going to bother to ask how you know that."

"What time should I come?"

"Don't come here," Janice said.

"Well," Paul said, "there's a public phone a couple of blocks north of you, near Fall Creek."

"I know it," Janice said.

"I'll meet you there," Paul said. "About nine?"

"I can't be sure of the time."

"I'll wait," Paul said. He hung up.

"Yeah," Janice said to the phone in her hand. "You do that." She hung up too.

Behind her Steve said, "So, where are you going to meet him?"

Janice jumped and turned and clutched her chest. "Oh, Steve," she said, "you frightened the life out of me."

"Thought I was outside, didn't you?"

"No. I mean, well, you went outside. You were banging on that old car. How is it?"

"I came back in," Steve said.

"So I see," Janice said.

"I heard the phone," Steve said.

"Yeah?"

"And I needed batteries for my flashlight." He held up a long black flashlight. He flicked its switch a few times. "See?" he said. "Dead as a doornail."

"Well," Janice said, "I don't have any batteries."

Steve slapped the flashlight on his palm. "What good's a big, heavy flashlight when all the batteries in it are dead?" He slapped his hand again. "I wonder." He slapped the flashlight into his hand twice more.

"Don't do that," Janice said. "It scares me."

"So, what time are you meeting Mr. Chinese Take-out?"

"I'm not meeting anyone," Janice said.

"You're right about that," Steve said. "But he's expecting you. And don't say he's not, 'cause I heard you making the plans."

"It's the guy who keeps making wrong number calls. He expects me at that old phone at the end of the street. But I never intended to go. I was going to get the cops on him."

"That's who you were dialing?" Steve said. "The cops?"

"I wasn't dialing anybody."

"Exactly," Steve said. He slapped his hand with the flashlight. "How stupid do you think I am?"

"I mean I was going to," Janice said.

"Oh sure, I really believe you were going to call the cops," Steve said. "So tell me, Jan, is this something you been doing a lot while I was away? Meeting guys at phones?"

"I haven't met anybody."

"You put your phone number up? They call you? You do business? Is that it?"

"I haven't met anybody. And I wasn't going to go out. I'm staying here tonight."

"Damn right you are," Steve said. He turned and headed for the door.

"Where are you going?"

"I have a date," Steve said. As he passed through the door he smashed one of the jambs with the dead flashlight.

The girl opened an old suitcase she kept on the floor by her mattress. She hunted through the objects inside it until she found a small flashlight. She flicked the switch. The light was still strong. She felt pleased.

When it was dark the girl retraced her route back toward the carrot garden. The night was moonless and lit only by stars and the city's lights. She liked the night. It gave her easy anonymity. She could walk almost anywhere and not be seen. But although she knew the way she used the flashlight frequently. She was hungry and wanted to find the Chinese food as soon as she could.

However as she approached the carrot garden's fence she heard dogs grumbling. She stopped to listen. She wanted to know for sure whether the dogs were in the old woman's garden. Usually they were in the house. Not being seen was one thing. Not being heard or smelled was more difficult.

But then another noise drowned out the dogs. People were arguing. She couldn't make out any of the words, but she knew the sounds well enough. She was reminded sharply of Auntie Vi and Uncle Artie and she covered her ears. Then she flashed the light in the direction of the noise, as if exposure might turn the dispute into silence.

In the garden the dogs heard the fight too, and barked. The girl could hear that there were at least two dogs. And they reminded her that she was not there to listen to a fight. She was there to find her bag of food. So she hunted for the place on the fence which she had cleared to run from the dogs in the first place. And there, by the fence, was her dinner, spiked in the weeds. The girl scooped most of the food back into the bag. She could sort it an out later at home.

And then she heard footsteps. Someone was running toward her.

The girl didn't know what to do. She crouched by a bush, hoping that she would be invisible. But the steps continued to come straight for her And they were heavy, the steps of a man.

Before she could do anything he was on her, crashing through the undergrowth. The girl jumped up and turned her flashlight on and shined the light in the man's face and shrieked.

The man screamed and threw up his hands and stopped in his tracks. Her flashlight beam caught his face for an instant and he looked terrified. He moved a step back in the direction from which he'd come, but then he froze, looking at the light.

The girl heard something heavy fall on the ground. The man looked in the direction of the sound.

The girl flashed her light off and then on again. The man moved past her, without turning away. "Who . . . who . . . who's there?"

It made the girl think of an owl and a ghost. She screeched, "Woooooooo!" in a scratchy high-pitched voice.

The man ran away as fast as he could.

The girl laughed aloud once he was gone. She laughed so hard she had to sit down. She had all but frightened the life out of him. And she'd found her Chinese food.

She dipped a hand into the bag of food and ate a few bites. It tasted wonderful. Perhaps the dogs smelled it too, because they growled again. So the girl got up. But before she left she decided to see if she could find what the frightened man had dropped. And she found it easily. It was a large, heavy flashlight. The light didn't work, but she might be able to fix it.

Somewhere in the direction the man had run from she heard a splash. The girl was curious, but she could come back in the morning. Food was what she wanted now. So she put the big flashlight under one arm and headed back to her house.

On Wednesday morning Adele went to Talbot Street to see if she could learn more about the young girl who was stealing carrots. She did not, however, return to Mrs. Preston's house.

Not many people in the neighborhood had seen the girl, but at one house Adele talked to a pair of sisters who did know of her.

"She look in the trash, don't she, Ewa," one sister said.

"Ya," Ewa agreed. "And so we put cookies there, don't we, Johanna."

"Ya, cookies," Johanna said. "And meat sandwich, and brown bread."

"Good for a girl," Ewa said.

"Do you know where she sleeps?" Adele asked.

"A house, we think," Ewa said. "Don't we, Johanna?"

"Ya," Johanna said. "Empty, but got a light at night sometimes."

The girl slept later than usual, but she felt good when she woke up. After a Chinese breakfast, she washed herself in the creek, and that reminded her of the splash she'd heard the previous night.

Splashes could mean things thrown away. Certainly it was worth a look.

When Adele found the derelict house the sisters had suggested, it looked empty. But she made her way onto the rotting front porch and knocked on the boarded up door.

From behind her someone said, "Hey!"

Adele turned around and saw a girl on the abandoned road. It was hard to assess her age but she looked, maybe, fourteen. A dirty fourteen. Adele said, "You scared me to death."

"What are you doing there?" the girl asked.

Carefully Adele made her way off the porch and approached the girl. "I was only just looking."

"Look at something else," the girl said.

"Is it your place?" Adele asked. "My name's Adele. What's yours?"

"Go away," the girl said.

"Funny name," Adele said. "But I've met members of your family before."

For a moment the girl looked puzzled.

"The Go-Away family," Adele said. "I've met a lot of you."

"You're a social worker."

"Wow!" Adele said. "I didn't know it was quite so obvious."

"I'm eighteen," the girl said. "I'm of sound mind and not a danger to myself nor to others. So I'm none of your business."

"You sure know the law," Adele said.

"My last social worker explained it to me."

"And where was that?"

The girl laughed. "Do I look stupid enough to fall for that?"

"What about telling me your name?"

"If I tell you my name will you go away?"

"I don't plan to move in," Adele said.

The girl shrugged. "Ros."

"Ros what?"

After she'd given it some thought the girl said, "Ros Brown."

"Well, Ros Brown, I'm Adele Buffington. Have you been here a long time?"

"Nearly two months."

"I'm impressed because not many girls can look after themselves like you do," Adele said. "And did you know this area before? Or did you find it by chance?"

Ros glared.

Adele knew she'd pushed for information too hard.

Ros said, "Do you want to see something?"

"What?"

"You'll want to see it."

"Okay." Adele wondered if Ros might be about to show off where she lived. But instead the girl turned around. She's leading me away, Adele thought. Protecting her nest.

"Where are we going?" Adele asked after a while.

"I saw it this morning," Ros said. She followed the creek's bank.

"I'm not here to do you any harm," Adele said. But Ros didn't answer. So as they walked Adele tried to work out where they were.

Somewhere near Talbot Street Ros stopped and then moved down the bank toward the water. "It's here," Ros called.

Adele couldn't see anything, but she made her way cautiously toward the water.

Ros was pointing to a heavy tree branch which was caught on some stones. "See?" she said.

"What?" Adele said.

"There."

At first Adele still couldn't see. Then she did. A man's body was floating in the water, snagged on the branch. "Oh, oh my good God!"

"I thought you'd like it," Ros said.

"Detective Sergeant Proffitt," Homer said.

"Homer," Adele said, "I've just seen a body."

"As good as mine, ma'am?" Homer said.

"A body, Homer. A dead body."

He sat up. "Where's that?"

"It's floating in Fall Creek. There's a wound on his head. I think he's been murdered, Homer. Murdered."

"Calm down, Adele. Please calm down."

Behind Proffitt Genghis Gordon said, "The girl friend, eh?"

Homer turned away from Gordon. Adele said, "I'm calling from a public phone at the end of Talbot Street. I came up here to talk to a girl who's been living in a derelict house, and she led me to the body. And it's her I want to talk about."

"Me too," Homer said. "How'd she know where the body was?"

"I have no idea," Adele said.

"You didn't ask?"

"No," Adele said. She felt exasperation. "Look, I called you instead of nine-one-one because I want to make sure this girl is not given a hard time."

"If she had something to do with it, ma'am," Homer said.

"What's this about a body?" Genghis Gordon whispered. He squeezed between Homer and the window he was looking out.

Adele said, "Getting information from her is one thing, but I do not want this girl subjected to excess aggravation by any of the blunt instruments you've got down there wearing badges."

"How old is this girl?" Homer said.

“A dead girl?” Genghis asked. “What? Raped and murdered?”

“She says she’s eighteen, but I don’t believe her.”

“If she’s eighteen —” Homer began.

“I’m talking about a child,” Adele said. “Someone who needs to be looked after. But I should have known better than to call a policeman, shouldn’t I?” She hung up.

Homer Proffitt and Genghis Gordon were at Fall Creek in less than half an hour. Homer left Gordon to supervise what was done with the body. He dealt with Adele. “So where is this girl now, ma’am?”

“What girl?” Adele asked.

“Please,” Homer said. “I promise I’ll do everything I can for her, but she found the body. We’re going to need to interview her.”

“Will you be the one who talks to her?”

“If I can, and I’m sure there won’t be a problem unless she’s involved in some way.”

“She’s not. She’s just a scared kid.”

“That should be all right then,” Homer said.

Genghis Gordon approached them. “Hey, Homer, what’s your little girlie friend doing here?”

“I’m nobody’s ‘little girlie friend,’ Officer Gordon,” Adele said, “and I never have been, not even when I was little and girlie.”

“And spunky with it,” Genghis said with a wink.

Homer said, "Adele reported the body."

"Yeah?"

"Genghis, why don't you begin working the houses along here. Ask the folks if they saw anything," Homer said.

"Sure," Genghis said. He blew Adele a kiss, spun on his heels and headed for the nearest house.

"Just keep that asshole away from Ros Brown," Adele said. "Please, Homer."

The first house Genghis Gordon went to was Mrs. Preston's. When the dogs inside responded to his knock, he made sure his truncheon was loose in its holster. That could be good. Quick draw and deflect one lunging dog this way and another that. Like the movies.

Mrs. Preston called, "Who's there?"

"Police. Open up."

"I didn't send for the police," Mrs. Preston said.

"Open the door, please," Genghis said. "And restrain your dogs. I don't want to have to do them any harm."

"What?"

"Open the damn door, will you? Jeez."

Slowly Mrs. Preston unlocked the door and opened it. Genghis kept hold of his truncheon as he showed his ID. "We've just taken a dead man out of the creek. Have you seen anything suspicious around here the last few days?"

"You should catch that girl," Mrs. Preston said.

"What girl?" Genghis said.

"She steals my carrots. I caught her at it last night. My boy, Gerald, planted those carrots for me. And if I ever catch her, I'll give her what for. I've got a bat. I'm not afraid to use it if I have to."

"This Gerald," Genghis said, "he isn't missing, by any chance, is he?"

"Gerald? Missing?"

"Does he live here, madam?"

"Who?"

"Gerald."

"Of course not. He lives in Little Acre. What are you asking about Gerald for? You should go catch that girl."

"So how old is this Ros Brown, Adele?" Francis asked.

"She says she's eighteen."

"Well then."

"I'm certain she's much younger, Francis. Fifteen. Maybe even less."

"But if she says she's eighteen and we have no other information about her . . ." He shrugged.

"So if a businessman accused of having sex with a twelve-year-old said she told him she was eighty, you'd be perfectly happy?"

"Yes, all right, I take your point," Francis said. "But raw emotionalism will get us nowhere."

"Doing nothing will get us nowhere too," Adele said.

"And has she seen the police?"

"Homer Proffitt talked to her," Adele said.

"And she said she was near the creek last night, and that she heard an argument, and that she saw a man running."

"A man?"

"It could have been totally innocent, a jogger or something. But remember, she led me to the body this morning. She didn't have to do that, so Homer let her go back to her house."

"What's known about the victim?" Francis said.

"There was a head injury. That's all I know. But the girl told me that she'd had a social worker before, Francis. So she'll be on that new computer of yours."

"Assuming she's from central Indiana, I suppose she will," Francis said.

"We ought to find out whatever we can about her, even if it's only to cover ourselves."

"Yes, all right," Francis said. "Ros Brown, you said?"

"The Ros might be right," Adele said, "but I'm sure she made up the Brown. To be safe you should go through all missing teenage girls who more or less fit the description."

Ros sat on a nest she had made from an old mattress and various bits of clothing taken from trash cans. It was the most comfortable place in the world. She was eating, a meal which combined some of yesterday's Chinese food with bread collected in the afternoon from behind O'Malia's Market. All the day's commotion was over. The social worker woman said so, and Ros wanted to believe her.

Somewhere outside a car door slammed. Ros stopped chewing to listen, but there was no other noise. Even so, she considered getting up to take a look. But she was comfortable, and hungry, so she didn't. Sometimes noises traveled on the wind from the other side of the creek.

Ros' thoughts turned to what else she had to eat. There were some apples, also from O'Malia's. She'd been particularly pleased to find them because Auntie Vi liked her to eat apples. She'd try to give her an apple when Ros wanted candy. "If you're hungry, have an apple." Or a carrot.

Before she'd run away Ros thought of such things as "rabbit food," but now she liked it when she had apples and carrots. She missed Auntie Vi. And maybe Uncle Artie would die, so she could go back.

Suddenly there were footsteps on the porch. But before Ros could stand up the front door burst open. A man came into the house and pointed a gun at her. "Police!" he shouted. "Hands up! Hands up!"

Another man with another gun rushed in. And then there were more men, and women, and bright lights. Ros didn't know what to do. She didn't stand up. She didn't put her hands up. She scooted herself away into a corner and tried to shield her eyes.

A man dragged her to her feet. He said, "I have

a warrant to search these premises for unlawfully acquired property, and if you want to confess to the murder, that's okay by me too. Do you understand your rights?"

One of the other men said, "Is that your personal version of Miranda, Genghis?"

Genghis Gordon said, "What the fuck's the point with the likes of her?" Then he said, "Go through all this trash, guys."

"What are we looking for?" someone asked.

"Just drugs, stolen property, and a murder weapon," Genghis said.

Another man said, "I don't know about drugs, but how's this for a weapon?" He held up the heavy black flashlight.

Adele caught up with Homer in his office in police headquarters downtown. "How could you, Homer?" she protested. "How could you let it happen?"

"I wasn't there, ma'am," he said.

"I asked you to look after the girl," Adele said. "I asked you not to let thugs like Gordon brutalize her."

"Unfortunately, I wasn't consulted, ma'am," Homer said. "Genghis did it on his own initiative."

"But did you make any effort to keep track of the case?"

"It's not how these things are done."

Adele banged a fist on his desk. "Oh, how could I be so stupid as to think a policeman could have feelings."

"Y'all don't have a monopoly on feelings," Homer said.

"I meant feelings for other human beings, not feelings for yourself."

"That's not fair," Homer said.

"Was the way Ros Brown was dragged out of her home and into a jail fair? Do we speak anything remotely like the same language?"

"Look, ma'am," Homer said, "the post mortem said that the guy was hit on the head and that he was alive when he went into the creek."

"And that makes it all right to terrify a young girl? That makes it all right to drag her screaming to jail?"

"The girl knew where the body was, Adele," Homer said.

"And she reported it!"

"Only because you came to her. So Genghis thought it was worth searching her place. And he came up with a big heavy flashlight. With dead batteries. Now, you tell me why your little innocent teenager has something like that."

"Is it a crime?"

"A big, heavy flashlight, Adele. And she knew where the body was."

"She's, maybe, fifteen at most, Homer."

"She says she's eighteen."

"I don't believe this," Adele said.

"That girl may be a homeless waif to you," Homer said. "But from where I sit we've got to ask, why is she there? Why did she leave wherever she came from? Why has she chosen to live alone? Why not come voluntarily to one of the agencies like yours? What is she hiding from? What kind of girl lives alone in an empty house?"

Adele said nothing in response.

Homer said, "Seems to me it could be the kind of girl who's turned her back on society. Maybe so far that she's taken the life of another human being. Even if maybe it was only because she was frightened."

"I want to speak to her," Adele said.

"What?"

"I want to see her."

"What? Now?" Homer said.

"Now."

He thought for a moment. "Yeah, all right. I can do that, I guess. See if there's anything she needs. And if you find out anything relevant to the case —"

Adele said, "I'll go straight to Genghis Gordon, who has obviously infected even you with the virus that makes policemen inhuman."

"Now that's not fair, Adele," Homer said. "You know that."

"Is Gordon an alien, Homer? Is that your excuse?"

"I'll have her taken to an interview room," he said. "It's all I can do."

Adele was waiting in Interview 5 when Ros was shown in. A young policeman in uniform released Ros from her handcuffs. He said to Adele, "You push the button if you need help, miss."

"I will," Adele said. The young officer closed the door behind him as he went out.

Ros stood in the middle of the room with her eyes focused on the floor. Adele was shocked at how pale the girl looked. "Do you remember me, Ros?"

Ros said nothing.

"Please, honey, sit down." Adele pointed to a chair.

Ros did not move at first, but then she retreated to the corner of the room farthest away from Adele. There she dropped to the floor.

Adele left her chair to sit on the floor too. She sighed. "It's awful in here, isn't it? I've been to the cells. Do they have you in one alone, or are there other people with you?"

Ros said nothing.

Adele said, "I am so sorry about what's happened. I tried to prevent it, but there was nothing I could do."

Ros said nothing.

Adele said, "I'm not asking you to be grateful or anything. I'm sure you don't like me. No one likes social workers, do they? They think we interfere when we shouldn't, except when something terrible happens and then they say we didn't interfere when we should. But, Ros, I am a social worker and not the police. Definitely not the police. We're different from them. The police try to convict people. We try to help them. We may not manage, but that's what we try to do. It's what I'll try to do for you, if you let me."

Ros said nothing.

"Well, I'd like to know more about you, Ros. So it's only fair that I tell you things about me. Don't you think?" Adele paused and took a breath. Then she said, "Well, let's see. I grew up in Indianapolis. I'm not married, but I was once, a long time ago. And it was a disaster, except that I got a daughter out of it, Lucy, and that's great even though she causes me more worry than anything else in the world. But these days I live alone, like you. I have friends, including boyfriends. I even thought that I liked a policeman for a while. I thought that he was different from the others. But I've learned better about that today. What about you? Have you got a boyfriend?"

Ros said nothing.

Adele touched Ros on the arm. "Look, I'm not going to go away. And I'm going to do everything that's within my power to help you."

Ros screamed, "I hate you! Leave me alone!" She jumped out of her corner and hit Adele on the arms and on her chest. "Leave me alone! I hate you! I hate you!"

Adele fended off Ros' flailing fists and then encompassed the girl with her arms. "Oh Ros," she said. "Oh, honey, it's all right. It's going to be all right."

Ros went limp. She said, "They took my shoelaces. And my belt."

"That's what they always do," Adele whispered.

"But my pants fall down," Ros said.

"I'll try to get them to give your belt back."

"I'm not nothing," Ros said fiercely. "I'm not nothing."

"Of course you're not," Adele said. "Of course you're not."

Homer was working at his desk when Genghis Gordon danced in. "Who's afraid of the Big Bad Genghis?" he sang. "The Big Bad Genghis, the Big Bad Genghis."

"Shut up, you barbarian," Homer said.

"I go out for coffee," Genghis said. "I come back with an identification."

Homer sat back. "Oh yeah?"

"Dead guy's mother ID'd him. Paul Montgomery — Monty to his friends. Twenty-three years young. Lived at home, just Monty, Mom, and Monty's computers."

Homer patted his lips as he thought about the new information.

"Now what I figure," Genghis said, "is that Monty hit on little Ros Brown, but she hit him back." He grinned.

"It's possible, I guess," Homer said. "But what was Monty doing by Fall Creek at night?"

"I'll think of something," Genghis said. "Meanwhile we've got to see if the girl's flashlight matches the hole in Monty's skull. So I'm off to forensic and that leaves you going to see Mrs. Montgomery and looking at the late, lamented's room."

"Yeah, all right," Homer said.

"I'll have this wrapped up with a bow in no time," Genghis said.

"Tell me something, Genghis."

"Anything, my flower."

"How'd you know to invite Paul Montgomery's mother to come in to make the ID?"

"Superb police work."

Homer waited.

"Monty's wallet was still in his jacket."

"Yeah? Any money?"

"Thirty-seven dollars."

"So," Homer said, "we're not talking robbery."

"No," Genghis said.

"Even though the girl was scavenging to keep alive."

"It's like I said," Genghis said. "A crime of passion and self-defense."

Mrs. Montgomery's house was flat-roofed, one story and in need of paint. When a tiny, pale woman with puffy eyes answered Homer's knock he said, "Mrs. Montgomery?"

"Yes," she said so quietly that he could hardly hear her.

"I am terribly sorry to disturb you again after your loss, ma'am, but I'm Detective Sergeant Homer Proffitt."

"Oh, yes," Mrs. Montgomery said. "That other detective said he'd be sending someone to look through Monty's things."

When Homer left Mrs. Montgomery's, he

went straight to the IFCA offices but when he asked for Adele, Francis Twilly came out to say that Adele wasn't there. So Homer felt obliged to show Francis what he had discovered in Paul Montgomery's room.

"That's astonishing," Francis said, leafing through the sheets of paper.

"They were sitting on the desk next to his computer," Homer said.

"That's astonishing," Francis said again. At that moment his intercom buzzed. "Yes?"

"Francis, you asked me to let you know when Adele came in."

"Have her come to my office, Mary Louise."

Almost immediately there was a knock on the door. Francis called, "Come in."

Two steps into the office Adele stopped, staring at Homer. "What are *you* doing here?"

Francis said, "Adele, look what your friend Homer's found in the murdered man's bedroom."

"Frankly, Francis," Adele said, "I couldn't care less."

"Oh, I think you'll be interested in these," Francis said. He held up a stack of computer printouts.

"They're social work case histories," Homer said. "The dead guy, Paul Montgomery, had them."

Adele took the files and leafed through them quickly. "But these are confidential files," she said.

"Exactly," Homer said.

"And they were where?"

"In the murdered man's bedroom."

"I think he hacked into our computer," Francis said.

"But what would he want with case histories?" Adele asked.

"That's what I'm here to find out, ma'am," Homer said.

"You're the longest-serving practitioner at this site, Adele," Francis said. "Maybe you can make something out of them."

"All I found," Homer said, "was that eight of the cases have been ticked. The ticks are all by women's names, but a lot of the ones without ticks are women too."

"All right," Adele said. "I'll look at them and try to work it out."

"Good," Homer said.

"If you release Ros Fryer."

"Who?"

"Ros Fryer. The underage girl who is still being held in police custody."

"You got her real name," Homer said. "Good."

"You release her, and I'll look at your bits of paper."

"I'm sorry," Homer said. "I don't have the authority."

"Too bad then." Adele dropped the computer printouts on Francis' desk.

"You must be joking," Homer said.

"Do I look like I'm laughing?"

"Adele," Francis said, "this hardly seems a constructive attitude."

"Tough," Adele said.

"Oh, great," Homer said. "Terrific. Wonderful. Well, ma'am, I'll just go and interview the eight damn women myself."

Adele wondered if Homer thought this was a threat that would make her cave in. "Good luck," she said, and opened the door to Francis' office. "Do you know your way out, Sergeant Proffitt?"

Homer paused. Then he stomped out.

Francis said, "Honestly, Adele, I am amazed at your attitude. And, frankly, I don't think it's something that I will be able to ignore when I report to —"

"She's fourteen, Francis."

"What? Who?"

"Ros Fryer is fourteen years old and she's locked up in a cell in the Indianapolis Police Department. Get her out."

"Hell, it's unfortunate of course, but —"

"Get her out, Francis," Adele said. "Act like the director of a social services agency is supposed to. Care, Francis. Or if you can't care, at least do something. Or it's something I will be unable to ignore when I make my report."

"Fourteen?" Francis said. "You're sure?"

"Your telephone is there, Francis," Adele said, pointing. She picked up the printout photocopies from his desk and left the office.

Janice was peeling potatoes when the doorbell

rang. She hoped that Steve would answer it, but when the bell rang for the second time all he did was call from the couch, "Someone at the door."

Janice was still wiping her hands when she found that her caller was holding up police ID. "Detective Sergeant Proffitt," he said. "Are you Janice Downs?"

"Yeah. Why?"

"A man was murdered near here last night, Mrs. Downs."

"Oh, yeah?"

"We took his body out of Fall Creek, near the end of Talbot Street."

"Oh," Janice said. She blinked twice. "So what's that got to do with me?"

"Were you out that way last night, Mrs. Downs?"

"Me? Don't be silly. I can't even swim." Her hands gripped each other. "Why? You can't think I had something to do with some dead man."

"His name was Paul Montgomery. That mean anything to you?"

"Nothing."

"Well, he had the names of several women, and yours was one of them."

"Mine was?"

"Can you think of any reason why he might have had your name, Mrs. Downs?"

"I told you, I never heard of the guy."

"Your name was part of a social work case history. Have you ever had a social worker?"

"No," Janice said. "Well, yeah. My kids did. Only they got fostered out. But I'm trying to get them back."

"So you have had a social worker."

"I just said so, didn't I?"

"But you can't think why Paul Montgomery would have your name?"

"No. I never heard of him. Don't you people understand English?"

"Well, if something comes to mind, Mrs. Downs," Homer said, "I'd be grateful if you'd contact me." He handed her a card.

After she watched Homer drive away, Janice went straight to Steve in the living room.

"Who was at the door?" Steve asked. His eyes stayed on the TV screen.

Janice turned the set off.

"Hey, I was watching that."

"That was a cop," Janice said.

"A cop?" Steve said. "What'd he want?"

"A guy was murdered."

"Yeah?"

"They found his body in Fall Creek. At Talbot Street."

"Yeah?"

"Last night."

"Hey," Steve said, "why are you looking at me? Don't look at me."

"Look at you? Now, why should I do that, Steve Downs?"

"I didn't kill nobody, Jan."

"Did I say you did? Just because you got in late

last night, covered with sweat from running so hard."

"It wasn't me!" Steve said. He stood up. Janice took a step toward him, her fists clenched in anger. Steve backed away. "It wasn't me!"

Adele rushed into Francis' office. She waved the computer printouts. "I think I know what links the tick marks. I think I've worked it out."

Francis said, "Adele, I prefer people to knock on —"

"The ticks are all the women who live alone. And none of the other women do."

"Alone," Francis said. "That's interesting. So what do you think this Montgomery was up to?"

"There's more, Francis," Adele said.

"What?"

"One of the women on the list is a woman I dealt with a few years ago. Janice Downs. Her husband went to jail, and then she couldn't cope with three young children. Eventually, we found long-term foster parents for them."

"I don't understand what you're getting at."

"Janice's husband went to jail for beating a man almost to death. He thought the guy was making eyes at Janice."

"But if he's in jail."

"He was paroled five weeks ago, Francis. He's back with Janice again. They live less than three blocks from where the body was found. Now, suppose Paul Montgomery was making approaches to women he thought were alone and maybe vulnerable."

Francis' jaw dropped as he understood what Adele was suggesting. "You think Montgomery might have gone to Janice Downs' house and found Steven Downs instead."

"Yes," Adele said.

"This is a police matter," Francis said.

"I know," Adele said.

"So, are you going to call your friend, Homer?"

"You do it, Francis," Adele said. "I think I'd rather go home and take a bath."

Adele was in the bathtub when the phone rang at about seven. Although there was a phone within reach she considered letting the machine take the call. But then she answered it. "Hello?"

After a moment, Homer said, "Howdy, ma'am."

"Oh. You."

"Is it a bad time?"

"I just got in the bath."

"I'll be right over," Homer said.

"I don't think so, Sergeant Proffitt," Adele said.

"Do you want me to call back?"

"If it's about work, tell me now. If it's not, then what say you forget it."

"Please, don't say that, ma'am."

"I just did," Adele said. "Are you still at work?"

"Yeah," Homer said. "There have been developments."

"Such as?"

"Genghis arrested Steven Downs."

"Already? Oh, I forgot. Your friend Genghis has a theory of policing that is arrest first and interview later."

Homer said, "Forensic came up with two of Steven Downs' prints on the flashlight we recovered from the girl's house."

"Her name is Ros," Adele said.

"Ros Fryer. I know her name," Homer said.

"That's what I call caring policing."

"You're going to have to put this behind you sometime, Adele."

"I am?"

"It wasn't my fault."

"No? Well, maybe not. But it is your job. Your ethos. Your mind-set. People like you and people like me should keep on our own sides, Homer. It just doesn't work."

"It seemed to be working to me."

"There's too much conflict of interest."

"I'm interested. It's no conflict. And if nobody ever tries —"

"Did you try? I asked you to. I even said please. But do you *ever* see people, not arrests? Problems, not evidence? The victims, not just witnesses? Do you ever deal with gray, not black and white?"

"We are not all of us the same, ma'am. And to act as if we are makes you blind to gray too, doesn't it?"

Adele sighed. "Maybe I was talking more about the uniform than you personally," she said.

"Well, you have seen me personally without the uniform on."

"Ugh. Don't remind me."

"That bad, huh?"

"My mother warned me. So did my daughter."

"I'll give up beer. I'll go to a fitness class. I'll eat lentils. Whatever you say."

"Yeah, well," Adele said, "you let me think about it, all right?"

"As long as you will think about it," Homer said.

"Sorry," Adele said. "No promises."

Thursday morning Ros Fryer was sitting in the sun on the bank of Fall Creek when she saw Adele walking her way. She stripped some stalks of grass and then turned back to the creek.

"Hi," Adele said as she sat down.

Ros threw the seeds toward the water.

"Am I late?"

"I don't have a watch," Ros said quietly.

"How are you this morning?"

"All right."

Adele brushed her hair away from her eyes and leaned on her elbows so the sun was bright on her face. She said, "Well, I talked with my boss about you."

"Oh, yeah?"

"We have what we call short-stay foster families. There's one just . . ." Adele squinted as she looked across the creek. "I'm not sure whether it's that brown house, but it's near there if it isn't. Do you see it?"

Ros looked in a different direction at first. Then she looked where Adele pointed. "I see the brown house," she said.

"The idea is that you stay there for a while. And you already know the neighborhood."

"I don't see why I have to go anywhere."

"Think about the winter, Ros. Think how cold it gets."

"Get me a heater."

"We can't do that," Adele said. "The house isn't yours — or ours. Anyone could get in there. You should be in school. All that kind of thing."

"I'm not going back to *him*."

"No one will make you. All I'm suggesting is that you meet these people. If you like them, fine. If you don't then we'll find somewhere else."

While Ros went back to the house to get her things together, Adele walked to Mrs. Preston's. When Mrs. Preston opened the door she said, "I know you."

"I've been here before, Mrs. Preston. I talked to you about the girl who stole your carrots."

"She's back," Mrs. Preston said. "I've seen her."

"I know," Adele said. "But I just wanted to assure you that she won't be stealing your carrots anymore."

"My boy, Gerald, planted those carrots," Mrs. Preston said. Her dogs began to bark.

When Adele got back to the IFCA offices she had a message to call Homer. "He said to tell you it was about work," Mary Louise, the receptionist, said. "He said I should be very clear when I told you that."

"Thanks," Adele said with a smile.

"I just wanted to let you know," Homer said, "that Steven Downs didn't do it after all."

"But I thought his fingerprints were on the flashlight."

"They were. They are. But unfortunately the flashlight was not the murder weapon."

"What?"

"Our pathologist seems obsessed by some wooden fragments in Montgomery's scalp. And he says that whatever hit Paul Montgomery was thicker than our flashlight. Genghis tried to get him to say that Downs might have hit Montgomery more than once with the flashlight and that's why the hole is bigger. But the pathologist says he would have to have done it with a wooden flashlight."

"So you've let Steven Downs go?"

"Not yet."

"Why not?"

"Downs admits he was on the scene the night of the murder. He had to have been for your Ros Fryer to get the flashlight. So Genghis is trying to turn up another murder weapon either at Downs' house, or on the route between."

"And what does Downs say?" Adele asked.

"He says someone else was fighting with Montgomery when he got there. He says he panicked and ran because of his record and because he's on parole. And he says that somewhere along the creek a ghost appeared in a burst of light and scared him to death."

"So when will Genghis interview the ghost? Before or after he's arrested it?"

"Downs figures he dropped the flashlight when the ghost appeared."

"At least that fits with what Ros said about finding it."

"I may have to talk to Ros again, ma'am," Homer said. "But I will make sure it's me that talks to her and not Genghis."

After a moment, Adele said, "What?"

"I said I will be the one to talk to the girl, to Ros, and not Genghis. Weren't you listening?"

"I . . . was thinking," Adele said.

When Adele knocked on Mrs. Preston's door again the first voices to answer were those of her dogs. Adele knocked a second time. From inside Mrs. Preston said, "Who's that?"

"I'm the social worker, Mrs. Preston. I need to talk to you."

"About that girl?"

"No, about something else."

"What?"

"Please open the door, Mrs. Preston."

Adele heard the locks being undone and eventually Mrs. Preston stepped outside. "Have you caught her? Have you locked her up?"

"It's not about the girl, Mrs. Preston," Adele said.

"Well, what then?"

"When I was here the very first time you told me about a man who'd been hanging around. You said he'd been using the telephone."

"No," Mrs. Preston said. "No more."

"And you said you had a bat," Adele said. "That would be a baseball bat, wouldn't it?"

"It was Gerald's bat," Mrs. Preston said.

"May I see it?"

"Why?" Mrs. Preston asked.

"I'd like to." Mrs. Preston didn't move. "It's made of wood, isn't it."

"Nothing to do with you," Mrs. Preston said.

"What happened, Mrs. Preston?"

"When?"

"When you saw the man by the phone again. Tuesday night."

"It was dark," Mrs. Preston said, "but you can still see at night, if you're used to it. I can see when that girl takes my carrots and that's at night."

"So what happened with the man? Did you go out to tell him to go away?"

"He was disgusting," Mrs. Preston said.

"How?"

"He said things."

"As you went to talk to him?"

"He touched me. He acted like I had come out so he could do it."

"And you hit him?"

Mrs. Preston looked toward the path to the phone. "He just lay there, and I thought, that'll teach you. But then he didn't get up again. And I thought, I can't leave you there. The dogs might get you. And if they did that then they'd come and say they were dangerous and take them away from me, no matter what Gerald said."

"So you dragged him to the creek?"

"He wasn't very heavy," Mrs. Preston said. "And it was down a slope. You see? And the dogs didn't get him, did they?"

"I'm going to have to use the phone," Adele said. "Will you stay here while I do it?"

"Are you calling my boy, Gerald? Is that who you're calling?"

"I will," Adele said. "But I've got to call my friend in the police first."

"Tell them about the girl," Mrs. Preston said. "She's been stealing my carrots."

Michael Z. Lewin has written sixteen novels, most set in Indianapolis and featuring private detective Albert Samson or police lieutenant Leroy Powder. A former science teacher and basketball columnist, he has also written several plays for both stage and radio. He lives in England.

Expert Opinion

Benjamin M. Schutz

It was winter when first call came in. That brief lull in domestic warfare that comes right before Christmas. No one wants to be in court that time of year. Not the lawyers, not the families. It has to be a life or death emergency to get on the docket. No judge wants to be playing Solomon in the manger.

I looked out my office window. The sky was gray and cloudy. The air cold and dry without a hint of snow. Walking to my office, the day had the look and feel of marble.

The phone rang twice before I picked it up.

"Dr. Triplett, this is Larry Fortunato. I'm an attorney in Lawrence, New Jersey. I'd like to use you in a case."

"I'm sorry, Mr. Fortunato, but I'm buried in work right now. I'm not taking on any new cases."

"How long until you can?"

"I won't be starting any new cases for another six weeks, maybe two months. Can I refer you to anyone?"

"Not really, Doctor. You're the one we want."

"Is one of the parents down here?" I asked, wondering why a New Jersey lawyer was so keen to use me here in Virginia.

"No, the parents both live up here. I did some research. Your name kept coming up as the best, so I figured we'd go with the best."

"That's very flattering. What kind of case is it?" May as well find out what I was best at. I wasn't going to take the case regardless of the answer.

"It's a sexual abuse case. Mother claims the father abuses the little boy."

"There are some very good people up your way. There's —"

"I know doctor, but believe me we called all of them. I asked them the same question. If it was your kid, who would you want to do the evaluation? You ought to feel pretty good about this. Your name is always the answer. Well, not always. Some shrink across the state isn't too crazy about you, but I heard you blew him away in court a couple of times."

"That is nice to hear. This is a hard area to keep a decent reputation in. People don't really want evaluations done. They want verification of what they already know is true. A lot of messengers get killed in this line of work."

"No problem of that here, Doctor. Neither of the parties would be retaining you. It's the little boy's —"

"Don't tell me. I don't want to know. Even if I took the case, I wouldn't want to hear anything without all the attorneys on the phone. These cases are like tar pits. You make one false move and you can't undo it. These cases are littered with the bones of evaluators who screwed up."

"Okay. I respect that. Let me ask you one question. Hypothetically, if you were to take the case, how much would it cost?"

"My hourly rate is two hundred dollars. Not knowing anything about this case, I'd tell you the range is eight to twelve thousand dollars. These cases are very, very draining. I can only do two or three at a time. They take at least two months to complete. If I was taking any more of these that is."

"Of course. Sounds like you need a little R and R."

"Yeah." I needed more than that. I needed a new how and why, but that was none of his business.

"Well, thank you for your time, Dr. Triplett. Take care of yourself."

I cradled the phone and surveyed the cases on my desk. First up Tiffany Pearlman. A child so damaged that she could scarcely go a day without harming herself. Overdoses, auto wrecks, pregnancies, poetry in her own blood. A walking death notice lacking only a date. The county had no money to underwrite treatment. The parents were bankrupt from trying to pin the blame on each other. She was a slow motion suicide heading downhill. If I was lucky, I'd get her committed the first week of January and buy her a little time. She, of course, thought that she was fine and it was the rest of us who were crazy.

The rest of the pile was more of the same. Their trials were strung out over the next month. After that I was going to take some time off. See if I could reinvent myself.

The envelope was on my secretary's desk a week later. She wasn't in on Wednesdays so no one saw who delivered it. A large manila envelope with my name typed across the front. I got these packages all the time. First thing a divorce lawyer tells their client: keep a journal.

Each parent documenting the outrages perpetrated by the other. Each hurt brooded over lovingly. No slight too small to remember or small enough to forgive. However long they spent preparing their case, it took at least twice as long to recover any sense of proportion. If they ever did.

I took the envelope into my office, I peeled it open and dumped out the contents.

The money was old and in wads held together by rubber bands. One fell on the floor. I picked it up and looked at the door. It was open. I felt naked and closed the door.

There was no letter in the envelope. Nothing. This was definitely not Publisher's Clearinghouse. I picked up a brick. All hundreds. Did banks ever give people hundreds? I thought they were for interbank transactions. I did a quick total. Six thousand. Twelve bricks. Seventy-two grand.

The phone rang. I picked it up and said nothing.

"Dr. Triplett. You received a package today." The voice was smooth and even and unknown.

"Who is this?"

"That package contained an amount of money twice what you would earn from your caseload for the next two months, am I correct?"

"Who is this? I'm not going to answer any questions until I know who this is."

"This is your new client, Dr. Triplett."

"Oh, no, you're not. I don't work like this. You tell me who you are and where to send this money. I don't want it."

"You can't return it, Dr. Triplett. No one will accept it."

"Then I'll give it away. I don't want it."

"If you give it away, it will be considered spent. Lie back and enjoy it, Doc. You've been bought and paid for." After a moment of silence the voice returned, softer. "Take a deep breath, Doctor. Count it again. That's a lot of R and R, Doctor. We'll be in touch."

I hung up the phone. My heart and mind were racing. I felt like I was swimming through Jell-O with my mouth open.

This was not happening to me. I looked at the money. Oh, yes, it was. I'm a psychologist. I don't even do criminal work. I obey the law. I don't even get traffic tickets. This is insane. There has to be something I can do.

I looked at the bricks of money again. Seventy-two thousand dollars worth of serious intent. Maybe I should call the cops. And tell them what? I was being forced at twice my hourly rate to perform unknown services, for an unknown person. I'm sure there is a crime in there somewhere. Any ideas, Officer? Sure. If they want you to do something illegal, or they threaten you with bodily harm, you call us. Gross overpayment won't do? No.

I had to talk to this guy the next time that he called. That's what I do best — talk to desperate people. People backed into corners, people who felt they had nothing to lose or everything to lose and no way to win. People who could not compromise or negotiate or yield. That's what I did every day. End conflicts, build bridges, put doors into corners. That's what put this guy onto me now. This time I was one of those people. I'd use my skills to get myself out of his life and him out of mine. I felt better already. I had a plan. I knew what I was going to do. I was good at this. The best, he'd said.

I looked at the money. First things first. This had to be put into the bank. I had to be able to return it and that meant guaranteeing its safety. My office safebox wouldn't do, neither would the one I had at home.

I scooped the money into the bag, put on my jacket, turned off the lights and locked the office door. Outside, I fiddled with my key ring, looking for the front door key. I found it and locked the dead bolt. As I withdrew the key from the sticky lock, I heard a voice.

"Dr. Triplett?"

I turned toward the voice. There were two of them. Left wore a butterscotch leather jacket over a chocolate turtleneck. His face was deeply pitted. Could have been acne, could have been shrapnel for all I knew. His hands were at his side. Right was the talker. His head cocked slightly to one side, a smile on his face. "Dr. Triplett, would you step this way please?" He turned sideways and pointed to a black limousine with tinted windows.

I looked from Left to Right. "And if I say no?"

Left reached up and pulled away his jacket to show me that the question had been rhetorical.

"Right here on the street. You'd shoot me?" I asked Right.

"In a fucking heartbeat, Doc. You have no idea how angry Mr. G is with you. Getting shot is the least of your worries. Step this way, please."

He stepped off the curb and opened the door. All I could see was a pair of legs in the middle of the rear seat and an empty bench facing backwards toward the legs. I stepped between Left and Right, holding my bag like it was my lunch. Right's cologne was cloyingly sweet. I ducked my head and slipped onto the bench with my bag of money in my lap. Right slid in next to me and pulled the door closed. Left came around the car, opened the other door and sat down next to me. I was pressed between them, feeling the pressure of their arms and legs against me from my shoulders to my shoes. I couldn't move.

My host stroked his beard slowly, rhythmically, like he was petting himself. He lifted his chin, pursed his lips in thought and then backhanded me across the face.

My eyes watered and my muscles tensed. The

pressure on me from both sides increased. I relaxed.

"Who the fuck do you think you are? Huh?" he asked. He was short and stocky, with black hair that swept straight back from a widow's peak. With his sharp, curved nose, thick neck and bulging eyes, he looked like a great horned owl. I felt like a field mouse. His hands were pale and square with short, thick fingers.

"I asked you a question. Who the fuck do you think you are?"

"I think I'm terrified, that's who."

"That's good. You should be. You should be wondering if you're ever gonna get out of this car."

He leaned back against the seat. "I called you and told you I had a problem. A serious fucking problem, and you were too fucking busy to help me. What do you think? You're too good for me?"

The pale hand flew and my head snapped back. I closed my eyes to stop the spinning.

"I came to you with respect." He said pointing a single finger at me. "We did our homework. You're the best. You gave us a price and we doubled it. In cash. Up front. But you're still too busy for me, for my problem. How'd you get so special, Mr. Terrified? You feeling special right now?"

"No," I whispered.

"So tell me, what is it? I ain't good enough for you? My money ain't good enough for you?"

I took a deep breath. Telling him that his attorney had never gotten around to giving me his name was not going to derail this tirade. "It had nothing to do with you or your money. I'm full. There's only so many of these that I can do at one time. I'm in the middle of three cases. I have to finish them. They've got court dates."

"So? You think we couldn't fix that? You don't think we could arrange a continuance or two? Talk to the lawyers, the docket clerks if that's what you needed? Did you come back and say that was the problem, could we work with you on that? No. Nothing. No interest. Just blew me off. Too busy. You busy right now, Mr. Terrified? I'll bet you are. Busy holding your water, is what."

My companions snickered.

"Since you're not too busy all of a sudden, let me tell you about my problem."

I smiled weakly. "Sure."

"When I was younger, I met this girl. You don't need to know her name. A stripper. Whew, God was she hot. Anyway, that's another story. She got knocked up. Said the kid was mine. Now I'm married. I got two kids of my own. Coulda been mine, I'm not saying that. But I tell her you push this and he's an orphan. Let it be and I'll keep an eye on him. I'll look out for him. She's a smart girl. I don't hear from her again. Until a few weeks ago. She calls me up outta the blue. Says my son's in trouble. I gotta help him out like I said. So I say okay, what's the problem. She says he's getting divorced. I start laughing. That's the fucking problem? No, she says the wife claims he's diddling the kid. Won't let him have no visitation. It's killing him. He grew up without a father, now he'll grow old without a son. Help him. Help him. You said you would. He's your own flesh and blood. Look at him, just see him once and then deny him. Look me in the eye and deny him. Fuck." He shrugged and rolled his eyes. "She gave me the address. I went by. Stopped me cold. I seen him walking down the street. It's like I'm watching myself. Little things. The way he walks. The way he laughs. He looks just like me at his age. Okay, he's my son. So I introduce myself to him. I tell him I'm a friend of his mother's, that's all. We sit down and talk. He tells me his wife, she's getting boned by her boss and she wants out. She says she's gonna take the kid. He pulls out his wallet, shows me a picture. What do I know? Kids, they all look alike. He tells me his name. The kid's got my first name. It was his mother's idea. Now so far neither of my other two kids are married. This is my only grandchild, a grandson. With my name. I say how's she gonna do that? She's sucking some other guy's dick and she's a fit mother, c'mon, am I right?"

I nodded in the understanding that passeth all reason.

"He says she's saying the boy don't want to go with him on visits. That when he comes back, he's got nightmares. He wants to sleep with her. That his daddy's mean to him. That he touched him where nobody should touch him. That his butthole's red and sore when he comes back. My son, he gets down on his knees. We're in a restaurant. He gets down on his knees and he swears on his mother's life that he never touched the kid. That it's a fucking lie. I tell him to get up, he's drawing eyes. I tell him I'll talk to her. Hear what she's gotta say. I'll get to the bottom of this."

He leaned back. "You got any questions. Anything else you want to know?"

"No. Not now. If I do, I'll ask, if that's okay, of course."

He smiled broadly. "Of course it's okay. That's why we're here isn't it? I tell you my problem and you listen and ask questions, right? I mean, I'm not paying 400 dollars an hour to a deaf mute, am I?" The smile spread. I was invited to reply and managed a wince of relief.

"Okay. So I go meet the wife. Jesus, what a bitch. I tell her how I'm Vito's uncle and I hear that they're having some problems, maybe I can help. Well, she unloads on him. He's never been a provider to her. He's always losing jobs. She's worked two jobs to make ends meet. She also says he's never been a real man in the sack. She thinks he's maybe a little light in the loafers." He wagged his left hand and pursed his mouth in distaste. "She liked the way he was at first — real gentle and all. But then she realized he was a mama's boy. His mother, she never let him out of her sight. She was always afraid he wouldn't come back, like the father. She was always running his life, calling him at all hours and him always going over there. She got tired of playing second fiddle to the mother. On top of that he was never interested in her as a woman. She had to get him drunk to do it and even then he wasn't flying at full mast. So I ask her about her boss. She says he's just a friend, that Vito's paranoid that she's sleeping around 'cause he wouldn't give her what she needed. She says they just talk. I ask her about the kid. She tells me the same story as Vito. I ask if there's anybody else has seen this stuff. She says no. She took him to the doctor's to check out his butt. She said they couldn't see nothing wrong. They stuck some camera up his butt, a colosto— something. I don't know."

"A colposcope. It's called a colposcope." My voice sounded like it was being piped into the car.

"That's right." My host smiled.

"That's good. It's a specialist's instrument. Somebody with some training took a look at him."

"Maybe, that's good. I don't know. All I know is my grandson has some camera shoved up his ass. He's three years old for Christ's sake. What the fuck is this?"

When I didn't answer, he went on. "She says she ain't gonna let Vito see the boy without a supervisor. A fucking supervisor. And not his mother. She doesn't trust his mother on account of their relationship. He's gotta go down to welfare and get a fucking social worker and pay to see his own kid. If he doesn't agree she's gonna call child protective services and have him charged with child molesting.

"Child molesting. My son molesting my grandson. Can you believe this shit? I asked if I can see the little boy. She asks why. I say I want to talk to him a second, that's all. She says she wants to be there. Okay, fine. She brings the little boy in. He's cute. He's got these big, dark eyes, in this little face. He looks like a little bird, you know what I mean? Very serious face. He's watching me. He's sitting on his mother's lap, holding on to her with both hands. I try to catch his eye, get him to come over, sit in my lap, talk. He keeps turning his face away. She says he's shy. I think fuck, she's gonna make him a freaking mama's boy just like she complains about Vito. So I take out a silver dollar I got in my pocket, that and a couple pieces of candy I brought just in case I want to talk to this kid. He looks at the mother and she says, go, it's okay. So he comes over and sits on my lap. I give him the dollar, tell him if he's a good boy he can keep it. I ask the mother to step outside, give me a little privacy with the boy. She don't like that, so I tell her to go to the front window, tell me what she sees. She goes over to the window, comes back, pats the boy on the head and leaves. Smart woman."

Left and Right chuckle with amusement at the memory.

"So I ask the kid some questions. His daddy, he ever stick anything in his butt? He ever touch his pee-pee? Why don't he like to go over his dad's house? Don't he know that if he's lying his old man could go to jail? Why would he want to do that?

"The kid just looks at me with those big eyes. He don't say nothing. I give him a piece of candy. He takes it and puts it in his mouth but he still don't say nothing. Now all this time, I'm very calm. He starts to cry. He wants his mommy. I tell him we ain't done yet. He can't see his mommy until we're done. He's gotta answer my questions first. The fucking kid starts to lose it. He gets down and goes to run to the door. I gotta grab him by the shirt. He's crying, I pick him up in the air and I shake him until he shuts up. I tell him I'm his grandfather and when your grandfather asks you a question you answer him. He just started screaming for his mother and he wouldn't shut up. The mother started screaming for the kid. This wasn't getting anywhere. I wanted to smack them both. I gave the kid back to his mother and told her not to talk to anyone about this, that I'd fix the problem.

"The bitch, she overheard me tell the kid I'm his grandfather. She calls Vito and tells him, 'You know that old man came by, your uncle, he's your fucking father.' Vito, he calls me, he says stay outta my life. You think you can just snap your fingers and make it all good. No thank you. I don't need your fucking help. You didn't have time for me, well now I ain't got time for you." He shook his head in disbelief. "So here we are."

Here we are indeed. Just click my ruby slippers three times and I'm gone. "What do you want from me?"

He looked at me incredulously, as if I had just barked or honked like a goose. "Ain't you been listening? I want to know what's happening here. There is no way anybody is gonna molest my grandson, no way. But if Vito ain't doin' it then there's no way he's gonna have a fuckin' social worker with him, watching him like he's some kind of pervert.

"This is my family. My son wants to be with his son, he's gonna be with his son. I gotta know the truth. What's happening. Then I know what I gotta do. I gotta know now. If my son didn't do it then he should be out in the park with his son right now, this minute, throwing him a ball, whatever they want to do. If he did do it, then it isn't gonna happen again, ever. That's what I want. I ain't waitin' two months for you to get around to me. I want the truth, and I want it now."

"What if you can't have that?" I asked, aware of a faint stirring of pleasure at his impotence.

"What do you mean?"

"I mean, what if the truth can't be known. Can't be proven. What if there's doubt about if anything really happened?"

"No." He shook his head rejecting that possibility. "It either did or it didn't happen. That's all you gotta tell me. I gotta know for sure. I can't be worrying the rest of my life, I made a mistake; that's he's sticking his fuckin' cock up my grandson's ass — you hear me? That ain't gonna happen." He got right in my face and jabbed home each word with the end of a finger, typing out his frustration on the keyboard of my chest.

I reached out and grabbed his wrist. "I get the point. Now you're paying me a lot of money to help you with this problem. Do you want my expert opinion or do you just want to break my ribs?"

Our eyes met like two dogs over one bone. Neither of us looked away. I let go of his wrist and he sat back. "Okay, what's your opinion?"

"When I asked you what you wanted, you said you wanted the truth. Suppose that isn't possible? Suppose you will never know without a doubt what happened? Can you accept that? Can you live with being wrong, with not protecting your grandson or with ending your son's relationship with his child for no good reason?"

"No, that's not acceptable. Those prices are too high. I want the truth. If I know the truth, I know what to do and what I do will be right."

"Then I can't help you."

"What do you mean you can't help me? You're supposed to be the best, you wrote the book, you know all there is about this shit. You're a fucking doctor, for Christ's sake."

"But I'm not God. Maybe I do know all there

is but that's a lot less than what we need to know.

"Even if I had an opinion about what happened, even if that was a result of all the research I know and all the skill I have, that would just be the best we can do right now, I could still be wrong. I can't guarantee you the truth, nobody can. If you can't accept that then I can't help you."

He shook his head like a buffalo beset by flies. "I don't get it. Why is this so hard? Okay, I don't know how to talk to little kids, but you do. That's your job."

I had to stifle the impulse to talk down to him, to rub his nose in his need, to hit him with fists of sarcasm, and remember that somewhere inside there was a confused parent trying to do the right thing for his kid, doing his best no matter how far it fell from being good enough.

It was also my best chance of seeing the outside of this car.

"This is why it's so hard. First, you have no witness. Whatever is or isn't happening, the only ones there are the boy and his father. He isn't going to confess. He hasn't. He denies it. Maybe it's the truth, maybe it isn't. What are you going to do? Torture it out of him? Even if he says he did it, you'll never know if that was just to end the pain. You can torture people into saying what you want to hear but not into telling you the truth. Pain trumps truth, unless you're a saint. There's no physical evidence. They checked out his butt and didn't find any fissures. But that doesn't prove anything. There's all kinds of abuse that doesn't leave physical evidence. He could be masturbating the boy or fellating him, or having the child do him. The nightmares, the fears, wanting to sleep with his mother, not wanting to go with his father, that means nothing. You see that very often with kids of his age when parents separate, especially if there's a lot of conflict. They don't want to leave the mother if she's been the primary caretaker, but after the transfer they have a good time with the dad. They return and they want to re-establish that closeness with the mother, they regress, they want to sleep with her. You don't have to have sexual abuse to explain all of that. That's one of the biggest problems. There's no set of symptoms that separates sexual abuse from other phenomena *and* that *always* shows up with sexual abuse. Sexual abuse is a complex thing. Is the violent rape of a ten-year-old girl by a stranger the same as a father masturbating in front of his sleeping six-year-old son? No, but sexual abuse covers both things. Some kids are abused, there's no physical evidence, they make no disclosures and no one notices anything wrong from the outside. That's why this is so hard. Not only that —"

"What about him telling his mother that his daddy touches him?"

"So far, all we have is her word that he said that. Suppose I interview him and he says nothing. Does that mean she's lying, or it didn't happen, or just that I couldn't get the information from him? Suppose he recants. He catches on that everybody's upset, that he might never see his dad again, that he loves his dad, that he wants his dad so badly he'll put up with that other stuff, that it isn't so bad after all. It takes a lot for a kid to give up on a parent, usually it's the other way around. Does that mean it didn't happen? No. I've had cases where the victim was in one room recanting to me, while next door the parent was confessing to the police.

"Suppose the kid does make a disclosure to me. I do a clean interview, no suggestions, no leading questions, I get a disclosure but not a lot of details, it's a little inconsistent, the affect's unremarkable. Not a great disclosure. Does that mean nothing happened? No. Kids are abused and may never give a 'great' account of what happened to them. You get the picture? This is a high wire act on a razor blade over a minefield. Very hard to keep your balance and anywhere you come down could blow up in your face."

My host sat silent and slack, pummeled by something he couldn't bully into submission.

"I'm not done yet. Let me throw a wrinkle into all this. Suppose I make a mistake, then what?"

"What do you mean?"

"You know what I mean. Suppose I tell you your son didn't do anything. That's my expert opinion. You tell the wife that he can have visits with his son. A year later they rush the boy to the hospital with a torn anus. What are you going to do?"

A smile appeared and disappeared, as enigmatic and unmistakable as the Mona Lisa's. "I'd kill you, you fucked up like that."

"Right. So the smart play for me is to tell you that your son did molest the boy. If I'm right, he doesn't get a chance to do it again. If I'm wrong, how will you ever know? The boy is being protected from something that never happened. And it keeps on not happening. I don't even need to do an evaluation. I just have to look out for myself and cover my tracks. You said it yourself. I'm the best there is at what I do. Who's gonna catch me? I go through the motions. I build a case. The evidence could go either way. I say your son did it. Now you have to worry about whether that's what I truly believe or what I want you to believe because it's best for me. You can't have certainty, it's not there. Not for you, not for me, not for anyone.

"This is not me being too good for you. This is not about me or you. This is about the truth. The truth is the same for all of us, you, me, everybody. Nobody can get a leg up on this one. What you want, I can't deliver. No one can."

"So, what should I do, Doctor? What's your expert opinion?"

"I think you have to accept that you may never know for sure what happened. That you can live with the possibility of being wrong. If you can, then an evaluation can be a useful thing to do."

"And if I can't?"

"Then raise him yourself. That's the only way to be certain." Like an open parachute on the ground, I quickly packed up my frustration before it blew me away.

"Or maybe you decide it isn't your problem. You don't have to fix this. Just because someone presents it to you doesn't mean you have to accept it. It's not your problem until you accept it as one. You said your son didn't want your help anyway."

He looked at me like I was a talking ferret.

"My son is accused of diddling my grandson and I'm supposed to nod my head and say my, my isn't that something. You all get back to me when you sort that out. It isn't my problem. You're in my prayers. That's what's wrong with you people. I hear this, it is my problem. I'm not gonna walk away from it. I'm gonna fix it. That's what I do best, Doctor. I fix problems. That's why people come to me. You think I'd be where I am today if I said well, that's tough, wish I could help you with that. Come back next time with an easy one. Sorry doesn't feed the bulldog, Doctor. Problems need fixin'. Tears and sympathy, that's for women."

He leaned back and reached into his pockets.

"So, what do I do with you? You think you earned that seventy-two grand?"

I pushed the envelope toward him. "Absolutely not. Here, keep it. I don't want any of it."

"Really? You sell yourself short, Doc. Maybe

you didn't solve my problem, but you cleared up my thinking. That's worth something. How long we been talking, Tommy?"

Left checked his watch. "About an, hour Mr. G."

"Okay, that's what, four hundred? Yeah. Tommy, get that out of the bag."

Tommy reached in and counted off four one hundred dollar bills and handed them to me.

"That was for services rendered, Doctor. That means that all of this is privileged and confidential, am I right?"

The question itself was a pardon and a release. "Absolutely. Not a word of this to anyone."

"Now, get out."

No one moved, so I leaned over Tommy, grabbed the door handle, unlocked it and stumbled out into the afternoon's fading light. I turned around and tempted fate. "Just for curiosity's sake, what did you get out of all this?"

"Watching you twist and turn on my hook reminded me that when you bring a problem to me, you make a problem for me. And there's a price for that, too."

I closed the door and the limousine pulled away. Low and sleek, it turned the corner and disappeared.

I had my life back, just as I left it. Or so I thought.

A week later, I was sitting on my patio, drinking a cup of coffee and eating a bagel. The sun was bright overhead, the air crisp and cool.

Winter and spring had a truce. I was skimming the newspaper. There it was, midway down page A8:

> Vito and Carla Battista were found shot to death in a parking lot outside Ms. Battista's lawyer's office, where the estranged couple had just left a meeting. Police believe the murders were a botched carjacking. The couple's only child, Salvatore, age 3, is in the care of his grandfather, reputed mob boss, Salvatore Giannini.

Benjamin M. Schutz's fiction has appeared in *Death Cruise*, *Unusual Suspects*, and *The Edgar Award Book*. His novels include *A Fistful of Empty* and *Mexico Is Forever.* He lives in Virginia.

Show Me the Bones

Carolyn Wheat

"He doesn't look like a bloodhound," the little girl said. Her hair was dirty and so was her sharp little face and so were her bare feet.

What was the mother thinking, bare feet on this hard desert ground with spiky plants and lizards and scorpions and God knew what else? I had on my day hikers, the hightops, and two pair of socks under that. But then I intended to walk as far as the track would lead me, and the kid meant to stay in her mean little yard, among children's toys left out so long their bright colors had faded long ago because it hardly ever rained out here.

"He's not a bloodhound, honey," I said in a syrupy tone I barely recognized as my own. Why I invariably called all kids honey or sweetie or some other cotton-candy nickname I couldn't say. Except, I suppose, that they made me nervous with their direct little eyes and blunt questions. "He's a Bouvier, and his name is Polo."

"Can I pet him?" She edged her dirt-smudged hand with its bitten nails toward Polo's curly black head. Her thin wrists were scarred, I hoped from cacti and not abuse. The long red-tipped tendrils of ocotillo had sharp thorns; maybe she'd reached in to touch the flowers and torn her skin on the long needles.

"Do you think he'll find my sister?" The little

girl's voice sounded squeezed through a thin tube, and she directed her gaze toward the ground instead of looking at me with her intense blue eyes.

God, I hope not, kid.

See, I never actually told the families what Polo was. They saw a dog, they figured "rescue." They figured tracking meant hunting for a living person on the move through the scrub. They didn't know Polo was a cadaver dog, trained to forget the living and find the dead.

I cleared my throat and said, "He's a good dog. He'll do his best, and so will I."

"Dogs always find lost people, don't they?" Now she gave me the full force of those blue eyes, gazing at me with a luminous innocence that pushed the breath out of my lungs. She looked both hopeful and scared to death, as if in some part of her eight-year-old brain she knew her sister wouldn't be found alive.

The ten-year-old had been missing five days now. Five long days and nights. The trackers worked all night; you didn't stop if you thought you might find a living child in need of medical care. But if you were looking for a body, you waited for first light.

There were four of us sheriff's department K-9 dog handlers gathered in the inky blue early morning. Devon had Kali, her black lab, on a long canvas leash. Kali roamed the perimeter, sniffing at each prickly pear, every cactus and bush, then looking back at Devon for confirmation that she was doing a good job. I always had the feeling the dogs were perpetually surprised to realize that their humans didn't actually smell the same things they did.

Scout, Jen's golden retriever, waved her feathery blond tail and sniffed the people instead of the bushes. Ruth's Daisy, the Doberman, wanted to do the same, but the child edged away as the Dobe headed toward her with a determined expression in her doggy brown eyes. Poor Daisy; she was as sweet as her name, but the Doberman reputation preceded her, and people often looked deathly afraid when all she wanted was to lick their faces.

We were waiting for one more team, and finally the metallic blue van with Nancy and Toby skidded into the dirt driveway. I even said to the kid, "Here comes a bloodhound," as if to reassure her that we were really taking her sister's disappearance seriously.

Blood drained from the child's face as Nancy slid open the door of her van and Toby bounded out. "A real bloodhound," she whispered.

"Do they smell the blood?" I had to strain to hear the words, then realized that in her ears, the word *bloodhound* carried sinister overtones.

But how to answer? How to say, well, no, it's not blood so much as the scent of a decaying corpse. Not exactly a reassuring reply.

Before I could formulate a suitable response, a deputy walked toward me and said, "We ready to get this show on the road?"

There were cops all over the place. The sheriff's vans and cars were parked farther along the dirt road, and they'd made a makeshift headquarters in the workshop at the rear of the little frame house. Radios crackled and guys milled around aimlessly while pretending to be incredibly busy. The real work was in the backcountry and everyone knew it. The cops who were still here were just waiting for news from the desert, news that would have them summoning an evac helicopter and a medic — or a crime scene team.

As the days and nights passed, the evac helicopter seemed less and less likely.

I didn't like being so close to the family of the missing child. I preferred law enforcement to keep itself separate from the grieving and the wailing, but out here in the middle of absolute backcountry nowhere, Ocotillo Wells, California — which called itself a town but was in reality a gas station, a hamburger joint, fourteen houses, and thirty mobile homes — there was nowhere to go that would insulate us from the little girl's devastating blue eyes.

Toby lived up to her expectations. She watched with undisguised fascination as the big brown animal loped along the hardpacked dirt, snout to the ground like a living vacuum cleaner, sniffing up every trace of scent. At one point, he stopped, threw back his head, and emitted his mournful howl.

The cops stopped talking. Jen and Ruth, who'd been gossiping in low tones, went silent, too, although they'd heard Toby's war cry a hundred times before. Something about that sound went right though a person, brought back tales of banshees and spirits of the dead crying from the grave.

The little girl burst into tears and ran toward the house. I wanted to stop her, to call out something that would reassure her, but I had no words. We were out here to find the body of her sister, and no sugar-coating was going to soften that blow.

It was time to get moving. Toby was ready, and that meant the rest of us were too. All the dogs were straining their leashes, eager to hit the trail and do the job they'd been trained for.

The sergeant broke us into smaller units. Each dog would accompany a sheriff's team heading in a different direction; we'd cover the backcountry near town first, hoping the child hadn't been abducted by a car and driven to El Centro.

Most of the other teams got into cars to be driven to a point of origin, but Polo and I would walk from the hamburger joint at the edge of town, right off Interstate 8. I would be with two deputies, one male, one female, both young and eager.

"First time you've worked with dogs?" I knew the answer by the way they eyed our animals, but I wanted to open conversation. They nodded in unison and introduced themselves as Don and Sarah.

When we reached the hamburger stand, which

wasn't open for business but still emanated a strong odor of cooking grease, Polo bounced on his bearlike legs and jumped on me. "No, babe, not now," I said. "We're going to work, Polo." I leaned in close and spoke directly into his tiny black ears with a deep-voiced seriousness that Polo had been trained to recognize as meaning business.

"Find the bones, Polo. Find the bones." Polo leaped and gave a single bark to tell me he understood. I unhooked his leash and let him race into the brush.

Bones. Saying "find the bones" instead of "find the body" made it sound clean and bloodless. But the kid was gone only five days, and that meant whatever we found, it wouldn't be nice clean bleached bones like the skulls in a Georgia O'Keeffe painting. It would be messy and bloated and there would be flies. And the dogs would love it.

I liked this job, in a strange and horrible way. I liked being out in the wilderness and I liked giving Polo a job. Dogs were meant to work; they went a little crazy if all they were expected to do was entertain their humans. And I liked being of help to people, which finding bodies was when you thought about it. People needed to know the truth about their missing children or parents or whoever, and they needed the comfort of bodies recovered and buried according to their rituals.

Polo and I were trained for tracking the living as well as the dead, but somehow it was the cadaver searches we were assigned to the most. Toby, on the other hand, almost always worked living cases, but Nancy had been out of town when this child went missing, so she wasn't available for the early search teams, and Toby had to make do with bones instead of sniffing the kid's sweater.

See, living people all smell different, and you use an item with a person's individual scent on it in order to set the smell, get the dogs familiar with the exact scent they're tracking. But dead people all smell alike. So all you have to say is "find the bones" and the dogs will let you know when they find any dead human.

It was the finding-the-body part I didn't like very much, and the main reason for that was that the dogs loved it as much as I hated it. Polo loved it on a pure animal level, reveling in the smells and the grue, rolling in the human goop caused by a badly-decayed body, trying to eat the flesh and, in one memorable instance, carrying a decapitated head in his wide maw. I loved my big black bear of a dog, but it was hard to pet him for a little while after that, and if his tongue touched my flesh, I washed immediately.

But I was back on the trail the next week, with a Sunday morning training stint in between. The work had to be done, had to come before my distaste.

We walked a good five miles, mainly in silence on my part, although Don and Sarah talked in low tones. It was as if the kid, the little sister, walked with me and I didn't want to seem frivolous in the face of her loss.

Polo raced ahead, plunged into the brush, sniffed everything, and then ran back to me, urging us to move faster. At one point, he lingered over a cholla cactus wound around with jimsonweed; I stepped gingerly into the desert tangle and made my way toward him, only to find a very ripe jackrabbit corpse.

"Polo," I said, deliberately sharpening my voice, "those are not the bones. Find the bones, Polo. Show me the bones."

He was reluctant to leave his prize, but he really did know the difference between lunch and his job, so he trotted away, albeit not without a few fond looks back at the dead jack. The deputies gave one another surreptitious glances that said, boy are we wasting our time out here with this big ragmop of a dog. Wish we had the bloodhound.

Well, Polo and I would show them.

I hoped.

The morning sun popped up over the horizon with incredible swiftness, and the desert took on a new and colorful persona. Wildflowers bloomed in profusion, thanks to recent rains; cactus flowers were an improbable fuschia and there were poppies and desert lilies and yucca flowers standing straight as sentries over six feet tall.

The heat was growing by geometric proportions. I'd drunk half my water already and soaked my bandanna in it to keep the back of any neck cool.

The desert plants didn't care about the heat. They didn't care about anything, with their prickles and their leather skins, the gray-green not-quite-leaves that didn't even look plantlike. There were wildflowers smaller than your tiniest toenail and big yellow blooms on the barrel cacti and the long red-tipped ocotillo. Hawks circled overhead, and for a minute I wondered if we waited long enough, would we see turkey vultures and then we wouldn't even need Polo, we'd just follow the carrion birds to where the child's body lay.

We were going to find a body. I knew it. The hollow place in my stomach knew it. Five days out here; the kid wasn't alive. She couldn't be.

The sound of rapid, joyous barks from up ahead stopped my musing and had me running toward the ironwood tree. Polo bounded up to me and circled me, bumping against me to move me faster. Bouviers are herd dogs, but instead of nipping at the heels of their cows, they push the animals into compliance, as Polo was trying to do now to me and the deputies.

"He found her?" Don asked, his voice carrying a world of skepticism.

"That's what he's telling us," I replied, moving as quickly as I could in the oppressive heat.

"Show me the bones, Polo," I said, the little shudder of anticipation turning into a full-fledged tremble. "Show me the bones."

Polo skidded on the edge of the wash and headed down the steep incline. I leaned over and had a look. The body lay at the bottom of the arroyo, sprawled in a posture no living creature could have tolerated. Polo barked and pawed the ground, circling the body in a gruesome dance of triumph, crowing over his find and nuzzling the body with his snout.

It was a man. A Mexican, probably an illegal trying to make it into the U.S. His black hair was matted with blood. There were flies all over the place and a smell you didn't have to be canine to recognize.

I stood in stunned silence, then reacted like a handler, reaching into my vest pocket for the goody box. I made my way with slow carefulness down the slope and joined the deputies at the body. I opened my tupperware box and took out a dog treat.

"What are you doing?" Sarah's gray eyes were wide with disbelief. "You think this is a good time to feed your dog?"

"I'm not feeding him," I replied. I leaned as close to the stinking corpse as I could, and held the dog treat in my open hand. Polo bounced and snatched it, then did another circle dance of triumph. "Good dog," I said with forced brightness. "Good Polo. What a good dog. You found the bones, Polo."

I turned back to Sarah. "I'm rewarding him. He has to associate treats with the scent of bodies if he's going to be a good cadaver dog."

"But it's the wrong body."

"He doesn't know that."

I could hear the crackle of Don's radio; he was calling our find in to headquarters.

Polo jumped up on me. "Oh, you good dog. Oh, you perfect and beautiful beast," I crooned, resolutely keeping my eyes locked on his sweet black face instead of looking at the dead man. I didn't want to see more of what I'd already seen — the horrible movement of the body, which meant that insect life was taking over inside the rapidly decaying corpse.

I was trying to breathe as little as possible. Sarah reached into her vest pocket and pulled out a tiny jar of Vicks. She scooped some out and pushed it under her nose, then handed it to me. I took it with a nod of gratitude and filled my nostrils with the strong scent of menthol, hoping to block out the overpowering odor of human rot.

Don's orders were to remain with the body while Sarah and I made our way back to Ocotillo Wells. We'd make a circle, continuing to search as we headed west.

I had to pull Polo away by brute force; every instinct in his body told him to stay with the dead man, to examine him fully and to — God forbid, but he was a dog, and dogs will be dogs — eat some of him. This I didn't explain to Sarah, somehow becoming as protective of her as I'd felt toward the little girl back at the frame house.

I walked for a while without giving a new

order, letting Polo adjust to the fact that he was now heading away from "the bones" instead of toward them.

I saw the child's guileless blue eyes before me. *Will you find my sister?*

"Sarah?" I stepped up my pace until I strode next to the deputy, who was moving with angry swiftness. "Any news from the base?"

"You mean was the kid at her grandmother's eating cookies and milk? Not hardly. They're sending a helicopter and two more dog teams. Anybody finds that kid, it won't be us. Thanks to that damn body in the wash."

I nodded. I'd known that had to be the case; if there'd been news, Don would have said so. But the little ghost girl walking next to me had to hear it for herself.

I didn't even know her name, yet she was as clearly part of the expedition as Polo and I. The missing girl was Melissa Sue. Ten years old. The child at the base was about eight, although I wasn't much of a kid person, so she could have been seven or nine.

Why didn't I know her name? Why hadn't I asked?

What the hell was I going to say to her if — when? — we found her sister.

I didn't have to say anything. That was the cops' job. But I knew that this time I would. This time I couldn't just load Polo into the van and head home for a much needed hot shower, leaving the body and the search behind me. Pretending to myself that this had been no more than a practice run, with Body in a Bottle instead of the real thing.

It was time to give Polo his new command. I bent down and spoke into his tiny ear. He reeked of creosote bush and cadaver. "Find the bones, Polo. Go find the bones for me, boy."

He gave his yelp of understanding and bounded into the brush. He was matted with cactus fishhooks and spine clusters and his paws looked as if they hurt from the hard ground, but he set off with an enthusiasm that put Sarah and me to shame. We were spent, demoralized by the body in the wash, and more than ready to pack it in — but for the need to bring the little girl home for her final rest.

We passed mesquite and pencil cactus, sun-wilted evening primrose and century plants, huge feathery palo verde trees at the edge of arroyos, prickly pears six feet tall with giant red balls ready to open into fleshy blooms.

Some people thought the desert was beautiful. I thought it was scary as hell, a dangerous place where only the strong survived, and I felt about as strong as a pillow.

How in God's name was a ten-year-old going to survive out here, even if she was born and brought up in Ocotillo Wells?

We were approaching the town. I could tell because I heard the Interstate's low hum and caught a glimpse of dust rising from the dirt road behind the hamburger joint. More sheriff's cars,

I supposed, come to join in what the newspeople would call the massive manhunt. Or maybe the newsvans themselves, each local channel out to get a sound bite for the evening report.

Massive girlhunt.

Where would a little girl go around here? This wasn't like my Michigan girlhood where there were creeks and parks and trees to climb, secret places only your best pals knew about. There was simply no shade anywhere, no honest-to-God trees to shelter you and let you climb into green, leafy hideaways.

My face was bright hot red despite the slathers of sunscreen and my straw hat. I was out of water, having given most of mine to Polo. We'd been out here five hours, and already we were ready to pack it in.

And Melissa Sue had been missing five days.

There was no way she could have carried five days' worth of water, and despite the recent rains, there weren't enough streams with drinkable water for her to stay alive.

Polo looked discouraged, too. He still sniffed the mesquite and the cactus, rubbed against the desert mistletoe and poked a very cautious nose into the ocotillo, but he moved more slowly and his tongue hung from his mouth as his craving for water grew more intense.

We had to stop. Sarah looked more than ready to take a shade break, and I didn't think there was much point in continuing the hunt. By now the town was in view; I could see the red roof of the hamburger place that was the town's only landmark.

Polo raised his head and sniffed the air. He stood, only his head moving this way and that, clearly trying to capture an elusive scent.

"Can't he hurry up?" Sarah's voice was sharp with fatigue and disappointment.

"I think he's on scent," I replied. "He may have something."

"Oh, come on, we're practically back at base. Every inch of this place has been searched already. It's probably another jackrabbit."

I ignored her and said, "Show me the bones, Polo. Show me the bones."

He gave his yelp of understanding and moved in the direction the scent led him.

You know the expression, being led around by the nose?

That's precisely what Polo looks like when he's on an elusive scent. His nose sniffs the air and he follows it. That simple. The shiny black nose catches a tiny whiff and he moves his head this way and that to make sure he's following the strongest odor.

Scent flows like water. If we could see what dogs smell, we'd see eddies and streams, scents blown on the air like twigs on top of a stream.

He was moving slowly. I liked that; it meant he had something and was being as careful as he could be to track it to the source.

"Show me. Show me the bones."

"There aren't going to be any damn bones."

I didn't usually tell sheriff's deputies to shut the hell up, but this was going to be an exception.

Polo barked. A single, sharp bark, and then he took off running toward a palo verde tree in the distance. I followed at the swiftest pace I could muster, while Sarah brought up a sullen rear.

He circled. He twisted his big black body and wagged his stub of a tail. His ears flattened and he bounded ahead, kicking up dust with his big bearlike paws.

"Find the bones," I called, which was pretty stupid because he was doing just that, but I wanted him to know I understood and appreciated.

Next to the palo verde stood an abandoned well. Polo circled it, then pawed the ground next to it.

"Oh, my God," I cried, racing toward the stone structure. "The kid's in the well."

Polo barked and pawed, lowering his muzzle to the dirt and then pawing again. His unmistakable signal that he'd found the bones.

The child's body was at the bottom of the long stone tunnel. Alice caught in the rabbit hole, forever in Wonderland.

Sarah called it in on her radio, her voice swelling with triumph, naively pleased at being the one to find the body. In this, she resembled Polo, who did his victory dance, although he was disappointed at not being able to get really close to the corpse. I took out my goody box and went through the reward ritual while I pondered the best way to break the news to the little girl back at the frame house.

And then I saw the jack.

Not a jackrabbit, but a little metal jack, the kind you scoop up after you bounce a rubber ball. I didn't know kids still played with jacks, and there was nothing to indicate how long the jack had lain in the gray desert dust, but the truth stabbed me like a pencil cactus thorn.

The child hadn't been hoping the bloodhound would find her sister. She'd been deathly afraid the bloodhound would unearth the truth. She knew where her sister was, but she'd been afraid to tell her parents.

Two little girls in the desert, playing wherever they could, using the thin shade of the palo verde and the stone well as their special place.

Had the child died instantly from the fall, or had she lain inside calling for help?

And why hadn't the little sister told her parents? Was the household so abusive that she was more afraid of the punishment than she was of her sister dying? Or was she simply too young to understand the consequences of falling into the well?

I would probably never know. I would go back into town and let Sarah do her cop duty, let the wheels of law enforcement turn with excruciating slowness.

I would put Polo in the back of my van, drive home and give both of us a long, scented bath to wash away the sweat and the smells, and I would write up my report and move on to the next search, the next body.

But I didn't think I'd ever go out tracking again without the little sister at my side, her blue eyes wide, her face pinched with the fear that the dogs would reveal hidden truth she was too afraid to face.

"Good dog, Polo," I said again, but it was hard to praise him for finding out what I hadn't really wanted to know.

Like many lawyers these days, Carolyn Wheat has put her legal skills, honed by the Brooklyn chapter of the Legal Aid Society, to good use in her novels, which feature Cass Jameson. Recent novels include *Mean Streak* and *Troubled Waters*. She takes a break from the law to examine a different side of crime in "Show Me the Bones." She has taught mystery writing at the New School in New York City, and legal writing at the Brooklyn Law School.

Copyright Notices

The employees of G.K. Hall hope you have enjoyed this Large Print book. All our Large Print titles are designed for easy reading, and all our books are made to last. Other G.K. Hall books are available at your library, through selected bookstores, or directly from us.

For information about titles, please call:

(800) 257-5157

To share your comments, please write:

Publisher
G.K. Hall & Co.
P.O. Box 159
Thorndike, ME 04986